Praise for
11 BEFORE 12

"Brilliant, laugh-out-loud hilarious, and heartbreaking
(in a good way), *11 Before 12* is probably the best middle
school friendship ever."

—**LAUREN MYRACLE**, *New York Times* bestselling author
of the Winnie Years and Wishing Day series

"Kaylan's first-person voice perfectly captures
the horrors of starting at a new school, from the
prospect of eating alone in the cafeteria to the
awkwardness of meeting a new neighbor boy."

—*KIRKUS REVIEWS*

"The voice is authentic, and this
book will entice those who want to read about
a relatable, funny young woman."

—*SCHOOL LIBRARY JOURNAL*

ALSO BY LISA GREENWALD

A FRIENDSHIP LIST NOVEL

11 before 12

LISA GREENWALD

KATHERINE TEGEN BOOKS
An Imprint of HarperCollins Publishers

For Aleah

11 BEFORE 12

ONE

"KAYLAN!" RYAN POUNDS ON MY door. "You overslept! School starts today! You're already late!"

I run to beat him over the head with my pillow, but I'm too slow. "Ryan," I shout down the hall. "You're a jerk! Karma's a thing, you know. Bad things will happen to you if you're not nice to me."

After five deep breaths, I call Ari.

"You want to go to the pool?" I ask her as soon as she answers.

She replies in her sleepy voice, "Kay, look at the clock."

I flip over onto my side, and glance toward my night table.

8:37.

"Okay," I reply. "I'll admit: I thought it was later. At least nine." I pause a second. "Sorry. Did I wake you?"

Ari sighs. "I'm still in bed, but you didn't wake me."

"Agita Day," I tell her. "August first, red-alert agita levels. I'm freaking out over here."

August 1 signals the end of summer, even though you still have almost a month left. August 1 means school is starting really soon, even though it's still twenty-nine days away.

"Oh, Kaylan." She laughs. "Take a few deep breaths. I'll get my bathing suit on and be at your house in an hour. I already have my pool bag packed because I had a feeling you'd be stressing."

"Perfect." I sigh with relief. "Come as soon as possible! But definitely by nine thirty-seven, okay? You said an hour."

"Okay. I'm up. And you're never going to believe this," she says, half distracted. "I'm getting new across-the-street neighbors."

"Really?" I finally get out of bed and grab my purple one-piece from my dresser drawer. "Describe."

She pauses a second, and I'm not totally sure she heard me. "They're moving the couch in right now," she explains. "I can't tell how many kids there are, but there's one who looks like he's our age."

"A boy?" I squeal.

"Yeah, he's playing basketball right now." She stops talking. "Oops, he just hit one of the movers in the head with the ball."

"Tell me more," I say, dabbing sunscreen dots all over my face. They say it takes at least a half hour for it to really absorb into the skin, and my fair Irish complexion needs all the protection it can get.

I only take after my Italian ancestors in the agita department, I guess.

"He went inside," she explains. "I think he got in trouble. I saw a woman, probably his mom, shaking her hands at him."

"Oops." I step into my bathing suit, holding the phone in the crook of my neck.

"Oh wait, now they're back outside. Taking a family photo in front of the house." She pauses. "He has a little sister. I think they're biracial. White mom, Black dad."

"Interesting," I say. "Maybe his sister is Gemma's age!"

"Maybe . . ." I can tell she's still staring out the window at them, only half listening to me.

"By the way, Ryan is insisting that red X thing is true. You haven't heard about that, right?" I ask.

"Kaylan!" she snaps in a jokey way. "No! He's totally messing with you. Okay, go get your pool bag ready, eat breakfast, and I'll be there as soon as I can."

I grab my backpack and throw in my sunscreen, a change of clothes, and the summer reading book I haven't finished yet. I'm having a hard time getting into *My Brother Sam Is Dead*, although from what I've read, it makes my life seem pretty easy.

I hear Ari's instructions in my head as I get ready, and I already feel calmer. Her soft voice—she's never really flustered by anything.

I stare at my watch again. 9:35. I wait for Ari on the front steps. I'm trying to stay as far away from my brother as possible. Ari still has two minutes, but I wish she was here already.

I stand up and look for her, but she's nowhere in sight. She is so going to be late. On Agita Day.

I learned the word *agita* from my mom. She's part Italian and she learned it from her grandmother, who was 100 percent Italian and apparently said it all the time. It basically means anxiety, stress, heartburn, aggravation—stuff like that.

I don't know what my great-grandma's agita was about, but mine is pretty clear.

Starting middle school.

A few minutes later, I spot Ari at the end of the block, and I walk down the driveway to meet her. She strolls toward me, hair up in a bun, with her favorite heart sunglasses on. Her pink-and-white-striped tote hangs over her shoulder like it's the lightest thing in the world.

"I brought you an extra hair tie," she says, showing me her wrist. "Since you always forget."

"Thanks," I say. "Let's go in so I can grab my stuff. I've had the worst morning."

"What happened?" she asks, after a sip from her water bottle.

I look around for my brother. "I can't even talk about it. Ryan and I got into a huge fight last night. I dumped a bowl of cereal on his head, that's how bad it got. Right as his friend Tyler walked in the door."

"Wow," Ari says.

When we get inside, Ari heads straight to the den and sits down in the brown recliner. It used to be my dad's favorite, before he moved out. I think about him every time I see the chair. I should be over it by now.

He doesn't miss the recliner. He doesn't miss us.

He hardly even calls.

"I've been thinking," Ari says, slipping off her flip-flops and putting her feet up on the ottoman. "I'm gonna go by Arianna when school starts."

My heart pounds when she says this, like more announcements and confessions are coming, like she's going to tell me stuff I don't want to hear. I pick at the mosquito bite on my cheek and try to listen.

She looks at me crooked and comes to join me on the couch. Ari, or I guess I should say *Arianna*, sits up straight, cross-legged, facing me. "Ya know, because, like, it's a new school. I should have a new name. Sound more mature. Sophisticated. That kind of thing."

I nod, but all I can think about is that I need a thing like that. I need to do something big, something to change myself before middle school. But I don't have a nickname people use, and I can't get a whole new wardrobe. Should I get a life-changing haircut or something? Nothing is coming to me.

"Just wanted to make sure you're okay with it," she says. "I know how you are with change."

I *psshaw* that away, but I'm kind of glad that she gets that about me, that she knows I'm terrible with change. "You're already sophisticated, though, Ar," I remind her. "I mean, you go to the ballet every year with your mom."

She laughs. "Um, yeah, but that's because my mom buys the tickets."

"Okay, well, you're mature—I mean, you babysit for Gemma all the time, and your parents are never worried that you two are home alone and gonna burn down the house."

"Kay." She puts her hands on my knees. "I get what you're saying, I'm pretty much ready for college. So I need a name that reflects that, shows my true self."

"Okay, well, if you think of something that I can do like that, *Arianna*, just let me know." I take a lip balm/sunscreen out of the pocket of my cover-up and rub it on my lips. "Do I have to call you Arianna, too? Or can I stick with Ari? I mean, I already know you're mature and sophisticated."

BFFs should be allowed to stick with nicknames

6

forever. It's like some kind of rule of friendship that everyone knows and accepts.

"Well, when school starts, around other people, use Arianna, okay? Otherwise, it'll be confusing. Ya know?" She puts out her hand so I'll give her the lip balm. "Just, like, try it a few times, so you can get used to it."

"Okay, Arianna." I laugh. "Ready for the pool?"

"I'm always ready for the pool," she says, picking up her neatly packed tote. She even remembered two bottles of water and the spray sunscreen.

I grab the still-damp-from-yesterday towel from the back of the bathroom door and throw it over my shoulder.

"Ryan, we're leaving," I yell as I'm running upstairs to get my bag, trying to get him to hear me over the beeping of his video game. "Your eyes are going to bleed out of your head if you keep staring at that screen all day!"

He doesn't respond.

"Do you think my brother got a personality transplant and didn't tell me?" I ask Ari on the walk over to the pool, loosening my backpack straps. I can never get it to sit right on my shoulders; it's, like, digging into my skin. I definitely need a new one before school starts.

She laughs, sliding her sunglasses to the bottom of her nose and eyeing me suspiciously. "Can you do that? It would be kind of cool if you could, actually."

I hold on to my backpack straps. "I was kidding, but yeah, could be cool. His crazy behavior has been going

7

on for a few weeks now, but I've been mostly ignoring it because I just wanted it to disappear."

"A magical ability to make things like that disappear would be cool, too," Ari suggests.

"Totally!" I think about it for a second. I wonder if there's a way to do that, like really control our thoughts and calm them down. "Ryan and I used to be friends, ya know? And now he's either being a jerk to me or ignoring me."

"I think brothers are like that," Arianna explains. "Probably the more you stress about it, the more it will seem like a big deal."

I look at her, but she doesn't meet my gaze. "That's what you say about everything."

She laughs. "Yeah, because it's true." She stops walking to get a pebble out of her flip-flop. When she comes back up, she puts an arm around me. "Kay, you stress too much. You know this, right?"

I mumble, "I guess."

"And also," Ari continues, "I don't know anything about brothers. I'm just making this up. Gemma still thinks I'm the coolest. But that's because she's eight. I'm sure she'll find me annoying, eventually."

"Probably."

We get to the pool and throw our towels on our favorite lounge chairs. They're not really "ours," of course, but I call them ours because we always sit in the exact same spot, by the steps to the shallow end. It's half-sun, half-shade.

The best spot at the pool.

Ari goes to the bathroom, while I lather on more sunscreen. I'm about to jump in the water when out of the corner of my eye, I notice Tyler sitting on the lifeguard chair. I look away and spend all my energy trying to focus on making sure every dab of sunscreen is smoothed in. I examine the little tan dots on my legs and inspect my chipping pedicure.

"Hey, Kaylan," he says.

"Oh, um, hey." I pretend that I didn't see him sitting there, when I clearly did. "I didn't know you were working here. I've been here, like, every day this summer and I've never seen you."

"I'm just filling in for August," he says. "I'm still training, really. I want to work as a lifeguard when I'm in high school."

I'm not sure if a kid only a year older than me, who's "still training" to be a lifeguard, should really be watching over the pool, but who am I to judge?

"Don't look so nervous." He laughs, pulling up his shirt to mop up the sweat on his face. I try to look at him as he talks, but all I see is stomach. Tyler's stomach. It's tan, golden brown, and it's right there in front of my face. It's like I can't see anything else. "Joey's keeping an eye on me."

Joey's the director of the pool and a lifeguard, too.

"All right, well, I'll be careful not to drown," I say and then laugh, not really sure if that was funny or not.

"Good plan." He gives me a thumbs-up.

Tyler blows his whistle at some kids wrestling in the shallow end. He looks so official, the way he sits there, leaning back in the lifeguard chair, like he has it all under control. His hair is just the tiniest bit spiky. He even has the white sunscreen lines on his nose and his cheeks, but it doesn't look dorky on him. It's like he was born to be a lifeguard.

My left eye starts twitching and all of a sudden my arms are really itchy. Like really, really itchy. Am I getting a rash from this new sunscreen? I can't stop scratching my elbow.

I think I'm breaking out in hives. He's just Tyler, Ryan's best friend since pretty much forever, but I can't look at him all of a sudden. I need to focus my eyes anywhere else.

Suddenly just talking to Tyler makes me feel like I'm about to pass out.

And seriously, why is Ari taking three hundred years in the bathroom?

Finally, she gets back. "Ari." I pull her close and whisper, "This is so random, but do you think Tyler's cute?"

She looks around like she can't find him, and I nudge my head up toward the lifeguard chair to show her where he is.

"Umm. Maybe?" She shrugs, sitting down at the edge of my lounge chair. "Never really thought about it. . . . Let me look at him closer."

"No! Don't!" I hit her on the arm.

"Ouch! Kaylan!" She gives me a crooked look.

"Sorry." I feel his presence in this odd way. Like I know he's close by. It's like an itch that's so super-itchy, but I'm not allowed to scratch it.

Ari nudges her head toward mine and whispers, "I'm sorry to tell you this, because Agita Day and all, but Brooke and Lily are here."

"What? Really?" I'm completely zapped out of Tyler thoughts. I scan the pool to find them.

"Yeah, I guess they're back from camp." Ari looks over toward the deep end. "They're over there with that group of boys—Chase Selnowitz, and I know a few of those other boys from Hebrew School."

Brooke, Lily, and Kaylan. We called ourselves *Blick* for BLK (kind of a dumb name, now that I think about it) and we loved each other. We met in a baby music class, and our moms became friends, and then we became friends, and I figured it would be like that forever. But then, overnight, it just wasn't. Brooke and Lily were scooped up by the Phone Girls (I called them that because they were the first ones to get cell phones), and I wasn't scooped. I was a freezer-burned pint of ice cream, left to melt on the counter—until Ari moved to our school in fourth grade.

"Is Tamar here, too?" I ask. "Are you guys still gonna be Tamari this year?"

Tamar is Ari's Hebrew School BFF. She jokes that Tamar's the *me* of Hebrew School, since Tamar doesn't go to school with us. People need a BFF wherever they are; it's a simple fact of life.

"I think we're done with Tamari." She laughs at the name combination they made up. "Are you still jealous about that, Kay?" She side-eyes me.

"No," I groan, and look away. "God, why are Brooke and Lily back already? And is one of them going out with Chase?"

Last summer, Brooke and Lily went to the same sleep-away camp as the Phone Girls, and they just *looooved* it. I overheard them talking about it all the time like it was the best thing ever and they were hanging out with celebrities or something.

Ari leans in close and puts her hands on my shoulders. "Come on, let's swim, it'll clear your head."

She takes my hand and leads me over to the pool, and we jump in together, holding hands, the way we always do. It's probably babyish, and I wonder if I should tell her that we should just jump in on our own from now on, or maybe even use the steps like normal, civilized people.

"They have mozzarella sticks at the snack bar today," Ari says, treading water and changing the subject entirely.

"What are the other specials?" I ask, even though eating is the last thing I want to do. My stomach is more knotted up than the rope we had to climb in gym last year. I can't think about Brooke and Lily. I can't talk to them, or ask them about camp, or anything without feeling totally embarrassed. It's easier when I pretend they don't exist.

Maybe there are things you just never get over. Like friendship endings, and your dad leaving, and who knows what else. Maybe I should make a Never Get Over list in my mind and just accept that some things need to stay there.

"Um, a turkey club and some blackberry smoothie," Ari explains. "Kay, let's race, okay? It'll be good for you. Crawl?"

I nod. "It's our best stroke, for sure." We take our places on the wall at the shallow end, and we ask Rebecca, one of the other lifeguards, if she'll tell us when to go.

Racing takes my mind off everything. For the few minutes that I'm trying to swim as fast as I possibly can, I'm not thinking about Brooke and Lily. I'm not thinking about Ryan being a jerk. I'm not even thinking about August 1 or agita or starting middle school.

My arms move back and forth like I'm an Olympic swimmer competing for the gold medal. My legs slice the water and it feels crisp and cool. My head turns to the side for a breath and I hear muffled sounds of children cheering and yelling. The water splashes behind me as I kick my feet. I turn my head again and hear the loudspeaker calling out the people who have food ready at the snack bar.

"Congrats," Ari says, all out of breath as soon as we touch the pool ledge. "I think that was your fastest yet."

"I think so, too," I say, smiling, as I catch my breath. "I feel like I could eat two full orders of mozzarella sticks after that swim."

"Go for it," Ari says, leaning back against the edge of the pool. "I wonder if those kids over there by the diving board are going to be in any of our classes. They look like they're our age, right?"

"Um, I don't think so. They look older."

"You think?" she asks. "Just because they're wearing itty-bitty bikinis?"

I glance over there, and crack up, and then look back at Ari. "Yeah, my mom would never let me wear that. Do you see how small the boobage areas are?"

Ari laughs so hard she has to dunk underwater for a second to calm down. "I actually have a bikini like that. My cousin gave it to me for a birthday gift, random. But I never wear it."

I stare at the Bikini Boob Girls and try to figure out their deal—boys and girls together like it's totally normal, and they're all best friends and hang out all the time.

Ari's still cracking up. "Boobage area! Is *boobage* a rea word?"

I shrug. "No clue. It should be, right? Let's just say it a lot, and it'll become a thing."

"Boobage," I whisper to her.

"Boobage," she whispers back.

"We can't say it without laughing!"

"I know," she shrieks.

We flick water at each other, and then flip over to practice our one-armed hand stands.

So what if this stuff is babyish? We're still having fun. And at least the boobage areas of our bathing suits actually cover our, um, boobage.

If it were up to me, we'd skip middle school and live at the pool forever.

TWO

WE'RE WALKING OVER TO THE snack bar to get lunch when we hear someone say, "Ari! Hey! Over here."

We look all around, not knowing where the voice is coming from, and finally we find the person. She's so tall, with the longest legs I've ever seen. She doesn't even have her hair pulled back; it's just blowing in the breeze, but not at all in her face. And she doesn't even look sweaty! We walk over to the section of lounge chairs in the sun, near the deep end.

"Oh my God, hi," Ari says, leaning in to give the tall girl a hug.

"Ari, you look soooo tan," the girl says. "B. T. Dubs, Tamar said she was coming later."

B. T. *Dubs?* Ew.

"Oh cool." Ari smiles. "I haven't talked to her since the

end of Hebrew, when she went away to camp. How was your summer?"

Ari's voice always gets super-high-pitched when she's excited about something, and now it's just, like, normal. I'm getting the sense that Tamari really is over. Good.

"It was amazing," the girl replies. "I was on this teen tour with Phoebe, you know her, right? We had the best time."

I'm just standing there, feeling really stupid because I don't know this girl, and Ari hasn't introduced me. I shift my weight from my left foot to my right foot and then back again. Should I go to the snack bar and meet Ari there? I don't want to interrupt, but I also don't want to keep standing here, like I'm hovering on the side of their conversation.

"That's awesome," Ari says. "Oh, do you know Kaylan?" She turns to me. "Did you guys ever meet? I can't remember. Jules moved here last year; we're in Hebrew together."

"I don't think we've met," I say to the girl. Jules, I guess. "I'm Kaylan, but duh, Ari just said that."

"I'm Jules. Also, duh." She laughs. "You guys go to school together?"

Ari nods. "Yeah, are you gonna be at West Brookside? I forgot where you said you were going. Doesn't the end of Hebrew feel like so long ago?"

Jules plays with the beads on her bathing suit top. "It

totally does. I'm not going to West Brookside, I'm going to East, but some of my other friends are going there." She looks back over at them. "I'll introduce you."

I say, "Introduce us after lunch, okay? I'm staaarrrr-viiiiinnnggg." I try to imitate this line I heard in a movie once, but neither of them get the joke.

"Oh, uh, sure!" Jules bounces on her toes. "See you guys later."

She goes back to her group, and Ari and I keep walking to the snack bar, not saying anything. We overhear Jules say, "Oh, that's Ari, she's cool, she's, like, the only reason Hebrew School is tolerable."

Ari and I look at each other then and raise our eyebrows. "That's, like, a major compliment?" I tell her, trying to imitate Jules's sing-songy voice.

"I know, right?" Ari squeals.

It's a weird thing to know that your whole life is about to change really soon but have no idea how that change will affect you. I mean, I've been going to school with pretty much the same kids since kindergarten, and in just a few weeks I'll be in this giant school with a bazillion kids I don't know. Okay, maybe not a bazillion, but lots of new people. It'll feel like a bazillion. Maybe even a bazillion plus one.

"Hello, Brookside Pool!" We hear Joey scream through the loudspeaker. "I said, 'Hello, Brookside Pool!'"

A few enthusiastic pool goers yell back, "Hello, Joey!"

"That's not good enough!" he screams.

So then we all yell, "Hello, Joey!"

Ari and I laugh at ourselves and everyone else for how seriously we take the Brookside Pool rituals.

"Who is ready for Freeeeeeezzzzze Daaaannnncce?" he asks.

Oh no. Not Freeze Dance. Not now. Not when we're in such a visible spot between the lifeguards and the snack bar. We were just going to casually get our lunch, and eat on our lounge chairs, and process that whole Jules interaction.

"Ari!" I talk through clenched teeth. "Our mozzarella sticks are getting rubbery. Come on, run!"

"We never miss Joey's Freeze Dance," she says, putting an arm around me. "Come on! We're amazing at it. We were reigning champs two years in a row!"

Joey turns up the music. *Because I'm happy, clap along if you feel*—Ari and I are dancing, totally getting into it, doing the twist down to the pool pavement and back up. Slapping hands and shimmying all over the place.

The music stops and we freeze instantly.

We are Freeze Dance rock stars, and we know it. A bunch of people get called out, but we're still in. We'll make it to the final round; I know we will.

Clap along if you feel like happiness is the truth.

We grab hands and dance around in a circle for the next round. It feels like everything is okay. A blanket of calm spreads over me. And all that matters right then is Ari and me and the pool and Joey's Freeze Dance competitions.

"'Because I'm happy,'" I sing along with the music.

"Oh my God," I hear someone say as they pass us. "What are they doing?"

"They're, like, way too old to be that into Freeze Dance," another person says.

My cheeks flash red. My stomach sinks. I freeze, and not because the music shut off. I look around. They were talking about us.

I glance in their direction. The bikini boobage girls? They're whispering behind their hands.

They were definitely talking about us.

"Come on! What are you doing?" Ari yells. "We're still in this! We can win!"

I wonder if she heard what they said.

I keep dancing with Ari, but my heart's not in it. Those bikini boobage girls are watching us, leaning against the wall to the bathrooms, heads close together, whispering and laughing.

"Okay, Kaylan Terrel, sorry to say this, but you are out," Joey says over the microphone. "Good effort. Good effort."

I walk over to a lounge chair and pretend I didn't hear what those girls said, that I didn't just lose Freeze Dance.

"Sorry, Kay," Ari says, all out of breath. "Those

eight-year-olds are fierce. We'll get 'em next time. Come on, let's go get lunch."

"Did you hear what the boobage girls said?" I whisper. "They were totally making fun of us!"

"They were?" Ari crinkles her nose, looking around to find them. "I didn't hear that."

"They were making fun of us for freeze dancing," I explain. "We're too old to be that into Freeze Dance, something like that."

She looks over to where they're sitting and smooths out the sides of her cover-up. "Well, that's rude. We're so good at freeze dancing. There's no age limit for it, obviously."

She hesitates, still staring at them. Finally, she pulls my hand to get me to stand up. "Come on. I don't want to walk alone to the snack bar, and I'm really hungry now."

We walk quietly, trying to avoid eye contact with the boobage girls and their guy friends as we pass them. "Ari, um, I mean, Arianna," I say under my breath. "We cannot sprint to the entrance when we hear the ice cream truck, okay?"

She looks at me crooked. "Huh?"

"If Eddie runs out of the chocolate-dipped pops, we'll just have to deal."

"Um . . . okay." I'm not sure why it's taking Ari so long to see where I'm going with this.

"We can't make fools of ourselves anymore." I pause,

and wait for that to sink in. "Okay? We need to be normal. Try to be normal."

Ari puts her arm around me. "I get what you're saying, totally. But on the other hand, we gotta be ourselves. Ya know? People who run as fast as we can, get the best ice cream. That shows determination and dedication and athletic prowess and—"

"Okay." I laugh. "I get it. I get it." I wriggle away. I'm too sweaty to be that close to another person, even if she is my best friend.

THREE

AFTER MOZZARELLA STICKS AND ice cream, Ari and I lie out on our lounge chairs to soak up some afternoon sun. Even if I hadn't looked at a calendar, I'd be able to tell that it's August 1. The weather is screaming August. It's like a complete change from yesterday, when it felt like it was 300 degrees and 100 percent humidity.

Today, there's a breeze. The sun isn't as strong. It feels like summer isn't trying anymore, like it's tired and can't work so hard at being hot.

"Do you know when we get our schedules?" Ari asks me.

"How would I know?" I scoff, not meaning to sound so harsh. My words just come out that way.

"Maybe Ryan told you or something. . . . I don't know." She eye-bulges. "Sheesh. Kaylan, you need to calm down or we're never going to make it through the next month."

I look over at the boobage bikini girls again, and then look away.

I don't know how to calm down. That's the problem.

When I was waiting at the dentist the other day, I made a list on my phone.

Things I Am Worried (More Like Freaking Out) About
1. *Changing classrooms for every period*
2. *Cafeteria lunch tables where people can sit wherever they want*
3. *Remembering my locker combination*
4. *Learning how to use a combination lock*
5. *Sweat showing through my shorts*

Lists are great because you can check things off and feel like you're accomplishing stuff. But a worry list is a bad idea—because it makes me worry that I will never stop worrying.

"I just don't feel ready for middle school," I admit. "Maybe I need another year in elementary. Do you think I can stay back?"

Ari laughs. "Um, you got all As except for a B-plus in gym, and they don't hold people back for that." She pauses. "Here's what we need to do. We need to come up with a plan." She taps my knee to make sure I'm listening. "Like my name-change thing. Arianna just sounds more middle school than Ari. We need to do more stuff like that."

I nod. I like where she's going with this. It's hard to stand still, to wait for something big to happen. It's better to take action; it's calming to take steps to prepare.

"Oh my God! Why didn't I think of this earlier?" I kick my feet against the lounge chair. "A list!"

"Kaylan, you and your lists . . ." She finishes the last drops of her iced tea.

"No, for real." I sit up. "Ari, you know lists always help me! But this is going to be a super-extreme list of only amazingness. The most phenomenal list in the history of lists!"

Ari leans over the side of her lounge chair a little to get closer to me.

I continue, "A list of all the awesome stuff we can do to be one hundred percent prepped and ready to rock middle school!"

"YES! You're totally right!" Ari claps. "This is going to be the best thing ever. Emergency sleepover tonight. My house."

"But Gemma always bugs us. Remember last time, she kept trying to sneak behind the couch and take videos of us?" I remind her. "We won't be able to focus."

"Oh, I already thought about that." She raises her eyebrows. "Gemma's sleeping at my grandma's tonight."

I high-five her. It's not that I don't love Gemma. I do.

She's super-adorable. I've always wished for a little sister, so I sometimes pretend Gemma is mine. But if Arianna and I are having an emergency sleepover to come up with a game plan, we can't be distracted.

"Perfect," I say. "This is going to be great. We have twenty-nine days to really get prepared. And the thing is, while I'm busy getting ready, I won't be fretting as much, ya know?"

"Exactly," Arianna says. "Having a game plan is always the way to go." She reaches over to get her book out of her bag. "I only have three chapters left and I'm still not totally sure I get what the book's about."

"At least you're almost done." I'm putting sunscreen on my leg in the shape of a heart to see if I can get a heart tan line when I feel someone standing over me.

I look up. It's Tyler.

"Hey," he says.

I rush to cover the sunscreen heart with my hand. "Hey."

"You know if Ryan's still home?" he asks me. "He didn't text me back."

I shrug. My heart's pounding but I smile, trying to play it cool. "No clue."

"All right. Later."

When he's gone, Ari raises her eyebrows at me.

"He's just Ryan's friend," I remind her. "He's slept over like a billion times. I mean, there are pictures of us running through the sprinkler together. I'm only wearing bathing suit bottoms. No top! How insane is that?"

"What? When?" Arianna gasps.

"Like a billion years ago, but still."

Arianna nods. "I just remembered something, actually. At the end-of-year Hebrew School party, some of the older girls were talking about him."

"They were?" My heart sinks for some reason. In a tiny little corner of my brain, I had this weird thought that Tyler was a secret that only I knew. "What were they saying?"

"I can't remember. . . . I guess that he was cute?"

"How can you not remember, Ari?" I continue with the sunscreen hearts, trying to calm down and focus on something other than Tyler or the boobage bikini girls or middle school. "That's like a major thing!"

She shakes her head. "You just asked me if he was cute for the first time today!"

"Right," I say, taking deep breaths.

We spend the rest of the afternoon on our lounge chairs. Ari finally finishes her summer reading book, while I pore over an old issue of *Seventeen* that I found near the snack bar. It claims to have all the info I need on how to "update my back-to-school style," but all their suggestions seem like they'll cost a billion dollars.

"Ready to go?" Ari asks after we hear the announcement that the snack bar is taking the last orders of the day. "I want to tell my mom you're sleeping over, clean my room, and pick up some good snacks."

"Sounds fabulous, darling."

We gather all our stuff and pack our bags. We link arms as we leave the pool and head to our houses.

We haven't even done anything yet to really prepare for middle school, but I already feel better. Like I'm on a path to greatness. I'm on my way to figuring everything out.

FOUR

WE STOP AT MY HOUSE first since it's the closer one to the pool.

"Be over at six," Ari tells me.

"Def."

We do our signature jump-in-the-air-while-trying-to-high-five thing that we've been working on since the end of fourth grade. We've pretty much mastered it, but the leg kick at the end could use a little work.

I walk inside all ready to change out of my bathing suit, take a shower, and get ready for the sleepover—and that's when I find Ryan and Tyler on the couch, hands in a giant bowl of popcorn, arguing about a video game.

I'm still in my bathing suit, barely covered up by this old Lake George souvenir towel, and I feel like I'm naked, like I'm standing in a storefront window with no clothes on. My stomach rattles. Oh God, I should've changed out of this wet bathing suit and back into my shorts in the locker room at the pool.

I wrap the towel tighter around my body and run down the hall, to the stairs.

Tyler turns around. Despite my best efforts to look away, we make eye contact.

"Guess you found him," I say.

Ryan turns around too now. "Who are you talking to?" he asks like I've gone crazy.

"Tyler." I glare at my brother and then look at Tyler, hoping he'll defend me. "He was wondering if you were home. But now he's here. So I guess he found you."

Tyler doesn't respond or even look up. He's too busy throwing popcorn in the air and trying to catch it in his mouth.

"Kaylan, get us some orange juice," Ryan demands, even though I'm already past the kitchen.

"No. Get your own orange juice." I find yet another one of Ryan's dirty socks on the floor and walk back into the den so I can drop it on the couch, right next to him. Maybe being forced to smell his own socks will keep him from leaving them all over the house. Probably not. But it's worth a try.

I go upstairs to shower and triple-check that the bathroom door is locked. I can't risk Ryan doing something terrible like stealing my towel or pouring ice cubes into the shower.

I spend forever in there, cleaning off the sunscreen and chlorine and shampooing my hair twice. There's probably nothing better in this world than a shower after a day at the pool or the beach. It's like the sun is amazing on its own, and then you get to come home and feel clean and smell like peach body wash.

I look at myself in the bathroom mirror and admire my bathing suit tan line. I know some people try to avoid them, but not me. I'm the opposite. I try hard to get them. I like to see the difference in my skin, from how it was at the beginning of the summer to how it is at the end. It's like visible proof of the passage of time, a marker of all the happy, wonderful summer days.

I change into my most comfy sweatpants and hoodie, and put my wet hair up in a bun. I'm packing my overnight bag for Ari's, appreciating this delightful, clean, sun-kissed feeling, when I hear clamoring downstairs. Pots and pans banging. Things dropping.

My mom is home.

She's one of those people who gets right to work on dinner as soon as she walks through the door. She doesn't take a break for a second. She says that if she stops she'll never be able to start again.

I walk down to the kitchen, a Brookside Road

Elementary School gym bag that I always use for sleepovers over my arm.

"Mom, I'm not gonna be home for dinner," I tell her, instantly regretting that I didn't choose to say it in a nicer way. "I'm sleeping at Ari's tonight."

"Um, okay." My mom forces a smile. "I wish you would've told me earlier. I bought salmon and I was going to make brussels sprouts the crispy way, your favorite."

"Sorry." I shrug. "It's really important."

Ryan barges in, ripping open a bag of chips. "What's so important about sleeping at Ari's?"

I don't look at him. "It just is. Okay?"

"Mom, Kaylan has gone bonkers," Ryan tells her. "Seriously. We may need to schedule an appointment with Dr. Noodleman."

Dr. Noodleman is our pediatrician. He has the best name ever. I think that's why we still go to him. But he's a good doctor, too.

"Um, Mom, Ryan was born bonkers and it's just gotten worse," I explain. "Dr. Noodleman already knows he's a lost cause."

My mom breathes in deeply and breathes out. "Okay, everyone, let's just relax." She sits down at the kitchen table and sips her water.

"Ryan, are you interested in salmon?" she asks him.

Tyler bursts into the room like someone's giving away

free Slurpees. "I'm definitely interested in salmon," he says.

She nods. "Great. We'll be eating at six thirty."

"Ry-dog, wanna shoot hoops?" Tyler asks him. "I bet you five dollars I can make a shot from the edge of your driveway."

"Deal." They shake hands, and Tyler leaves the kitchen. I hear the sound of potato chips crunching, and three seconds later the crumbs are mushed into my perfect, after-shower, clean hair.

"Ryan!" I scream. "Are you kidding?"

This is a war of dropping things on each other's heads. Where can I find some molten lava?

Ryan runs out the door, and I flip my head over to get the potato chip crumbs out. "I'll Dustbust, I promise," I tell my mom.

She pulls out a kitchen chair for me and pats it to get me to sit down. "Everything okay, Kaylan?"

"Um, no. Ryan is torturing me. Can't you see that?" I shriek.

"Yes, I do see that, and I'm working on it. But . . . this whole important sleepover with Ari . . ." She looks at me. "I worry about you."

Ever since the whole Lily-and-Brooke debacle, when I refused to go to school for a week, my mom is always on edge about me having friend catastrophes. I guess that's what moms do. They stress.

"Oh no, it's nothing to worry about," I assure her. "I promise."

"Okay." She puts her hand on my hand and smiles all gentle, in a way that feels way too dramatic for this moment. Like the end of an episode on some sitcom where cheesy music is playing.

I smile anyway. "Okay, gotta go get ready."

I run back upstairs to double-check that all the potato chip crumbs are out of my hair.

This list is going to be awesome.

The Ari and Kaylan BFF Prepare for Middle School and Completely Rule the World list. Okay, maybe that's too long. The Ari and Kaylan Crush West Brookside Middle School list. But that sounds kind of violent. And why is Ari's name first? Maybe mine should be. Or maybe it should be alphabetical order.

So I don't have the perfect name yet. But it's the perfect idea.

We are going to rock this and I can't wait to get started.

FIVE

"HEY, MRS. ETISOF," I CALL out as I pass her house. She's been my next-door neighbor my whole life, but I've only been inside her house a few times. I think it's because she's always outside. She's either gardening or sunbathing or getting ready to swim or kayak. She told me once that the world can be divided into two groups: indoor people and outdoor people.

It's clear which category she's in.

"Kaylan, my girl!" she calls back. She's kind of old, but I think she talks like a teenager. "How are you? Going to Ari's?"

She meets me at the end of her driveway, all dressed in her wetsuit and her kayaking booties. Her kayak is strapped to the roof of her car. "Yup!"

"Great. I'm going out for an evening paddle," she says.

"Come over soon, we'll make s'mores on the fire pit."

"Sounds great!"

I run around the corner to Ari's because I'm so excited to start the list. I get there at six on the dot and find her drawing on her front steps with sidewalk chalk, like she's deep in thought.

I don't have the heart to tell her that's not a very middle school thing to do. But maybe it doesn't matter. We're not in middle school yet.

"Hey," she says, not sounding as excited as I expected her to be. "I found this in the cabinet in the garage." She shows me the box of chalk. "Remember when we used to try to cover the whole path to my front door in chalk?"

I nod. She makes it seem like it was something we did a really long time ago, but truthfully we did it just last summer. I remember because I was so proud of our work, and so excited to show my parents when they picked me up at Ari's house. But as soon as they got there, I knew something was wrong. It was only my mom who was in the car. I could see bad news all over her face. That was the night she told Ryan and me that my dad had left and they were getting divorced.

It felt like someone had poked a hole in a perfect, air-stuffed, foil birthday balloon.

"Those girls at the pool were so rude," Ari says, as we're putting the chalk back in the garage. "I heard them, too;

I just tried to convince myself they were talking about someone else."

We walk back inside. "I know; I mean, it's Freeze Dance. Everyone loves Freeze Dance."

"Well, on a happier note, Mom said we can order pizza," Ari tells me as we run up the stairs to her room.

"Obviously pineapple on half, anchovies on half."

"Ha-ha." Ari forces a laugh. "But seriously—mushrooms on half. Cool?"

"Cool."

"Okay, I'll go tell my mom. You wait here, and look through my closet and see if anything you see screams first-day outfit, 'kay?" she asks.

I nod. "On it."

"Pizza's ordered," Ari says when she gets back to her room. "So let's get to work." She hands me a lined notepad and a pen. We sit facing each other in Ari's purple beanbag chairs.

"Okay, we need to start with a declaration!" I stand up, like I'm at a podium, making a speech. "I declare that this list is the best list in the history of lists!"

Ari stands up, too, and puts her hand on her heart. "I solemnly swear that this is the best project in the history of all best friendships ever to exist."

We double-high-five.

"And so it shall be," I say, because I think I heard that

in a movie once. "But in all seriousness, I don't think any-one's ever thought of something like this before."

"Geniuses!" We grab hands and squee, our faces tight and our eyes squinty.

"Okay, I'm going first," Ari insists as we sit back down.

"Wait!" I tap my pen against her knee. "First order of biz, we need to know how many things should be on it!"

She shakes her head. "No! We'll know when we finish it how many things should be on it. We can't decide the number in advance. Can we?"

We stare at each other, thinking for a second. "Okay, we'll come back to that," I tell her.

Ari folds her hands in her lap like she's about to medi-tate. "Here's my first thing. Ready?"

I nod.

"We need some guy friends. The groups of girls at the pool who all seemed older than us, it was because they had guy friends with them, too. Elementary school was for all-girl birthday parties and stuff like that. When I think middle school, I think girls and guys hanging out, like it's totally normal."

I nod. "Yeah, definitely. But that doesn't seem like such an easy thing to do. We can't just walk up to guys and be like, 'We need guy friends. Interested?' Ya know?"

Ari laughs. "That would be really funny if we did that. Maybe it would work? Guys do like confidence. I mean, that's what my cousin Sally says. But who knows if she's right. She thinks she knows everything."

I shrug, and lean back in the beanbag chair. My agita is bubbling up, like it was just resting under the surface and now it's going to overflow. Ari's idea to make a game plan was a good one, and lists always help me, but now I can't think of anything to add, and Ari's plan will be really hard to accomplish.

"I'm just gonna write down *make a guy friend*, and we'll figure out how to do it later," Ari says, writing in her perfect handwriting.

I hate my handwriting. I should probably add that to the list. Handwriting makeover. And that's when it comes to me: the second thing we need to do.

"Here's one," I say. "Makeover."

"You mean go to the mall and go to one of those makeup counters and pretend we're going to buy all the expensive makeup and get a makeover?" Ari asks. Clearly she's been thinking about this, too.

"Well, no," I reply. "I mean, sort of."

"Huh?"

"Okay, so I realized that one thing I'd like to make over about myself is my handwriting." I look at Ari and see her cracking up. "Don't laugh. Seriously. You know how much I hate my terrible handwriting."

"I know," she says. "It is bad."

"Thanks. So, I want a makeover, but, like, a *Whole Me Makeover*. Not just a new haircut or some new lip gloss or a plan to only snack on carrots. Though obviously those are good things. I'm talking complete makeover. From handwriting to jogging three times a week to drinking more water to volunteering in the community and really making a difference."

Ari nods and starts writing stuff down. "Okay, so far we have *find a guy friend* and *get a Whole Me Makeover.*" She chews on the end of her pen. I'm mentally adding that to the list for Ari's makeover. She can't keep doing that.

I close my eyes for a second, thinking about the fact that a million things can make up a Whole Me Makeover. "I'm tired. Let's go get a snack and see if the pizza's here."

"Sounds good to me."

We get down to Ari's kitchen and her mom has the pizza cutter out, about to start slicing.

"What are you doing?" Ari asks her.

"What?" She looks at her hand and at the pizza and then back at us. "Oh my goodness. I was thinking this was for Gemma. She still likes her pizza in half slices. What am I doing? Sorry, girls!"

Ari rolls her eyes and mouths *she's crazy* to me.

"Can I get you girls anything to drink?" Ari's mom asks us. "I have pink lemonade, yellow lemonade, fruit punch, water . . ."

"Mom! We can take care of it."

Ari's mom's lips curve up into an excited smile. She says, "Okay, well, enjoy, girls. I'll be in the basement doing laundry if you need anything."

"We're fine, Mom."

Ari always gets annoyed at her mom because she can be over the top in trying to be perfect and making everything wonderful for Ari and Gemma. I can see how it gets annoying. But sometimes I'm jealous. Not that my mom doesn't try. She does. She tries really hard. But she's on her own now and she works full-time and she's tired. I can tell she's tired. She doesn't complain or anything. I can just tell.

So I sort of think Ari should be more appreciative of her mom, more grateful. But I don't tell her that. Maybe I'll sneak it in to Ari's Whole Me Makeover, though. That seems like a good place for it.

We eat our pizza and keep discussing things we can do.

When I get to the crust part, I bend it over my mouth and hold it there with my top lip. "Should this be my new back-to-school look?" I ask Ari.

She cracks up. "Pizza-crust mustaches! That is part of your makeover. For sure."

I try to hold it in place with my lip while saying, "I need more crust for my goatee."

I take another piece of pizza, and try to think of ideas.

Ari adds, "Ya know, we can probably meet guy friends at the pool. There's that group of boys who are always playing Ping-Pong. . . ."

I nod and keep chewing. "Well, if they ever take a

break from Ping-Pong. I think that's all they do."

"Oh! And my new neighbor." Ari jumps up from the chair and looks out the kitchen window.

"What are you doing?" I ask her, after I swallow a bite of pizza.

"Spying on him, duh." She smiles all sneaky. "I thought he'd maybe be outside."

I sip my lemonade. "Ari! What if he sees you? On the first day he moves in, you're already the creepy neighbor?"

"He won't see me!" she screeches, still staring. "Plus, so what, I should take initiative, welcome him to the neighborhood."

"Come on, Ar. I've had Mrs. E. next door my whole life, and she's great, but this is an actual kid our age, and a boy, too! We can't mess this up."

"Okay . . ." She comes back to the table and finishes her slice. "So maybe we can try to chat it up with him, too? Maybe he'll show up at the pool?"

"Maybe." I shrug. "I don't know how to just go and *chat it up*, though."

"You know how to talk," Ari reminds me. "So you'll just, like, pretend you're talking to me."

"Um . . . it's not that easy for me to talk to other people, besides you. I mean, it was awkward with that Jules girl, before."

"Yeah, but I think it's because you were hungry." Ari

nods. "Here's the thing about Neighbor Boy: he's cute, but not like *freak out he is soo cute*, so it's not like we're going to have crushes on him."

"You saw him for three seconds. How do you know he's not that cute?" I laugh out loud, almost spitting my lemonade all over the pizza.

"I'm just saying he's a good candidate for guy friend," she explains.

"You make it sound like he's running in some kind of election. Imagine if all the guys in our class last year were competing for our friendship? They'd have to make campaign posters and speeches and stuff? That would be hilarious. It could be some kind of reality show."

Now Ari's the one laughing out loud. "I can email my Uncle David about it, he's some big producer in LA. . . ."

We spend a good few minutes discussing how funny this would be when Ari brings up another thing.

"Okay, on the subject of campaigns. I have another idea."

"I don't think we can run for president before middle school," I joke. "I mean, the limited amount of time will be an issue, and also I'm pretty sure you need to be thirty-five to be president of the United States."

"Duh." She glares. "Not that. But close. We need to get on TV!"

"What? Okay, Ari. Now you're the one going crazy," I say. "What does getting on TV have to do with us being ready for middle school?"

"Just think about it. We're on TV for something good. Not for something terrible, like we've been hit by a bus or something . . ." Her voice trails off and I can practically see the thoughts spinning around in her brain. "And then, like, everyone at school knows about us! We're kind of famous. Everyone wants to talk to us about it and find out all the details."

"That would be incredible," I say. "People just coming up to us and talking, and we're just, like, sitting back all cool, like it's no big deal."

"Totally!" She taps her nails against the table. "And everyone's like, 'Did you hear about *Ari and Kaylan?*'"

Ari's coming up with a plan.

And it's a good one.

SIX

AFTER PIZZA, WE KEEP WORKING at the kitchen table, trying to think of more things to put on our list.

Ari's mom appears at the doorway to the kitchen. "Girls," she says, all cheerful, the way she always talks. "I put s'mores ingredients on the outside table. I can help you make them on the Chiminea."

We both hop up from our seats.

"Mom, we know what we're doing," Ari groans. "We're not gonna burn the house down."

"Ari," her mom says, holding the door open for us. "Let me help. I'm still your mother."

Truthfully, I'm glad that Ari's mom is out here to help get the fire started because it's actually kind of hard with the logs and the newspaper and getting it all to work.

"I'm going to do some laundry," Ari's mom says after

the fire is going, and we've found acceptable s'mores sticks. "Let me know when you're done, and I'll come out and clean up."

Ari rolls her eyes, though I'm not sure if her mom can see that in the dark.

"Thanks so much," I say. "I love s'mores."

Ari and I eat three each, and after that we're totally stuffed, maybe too stuffed to talk. We're just sitting there, quiet, watching the flying embers.

"Maybe we're being too self-centered," I say, gazing at the fire. The flames have a way of bringing the soul-searching out of a person. "We need to help humanity somehow."

"Right now?" she asks. "We're in pajamas."

I crack up. "No. Not right now. But I mean, in general. That should be on our list. We need to think about others besides ourselves. It will make us better people."

"Very deep, Kay." Ari nods and writes it down. "I like it."

"We can start by helping some of those exhausted moms at the pool," I suggest, pulling my knees up to my chin. "They have all those kids, and they're trying to put on the sunscreen and the water wings and the kids are running away. You know? I mean, I think they can use help. And I like kids."

"Yeah, tired moms are definitely part of humanity," Ari replies. "Speaking of moms, here's another one. We need to have talks with *our* moms. We can't start middle school with them hovering all the time. We're gonna have a million things to deal with, and we can't be struggling with mom drama."

I think I see where Ari's going with this, but I'm not entirely sure. "Mama Drama, we can call it."

She nods and goes on. "I mean, both of our moms are super-overprotective. That needs to stop."

Right at that moment, Ari's mom comes back out. "I'm just cleaning up a little, girls." She yawns. "Let me know when you're going to bed, and I'll make sure the fire is out. Remember to brush your teeth."

"See what I mean," Ari whispers, and eye-bulges at me.

I try not to crack up, but that timing was just too perfect.

"We know, Mom," she yells. "We're eleven, not four."

"Ari, watch your tone."

"It's Arianna! How many times do I have to tell you?" Ari yells.

"You don't need to be so mean to her," I remind her, after her mom's gone back inside.

"She's so annoying."

"Yeah, but she's trying." It makes me nervous when they argue.

"Okay. Moving on." Ari looks down at the notepad. "I just remembered something that happened at the pool that I forgot to tell you!"

"What?" I squeal, putting another marshmallow on the stick.

"So I was in the bathroom, and that girl Cara was there," she starts, leaning over the arm of her Adirondack chair. "Remember, the one who's a year older than us? We hung with her a little last summer."

"Oh yeah," I say, toasting my marshmallow by the fire.

"So she was like, 'Did you get your hair highlighted?'" Ari flips her head over to show me the bottom and then flips back up. "I was like, 'No,' and then she said she totally thought I did because it looks so red!"

I go back to the chair with my charred marshmallow, curving my neck around to get a closer look. I guess it does look kind of red, maybe from the sun? It's a little hard to see in the dark. Maybe it's been getting redder all summer and I just hadn't noticed.

"It does look a little red," I tell her, assembling my s'more.

"So I think we should add highlights to the list!" She combs her fingers through her hair. "How awesome would that be? Starting middle school with fabulous hair!"

"Yeah!" I clap. "Add highlights. Why not? Could you see me as a blonde?" I crack up, and suddenly can't stop laughing. "Wait, does that count as part of our Whole Me Makeover, though? Is it a separate item?"

Ari twitches her nose from side to side, thinking for a minute. "Ummm. I think it is separate. Whole Me is more big picture—like who we want to be in middle school.

This is about fabulous hair, but, I mean, we need to go to a salon to do it. It needs to be its own thing."

I nod, stretching out my legs. "Yeah, you're right." I hesitate a second because we'll obviously need our moms' permission (and money) to do it, and Ari was just rude to her mom. What if she says no now? See, gotta be nice to moms. It's just the way to go.

Eleven-year-olds can't get highlights on their own . . . or can they? I mean, maybe we could sneak out and do it?

Right then, a major, important, huge component of the list comes to me. Out of the blue. A total cartoon-lightbulb-in-the-air-above-my-head kind of moment.

"OMG. Eleven," I say, clapping. "Eleven. Eleven. Eleven."

"Eleven," Ari repeats. "Why eleven?"

"Eleven things we need to do before we turn twelve!" I stand up and tap-dance with excitement. "Get it? Eleven Before Twelve!"

"Genius!" Ari hops up from her chair and hugs me and we jump up and down a few times. "That alone can get us on TV! We can start a movement. A guidebook for girls to follow before they turn twelve! This is huge!"

"Okay." I laugh. "Imagine if we did start a movement? And we had meetings with eleven-year-olds from all over the country to help them start middle school, too. We'll be experts after this year!"

"Yeah!" Ari says. "See, we can totally do this! Look how much we've accomplished already."

I sit back in my chair and stare at the flames, and sigh. Maybe Ari's right. Maybe we actually can do this and rock middle school and be happy. Maybe I won't need my worry lists—my agita will just fade on its own.

"And the fact that we're completing it by the time we turn twelve," Ari turns to me. "That's huge, too. We'll celebrate that we completed the list with our joint birthday party! I mean, we've only been planning it since, like, the day we met."

We discovered pretty soon after we met that Ari's birthday is the day after mine. Our moms had decided to bring in cupcakes for the class, and since Ari's birthday was falling on a Saturday that year, our moms were coming on the same day. At first I wasn't thrilled about sharing my birthday in-school celebration, but then it actually seemed great. Her mom brought all pink frosted cupcakes, and my mom brought all vanilla.

"YES! YES! YES! It's going to be the best ever." I jump up again and pop another piece of chocolate in my mouth. "We could have a bonfire! Here! At your house!"

"But my mom . . ." Ari's voice trails off. "That could get annoying."

"Your house is awesome, Ari. I think it's the perfect place for a party."

"True. And I mean, she could be better by then, after we have our talks with our moms, ya know, the heart-to-heart." Ari smiles. "I'm so glad we're doing this together.

I'm so glad we can help each other through this."

"Me too," I say.

She scootches over to the side of her chair and pats the seat so I sit down. Soon we're side by side, squeezed in on the red Adirondack chair. We're staring at the fire, and we're cuddled together. I don't want the fire to go out because I kind of want to stay in this moment forever and ever. But in a way, I do kind of want it to go out, because that means we can go to sleep and then wake up tomorrow and get started with this list.

When something this exciting happens, it's just too hard to wait to jump in.

When the fire is out completely, we go back inside and up to Ari's room. By the end of the night we have a complete list.

Eleven Fabulous Things to Make Us Even More AMAZING Before We Turn Twelve

1. Make a guy friend.
2. Do a Whole Me Makeover.
3. Get on TV for something cool we've done (not because we got hit by a bus).
4. Help humanity.
5. Highlight our hair.
6. Do something we think we'll hate.

7. Fulfill lifelong dream to kayak at night to the little island across the lake. (First step, find a kayak.)

8. Kiss a boy.

9. Get detention.

10. Have a mature discussion with our moms about their flaws.

11. Sabotage Ryan.

SEVEN

WE'RE SIDE BY SIDE ON Ari's trundle bed, and I can't fall asleep. I keep tossing and turning under my blanket. I try to sleep on my side, and then my back, and then my stomach. Nothing feels comfortable. "I'm overwhelmed," I say out loud, trying to see if Ari is still awake.

Thankfully, she is. "I know," she mumbles, half-asleep. "That's why we came up with the list in the first place. Remember?"

"Right. I know. Lists always help. But we're not going to be able to accomplish all of this before school starts."

Ari sits up in her bed and throws a pillow at me. I'm not too far from her, so it's pretty easy for her to hit me, even in the dark.

"Hello? Are you losing your mind? Remember your whole idea—eleven before twelve? We don't need to do it all before school starts. We have until November, our birthdays."

I sigh with relief. Even though it was my idea, I'd kind of forgotten that. I don't know what's wrong with me. My mind is spinning in so many directions and it's hard to stay focused.

"You're right. You're right. I feel better now."

"We can start sabotaging Ryan right away, though." Ari laughs. "I don't like what a doofus he's becoming to you. He used to be nice."

"He did, right?" I ask. "Now he's like a champion doofus. Like he won a contest against all the doofusy guys in the world."

Ari laughs and then yawns. "Okay, I'm going to sleep now. For real."

"For real for real?" I cozy up under Ari's pink comforter, trying to get ready for sleep, too.

She laughs. "Yes. For real. For real."

Five minutes later, I flip to my other side and see that Ari's wide-awake, staring at the ceiling.

"I can't sleep," she says.

"Me neither." I push down the comforter and throw my legs on top of it. "I never knew that you, like, wanted to get detention. Is that something you've been thinking about for a long time?"

She hoists herself up on one elbow. "Oh, well, it's just that we've spent so long being perfect, doing everything our moms ask us to. Ya know?"

I nod. "It's true. We do always follow the rules. I mean, remember in fourth grade when I got in trouble for talking and I had to go five minutes late to lunch? I practically passed out from the stress."

"Exactly!" Ari lies back down. "This will help us handle when bad things happen. Like, we'll get in trouble, but we'll be able to deal with it. And we won't do anything really bad. We won't cheat on a test or publicly humiliate anyone," she explains.

"Okay, we won't publicly humiliate anyone. Except Ryan, of course." I laugh and then get quiet.

"What?" she asks.

"Truthfully, the detention thing makes me nervous." I lie back down. "That's not really me, ya know? I think I'm okay with being a rule follower."

"It'll be okay." She pats my shoulder. "We won't get expelled or do anything that will end up on your permanent record."

"Okay, I'll trust you," I say. "For now. *Dun dun dun*."

"Kaylan! Of course you can trust me." She throws one of the smaller pillows at my head.

"Ouch!" I throw it back at her. "And kissing, um, that is scary, too. I have no idea how to kiss!"

"Well, duh, because you haven't done it," Ari says. "I mean, I guess everything is scary before you do it."

I stare at Ari's ceiling fan, spinning around and around

and around. "Does anyone know how to kiss before they actually do it? I mean, there isn't a kissing course you can take. YouTube videos?"

"Ew, Kaylan! That sounds really gross." She elbows me. "Can we please go to sleep now?"

"Fine. Good night." I cover my face with the pillow. I guess I have time to figure all of this out. Until November, at least.

And it's not like I have the boy picked out. A first kiss can't be with just any old boy. It has to be with someone special. Someone meaningful.

I hope.

EIGHT

"JASON! HEY!" ARI CALLS AS we're walking through the pool gate. Big, puffy clouds are overhead, but I don't really mind it. Sometimes I need a break from the sun.

We're late today because I had my annual checkup with Dr. Noodleman. It went fine, but getting to the pool this late is like against my religion. I didn't have a choice; my mom made the appointment. I hope no one stole our lounge chairs. Jason's up ahead and I don't think he hears her. "Jason!"

"What's going on?" I whisper. "Neighbor Boy? You talked?"

"Yeah, he's chatty. I'll explain later," she says to me, under her breath.

He turns around, finally, and gives us a wave. Then he

does this weird thing where he walks backward to get to us. I keep expecting him to trip over one of the plants or the pool noodles that are left lying around, but he's actually kind of good at it.

"Arianna! My neighbor!" He reaches out to hug her. Is this a thing new neighbors do now? Just reach out and hug each other?

They pull apart from the hug and Ari makes a confused face at me.

I shrug, trying to indicate that I don't have a clue what's going on either.

"Jason, this is Kaylan," Ari says, pointing at me. "Kaylan, this is Jason."

I nod. "I got that, from the 'Jason! Hey!'"

He bursts out laughing.

"Nice to meet you," I say.

"Same! Listen, I gotta run ahead. I said I'd play in the water volleyball game." He reaches a hand up to high-five both of us. "Catch you later, though?"

We nod, and mumble *later*. Didn't he just move here? How is he already in a league at the pool? Everything surrounding Jason is very mysterious.

We stop in the bathroom to make sure our bathing suits are on correctly. I turn to Ari at the full-length mirror. "You didn't tell me you talked to Neighbor Boy!"

"I know." She inspects her hair, still thinking about the highlights, I'm guessing. "It happened this morning. He was outside playing basketball while my mom was having her coffee on the porch. And then the moms started talking, and you know how it is. . . ."

"He seems nice. Friendly."

Ari loosens her towel so she can tighten it again, and that's when I see the bathing suit that she's wearing.

"What?" she asks, when she notices me looking at her.

"A boobage bikini?" I shriek.

"Shhhh." She hits me on the arm with her sunscreen tube. "Stop!"

"I can't believe you're wearing that," I shout-whisper.

"I know." She spins around in a circle, showing it off. "I just found it, and all my other suits were dirty, so I figured, why not?"

I shrug.

"Why? Does it look bad?" she asks.

"No. It looks great." I pick my backpack up off the floor. "I just can't believe you're actually wearing it! Can we go to our lounges now? We need to decide what we're doing first on the list."

"Highlights. Duh," Ari says as we leave the bathroom. "We already know where to get it done. We want to have a fresh look for middle school. And we can't wait too long to do it, because what if it turns out completely horrible and then we need to have it fixed before school starts?"

"Yeah, but hello—major obstacle in our way." I glare at her as we walk to the lounges. "Well, two, I guess."

Our moms.

"Okay, here's the plan," Ari says, once we're comfy on our lounge chairs. "We'll all go together. We'll get lunch first. You talk to your mom at dinner tonight and I'll talk to my mom. We need to really stress the fact that this is going to be a bonding experience for us and our moms."

"They do love lunching with us," I add, feeling grateful that Ari always has a plan.

"I know," Ari continues, "they love to do anything with us." She laughs. "I mean, are we even that great?" She turns to me.

"Um, yes!" I look up to the lifeguard chair; Tyler isn't there. "We are amazing."

"You're right. We are."

I ask, "Your mom dyes her hair, right?"

"Yeah, for sure. Yours does, too, right?"

I nod.

"So obviously they'll let us do it," Ari says all matter-of-factly. "They really can't say no. And I mean, we're just going for highlights. Nothing even that crazy."

After ice cream sandwiches and three games of Would You Rather, Ari and I are back on our lounges.

She elbows me when some of the bikini boobage girls walk by. That girl Cara is with them. "Look at her hair," Ari says through her teeth. "I want mine to look exactly like that."

I look over, and think about it for a second. "Yeah, it

looks really good. I see what you mean." Suddenly I get a bubbly stomach—like all of our hopes and dreams are wrapped up in our hair.

"Hey, Ari," Jules says, walking by with a crew of two girls and two boys. I wait for her to say hi to me, but she doesn't. Does she even remember that we met?

I pretend to be really busy with something on my phone.

"Hey," Ari says back.

"By the way, I heard my friends who are going to West Brookside got their schedules," Jules tells Ari. "So when you get yours, let me know. I'll hook you guys up!"

"Oh, cool, thanks!" Ari smiles, stretching out her legs.

"Oh, I love that bathing suit!" Jules squeals. "Where did you get it?"

Ari laughs. "I just found it in the back of my drawer. . . ."

I roll my eyes but try not to make it visible. Who is this Jules girl, and why is she always around all of a sudden?

Right then, as if it's a signal from God, I hear the loudest crash of thunder I've ever heard in my entire life. And then the heavens open up, and in three seconds we're completely soaked with rain.

Jules and her friends cover their heads with their arms and scurry over to their lounges.

"Brookside Pool is closing early due to thunder," we hear Joey say over the loudspeaker. "Stay safe, my friends."

"Run!" Ari screams, grabbing all of her things. "Come on!"

I stuff everything in my backpack and follow her, and soon we're sprinting home, flip-flops falling off, mud painting the backs of our legs, our towels stuck to our bodies.

"Come to my house; it's closer," I say, as we're running through the rain.

"This is terrible!" Ari screams. "I can't even see!"

"We're almost there," I shout, wiping the rain off my face with my arm.

"Do you want to come in?" I ask her. "I can lend you clothes."

"I think I'm just gonna go home. I'm already soaked." She reaches out for an air hug. "So you know the plan?"

"Yup."

"Good. Call me as soon as you finish dinner. You guys always eat later than we do. If all goes according to plan, we will be making hair appointments first thing tomorrow morning." She does her little Ari excited dance.

I nod. My stomach swishes as I walk inside my house. We're just talking about highlights here. I need to get hold of myself.

"Kaylan, thank God you're home. That was some storm!" My mom's wearing an apron, peering out the window. "Although it seems to have stopped now. Weird. How was the pool? Before the rain, I mean."

"Fine." I smile. "How was your day?"

I remind myself to be extra-nice.

"Busy, but good." She kisses me on the forehead. "Okay, go change into some dry clothes. Dinner will be ready in a half hour."

I can smell Mom's spaghetti and meatballs. "Mom, dinner smells great!" I call as I'm running up the stairs.

As soon as I get up to my room, a basketball hits my window.

"Sorry, Kaylan," I hear someone yell.

It's Tyler. He's outside with Ryan and they're soaking wet. A tiny little part of me perks up, more excited for dinner than I was just a few moments ago.

My heart does that pat-pat-flutter-flutter thing it always seems to do now when I'm around Tyler.

I wonder if he was at our house this much before and I just didn't notice it. It seems like he's here all the time now. Maybe he moved into the basement and no one told me.

I change into my faded-on-purpose gray V-neck and my favorite cutoffs. Normally I'd just wear a big night-shirt for dinner after coming home from the pool and a rainstorm, but with Tyler here, I feel like I have to at least look sort of normal and maybe even a little bit cute.

I'm coming down the stairs for dinner when I hear Tyler say, "Later, Mrs. T."

I open my mouth to say good-bye to him, but no words

come out. My whole body feels sulky after that. Disappointed about something I'd only just started to care about.

I take a deep breath and prepare.

I can do this. I can convince my mom that not only should I be allowed to get highlights but that they're a good idea. And she's excited about it, too.

Ryan's changed into dry clothes, and he sits down at the table and continues texting. He doesn't look at me or my mom, even after she brings over a steaming bowl of spaghetti and the pot of meatballs in the sauce.

"Ry, put down the phone," Mom says, sounding tired. "Please."

"One minute!" he yells.

We stare at him and he finally puts the phone in his pocket.

"Thank you," Mom mouths, and I wonder why she's letting him talk to her like that. I want to call her out on it, but I let it go. I can't upset her. The time for buttering Mom up starts now.

"Mom, your hair looks amazing," I say, nodding to help my words seem more believable. "Did you get it cut today or something?"

She gives it a gentle stroke. "No, I didn't even wash it today." She laughs a little and scoops some meatballs and spaghetti onto my plate, and then some onto Ryan's. "Must be the natural oils working their magic."

"Could be," I say with enthusiasm.

"Speaking of haircuts," my mom says, "Ryan, what's happening with your hair? It's in your eyes. We gotta do something about this."

"I'm letting it grow," he mumbles with food in his mouth.

"Forever?" I shriek. That would look beyond gross; he'd probably never wash it.

"Not forever, dimwit." He puts down his fork. "But for a while. I think I'll look cool with long hair. And I'm trying out for the jam band. I need to have the right look."

"Jam band?" I ask.

"I play guitar," he says, like I didn't already know that. "Tryouts are next week. That way we can start practicing as soon as school starts."

The way he talks—it all sounds so passionate and intense. Like he actually thinks he's going to be a professional guitarist or something. Part of me feels bad for him because he's honestly not that good. Like when someone has food stuck in their teeth and you're not sure if you should tell them or not.

I need to get this dinner conversation away from Ryan's hair and on to my need for highlights.

"Well, you'll need a trim," Mom says after a sip of water. "You can't start school with hair in your eyes like that. You won't be able to see the board, your papers, the computer, your music for jam band—"

"Mom, I get it," Ryan groans. "Let's just drop it for now. I thought you guys would be more excited about me trying out for the band. Guess not."

He looks down into his plate. Sulking. It's a forced sulk. I can tell.

"Ry, we are excited," Mom says and then looks at me. "Right, Kaylan?"

"Right. I'm so excited," I force.

But I'm not excited at all. Ryan's terrible on guitar and now I'm going to have to hear him practicing 24-7. "And actually, speaking of hair . . ."

I pause for a second and smile, trying to give everyone the feeling that we're on the same team, looking out for each other, encouraging new hairstyles.

"Yes?" Mom asks.

"Well, Mom, I thought that this Saturday, you, me, Ari, and her mom could have a really special girls' day—ya know, lunch, walking around in town, stuff like that, and then Ari and I could get our hair highlighted." I run the last part together really fast.

"Wait." Mom side-eyes me. "Say that again."

"She wants to get her hair highlighted," Ryan groans, scooping more food onto his plate. "Obviously she realizes she looks horrible and is causing everyone she sees to go blind, and needs to do something to fix herself."

"Ryan," Mom warns. "Stop that talk this instant."

"It was more than that," I mumble and try to ignore

Ryan. I turn to face my mom. "Ari and I want to have a girls' day with our moms! We want to spend time with you guys! And we want to get highlights. Nothing crazy. Just a little bit of a change before we start middle school."

"Oh, Kaylan, I don't know. . . ." She sighs. "You're only eleven. That seems awfully young for hair dye. Doesn't it?"

I'm not sure who she's asking. Clearly I don't think it's young. And Ryan doesn't care. My dad's not here, but he never paid any attention to hair rites of passage. I guess she's asking herself. Or asking the universe. Does the universe care about highlights? I doubt it.

"Eleven is not too young for highlights," I answer, finally. "Plus they have organic, like, healthier hair dye. I checked. And honestly, I know tons of girls who have gotten highlights. That girl Cara from the pool. Remember her? Mrs. Etisof's daughter even got highlights when she was younger! Middle school is a time for change, new starts. You need to realize that I'm not a baby anymore."

Her face sinks a little bit after I say that, and I'm instantly plagued with guilt. I shouldn't have said that. Not now. Not after she's had a tiring day at work. "I mean, I'm eleven. Ya know? I'm getting older." I put an arm around her and whisper, "But I'll always be your baby."

Sometimes you have to tell a mom what she wants to hear.

Especially when you're trying to get what you want.

NINE

OUR MOMS DECIDE TO HAVE a face-to-face chat about the highlights on Saturday morning. They've talked on the phone about it, but apparently that's not enough. Moms tend to overdiscuss things. I wonder if I'll be like that when I'm a mom. Maybe it's something that just happens to you as soon as you have a baby.

When Ari and her mom ring the doorbell, I make sure the muffins are artfully arranged on a plate and our tea box is open. Ari's mom's a tea drinker. My mom is a 100 percent coffee drinker, but she has this fancy box of tea she received as a Secret Santa gift once. (She had a really bad Secret Santa that year, but whatever.) So we bring it out for guests.

I want to do all that I can to make this highlights thing happen. It's the first thing on our list. If we can't reach our first goal, I'm not sure we can do the others, either.

The moms sit down in the living room, and Ari and I go up to my room.

"I typed up the list and made two copies," Ari says, unzipping her backpack. "And then I begged my dad to take it to work and get it laminated. He agreed."

She hands me a hot-pink, laminated piece of paper with our list printed in a pretty curlicue font.

"Everything is better laminated," I tell her. "Don't you think?"

She cracks up. "Where do you get this stuff, Kay? You have, like, a treasure chest of random sayings in your brain."

"Brain treasures!" I laugh. "That's me!"

"So our deadline is November second," Ari reminds me.

"Your twelfth birthday," I reply, as if she doesn't know.

She continues. "Right. We need to give ourselves the extra day for my birthday, because otherwise I'll still be eleven when we finish, ya know?"

It always seemed like twelve-year-olds were really independent—they could ride bikes all over town, wherever they wanted to go. They could stay home alone, too. Maybe even be allowed to order pizza. Plus kayaking—our parents always said we could paddle to Arch Island by ourselves when we turned twelve. It sort of seemed like they pulled that age out of nowhere, but whatever, we remembered it. And we're taking it to the next level—we're going to kayak at night.

Twelve is the dream age.

"I'm just getting this feeling," I start. "Like if we don't do the list, everything on it, something bad will happen." I sit down on my bed, and Ari follows.

Fake-spooked, she says, "Like what? We turn into elves or something?"

I laugh and shake my head. "No, I mean, nothing weird like that. But, like, we fail middle school. We're social pariahs. Ya know?"

Ari rolls her eyes. "Why are you so freakishly superstitious? You're just making it up!"

"My grandma really believes this kind of stuff, and so I do, too." I shrug. "Maybe I'm wrong! But maybe not. . . ." I tap my fingers against each other. "Come on. Let's go eavesdrop on our moms and see if they're coming around to the highlights."

"Ooh! Good idea!"

We open the door to my room, careful to do it slowly so it doesn't creak. I've had a creaky door forever, and nothing has made it uncreaky. My dad tried to fix it, but I realized at a pretty young age that he's just not so good at fixing things.

Ryan sees us right away. "Why do you guys look like you just broke a lamp?" he asks, all sweaty. He has that terrible, outdoorsy-metal-y smell, and I almost gag.

"Broke a lamp?" I cover my mouth to try and get Ryan

to stop talking and also to avoid the stench.

"You two are crazy," he says. "I'm going to Tyler's to shoot hoops. Tell Mom. Bye."

I nod, grateful that he's leaving the house with that stink.

We make it to the top of the stairs, and put our ears against the railing.

"It went so fast, didn't it?" I hear my mom say. My throat tingles. Sometimes I look at my mom and feel bad for her. I think she really enjoyed having little kids, and we're not little anymore. There's nothing anyone can do about that.

"It did," Ari's mom says. "I try to hold on to Gemma staying little as hard as I can."

Ari rolls her eyes. "Oh, here we go. They're not even discussing highlights!"

"What should we do?" I whisper.

Ari thinks for a minute. "We need to prove we're responsible and grown-up." She looks at me.

"You're right, that's definitely a thing that moms look for." I look around to think of something.

"Any chores that need doing?" Ari asks, hands on her hips.

"Chores, hmmm." I know my mom asks me to do stuff all the time, but at that second, nothing is coming to me.

"Oh!" Ari says too loud, and then covers her mouth. "Your mom has been asking you to go through the toys in the basement and sort them into bags so you can donate them."

"I love how you remembered that and I didn't." I cover my face in embarrassment. "Genius, Ari!"

Ari brushes the hair away from her face. "We can start that, and we don't have to do it all today." She looks down at the list. "And that falls into the help-humanity category, too. Doesn't it?"

"I think it does!"

We tiptoe down the stairs to the first floor and then down the flight to the basement. Our moms are still gabbing away about motherhood and who knows what else. I don't even think they notice us.

"Wow, it really is a mess down here," Ari says.

"Thanks, Ar." I roll my eyes. "That's why my mom has been begging Ryan and me to clean it up. We've been avoiding it, obviously."

Ari walks around and surveys the scene. "Okay, go grab some garbage bags and let's get started. But some things you need to save." She picks up a crate of Barbie dolls. "Like these. Your daughter could play with them, the same way I play with my mom's Barbies."

"Okay. That's true."

I run up the stairs to get the garbage bags from under the kitchen sink, and I hear my mom say, "We should let them get the highlights. I'm sure the ladies at Ambiance will know to keep it on the mild side."

"Oh, I'm sure," Ari's mom replies.

My heart flutters around like a butterfly. They're saying yes! We're getting the highlights! I don't know if I should tell Ari or let her be surprised.

We would have survived if they had said no, but the fact that they're saying yes symbolizes a huge victory! They're seeing us as mature and grown-up. They understand that we need to have a new look for middle school.

We're accomplishing our goals!

I grab the garbage bag and run downstairs, all hyped up to organize these toys.

Ari sees the huge smile on my face. "What's up?" she asks.

"Oh, nothing."

"Kaylan! You're lying! What is it?"

I shake my head and put some old Disney figurines into one of the garbage bags.

"Did you just see Tyler?" Ari asks.

I'm caught off guard. "Huh? No. Why?"

"That smile on your face," she says. "It's weird. I've only noticed it after Tyler has been around."

"Not at all," I reply. She's noticed that? I don't even know what that means. "I don't know what you're talking about. I heard our moms talking when I went to get the garbage bags."

"And?" Ari asks.

It's mean, but sometimes I like to have her sweat

things out a little bit. She's so calm that it's good to see her get a little nervous every once in a while.

"Tell me, Kaylan!"

"They're gonna say yes!"

We dance in place and do a silent cheer for a second. And then I say, "I guess we still need to organize these toys, huh?"

"Yeah, we should," Ari says.

"Okay, let's find a way to make it fun," I tell her. "I'll hold out the trash bags, and you throw stuff in." I turn up the music on my phone—a playlist I made called Summer Sensations.

Ari throws in a miniature poodle figurine. "Score!" she shouts when she makes it in.

"What are you girls doing down here?" my mom asks us, coming down the stairs. "You haven't played in the basement in forever."

We stand with our hands on our hips, letting them see for themselves.

"You're organizing the toys?" my mom shrieks. "Really?"

"Well, you did ask me to do it, like, three weeks ago, and you asked Ryan, too, and he hasn't touched his side. . . ."

My mom comes over to me and wraps her arms around my shoulders. "Thank you, Kaylan." She rubs her eyes, and I realize she's crying. Whoa. Too much. "Sometimes I feel like no one listens to me around here."

Okay, really too much. Way, way, way too much. Especially with Ari and her mom here.

"Mom, it's okay. I know I'm the best daughter in the world. We all do." I laugh a little to break the awkwardness that's spiraling around in the air. "And I do listen to you."

I bulge my eyes at Ari, who looks a little concerned and a little confused.

My mom sniffles and says, "Okay, well, I'm very impressed with the work that's being done here. Thanks, Ari, for your help. And we've decided that we'll let you girls get the highlights."

"You will?" I pretend to act surprised, and Ari does, too.

The moms nod.

"Yay!" We shriek. "Thank you. Thank you so so much!"

"And the cherry on the sundae," Ari's mom adds, "is that we can go this afternoon."

"What?" Ari and I grab hands and jump up and down.

"We called the salon, and they happened to have a cancellation," Ari's mom continues.

After a few more minutes of jumping and talking, our moms head upstairs.

"That felt almost too easy," I say to Ari, when I'm confident our moms are out of earshot. "I thought it was gonna be way harder to convince them. When it's easy, does it count as much? I mean, I know it's the first thing we've done, but . . . ya know? Do the things on the list need to be hard to accomplish?"

We squint our eyes at each other, feeling all suspicious.

"Yeah, and I mean, it's helping your mom, which is great, obvs. And she is human, but do you think we should be helping more of humanity? Like beyond our immediate families?"

I shrug. "Maybe, but what if we never think of anything else we can do that counts as helping humanity?" I ask.

"Relax, Kay." She puts her hands on my shoulders. "We just had a major victory. We're gonna figure this out."

I need to trust her. I'm too excited about the highlights for anything to get in the way of that.

TEN

OUR MOMS MAKE A WHOLE plan to take us to lunch at Fleetwood before our hair appointments. It's this old-fashioned ice cream parlor that has sandwiches, too, and it's the best restaurant in the world. Honestly. It's been featured on all those Food Network shows, and there's usually a line out the door.

But my mom grew up living next door to the owner—so we have connections.

Take 'em where you can get 'em, ya know.

"Girls, this is so lovely," Ari's mom says as soon as we've ordered. She folds her hands on the table and smiles at each of us. She'd probably make a good politician. I swear she's always smiling.

I lean over to sip my root beer and wait for someone else to say something.

"It's just a treat to spend time together," my mom adds. "We're all so busy these days, running around and everything."

I nod. "Well, thanks for taking us."

"Yeah, thank you," Ari adds.

After that awkward moment of appreciation, the moms start discussing some battle that took place at the PTA meeting over standardized tests.

Ari takes the list out of her backpack and rests it on her pants leg.

"Sometimes I just like to look at it," she says. "To remind myself of its awesomeness."

"I agree," I whisper, and look up to make sure the moms are still deep in their boring conversation. I put my arm around Ari, and we gaze at her list together like it's a beautiful painting.

"What should we do after highlights?" I ask Ari. "We need to figure out the next most important thing to do before middle school starts. Ya know?"

She looks down at the list and back up at our moms, to make sure they're not listening to us. "Shhh. They can't hear this."

I put a finger to my lip. "Right."

"Definitely guy friend," Ari says. "I mean, maybe it's Jason? He's nice, right? And he lives across the street?"

I nod. "Yeah. And we should save first kiss for near the

end, because, like, we'll meet new people when school starts—"

"Who's talking about a first kiss?" my mom asks. Our heads jolt up.

"Ummm," I reply. "Oh, not us. . . . These girls at the pool were all talking about it. . . ."

"And?" Ari's mom asks. "I think my first kiss was when I was eleven. I was at camp, and it was after Israeli Dancing, Louis Goldfarb—"

"Mom!" Ari shrieks, reaching across the table to smack her hand. "Stop!"

"Ari," her mom warns, laughing. "It's okay. . . . We're your mothers. You can talk to us. Right, Kaylan?"

"Well." I sip my water and try to think of something to say. "To be honest, I think we'd rather discuss something a little more intellectual, maybe the upcoming midterm election?" I pause and wait for laughter. "The rising prices at Starbucks?"

My mom laughs and shakes her head at me. "Oh, Kaylan." She looks at Ari's mom. "Always with the jokes. Always with the jokes."

Ari and I glare at each other, silently praying this conversation is over.

"What are you guys looking at?" Ari's mom asks, peering under the table.

"What?" My voice catches, heart pounding.

"What are you two plotting? What is that list?" Ari's mom's eyebrows curve inward.

Ari kicks me under the table. "Oh, just a list of things to get before middle school, like new backpack, new shoes, binders . . ." I nod like she has no choice but to believe her. "Just a to-do list."

"Yeah, we made it together. Just stuff we need to get ready." I look over at my mom.

She crinkles her eyes like she doesn't believe us. "Okay, well, we'll talk about what you need," she says. "And you know we're always here for you."

Ari and I look down at our feet. Why is this food taking so long?

Ari's mom adds, "Some girls aren't lucky enough to be close with their mothers, and it's very important, especially at this challenging time—"

"Mom," Ari groans for the millionth time. "Please."

"Ladies, enjoy your lunches," the waiter says, putting down our plates.

Finally!

"Thank you so much!" I say to the waiter, tempted to get up and hug him. "Really, thank you! This looks amazing!"

After sandwiches, sodas, and an ice cream sundae with four spoons, we head straight to the salon.

"Let's do this," I say.

Ari high-fives me. "Highlights, here we come!"

We arrive a few minutes before our appointments. Our moms sit on the leather couch and read magazines while they wait for us. I decide on blond highlights and Ari decides on red.

My hair is brown, but it has hints of blond, so I feel like the highlights will only help accentuate what's already there.

We sit side by side as the stylists paint our hair with the highlights and then cover them with foil.

"Eeep," I squeak and grab Ari's hand. "This is really happening."

"Do you think we're going to look so different?" she asks me. "Like, will people freak out at school? They're gonna notice we have a new look, right?"

I think about it for a second before I answer. "Ummm. I think people will notice, if that's what you're asking. I think Brooke and Lily will be totally jealous."

Ari looks down at her feet.

I look over to make eye contact, and Gina, my hair-stylist, keeps trying to push my head back.

"Keep your head back, sweetie," she says.

It's kind of hard to talk during this process. And it's a challenge to keep my head still.

"I mean, I don't care what they think. But ya know, they'll just be jealous."

"Right," Ari says. "Totally."

"Sweetie," Gina starts. "Every time you talk, your head

moves, and I'm worried this is going to come out uneven. So maybe let's stay quiet for a little bit."

I can't argue with the woman making my whole back-to-school look perfect, so silence it is.

It's kind of nice to have quiet. To daydream about my new look and how awesome it's going to be.

Good-bye, Elementary School Kaylan.

Hello, new and improved Middle School Kaylan.

ELEVEN

WE SPEND THE REST OF the evening staring at our-selves in the mirror in my room. I'm not even kidding. We just can't tear our eyes away from the magic that is blond highlights and the power that is red highlights.

"We look so much more grown-up," Ari says, for the billionth time. "We do, right? I'm not just making that up, right?"

"Oh, totally," I say, still staring at myself. "Honestly, we're really beautiful. I mean, we always were, but now, it's like there's just no denying it."

"Sorry to burst your bubble, ladies." Ryan appears out of nowhere, standing in the doorway to my room. "But it's gonna take a lot more than highlights to make you two look grown-up and beautiful."

He bursts out laughing after that, and throws a Nerf

ball at me. But he's not so good at throwing, and instead of hitting me, it hits the glass of fruit punch on my desk, and it spills all over the new white shirt mom bought me for the first day of school and directly onto the 11 Before 12 List.

"Shoot!" I say, grabbing gobs of tissues and trying to mop it up. Thank God it's laminated! "That's it," I say. "We're moving number eleven to the top of the list."

"Number eleven?" Ari asks, slightly confused. She's still staring at herself, stroking her hair. I wouldn't be surprised if she didn't even realize what just happened with Ryan.

I put my hands on her shoulders to reel her back in. "Ari! Why aren't you paying attention? Fruit punch just spilled on my shirt and on the list, and you didn't even notice!"

"Sorry," she says half-heartedly. "I just love these highlights."

"Sabotaging Ryan," I remind her. "It needs to happen. It needs to happen now."

"Okay." She smiles. "I'm game."

I guess not much is at stake when it comes to Ari and Ryan. But for me a lot is at stake. He cannot just, like, go on treating me this way, being the biggest jerk in the entire world, and then, nothing happens. Come on.

Enough is enough.

"So what's your sabotage plan?" she asks, finally

tearing herself away from the mirror.

"Jam band tryouts are next week," I tell her. "Ryan really wants this. Really, really wants this. He's even growing his hair out for it."

"And?" Ari asks.

"We'll cut a guitar string when he's asleep tonight." I raise my eyebrows. "Hide his extra strings."

"Really, Kay?" Ari chews her bottom lip and looks at me sideways. "So won't this ruin his chances of making it?"

"Well, maybe, if he's not smart enough to practice before. If he practices, he'll notice the broken string, and he can use his allowance to buy more. And he'll be fine."

"And if he doesn't?" Ari asks.

"He'll learn an important lesson!"

She shrugs. "I dunno, just kinda seems mean."

"Well, sabotage is sabotage, ya know?" I pause. "And a broken string isn't the end of the world. Like, he could still make it work. But it will mess up his audition. Make him all flustered and stuff."

"I guess," she says and goes back to the mirror.

"Since when do you have such a guilty conscience?" I ask her. "Remember that sleepover when Gemma wouldn't stop playing the electronic saxophone that sounded like a dying cat?"

"Yeah . . ." Ari laughs.

"You didn't feel guilty about hiding that from your sister!"

"It was the worst sound in the world," Ari defends. "I guess you know what you're doing."

Later that night, when I can't fall asleep, I go back and forth about cutting Ryan's guitar string.

Ari's sleeping soundly next to me, so I can't even talk to her about my dilemma.

I feel so good about my highlights that I don't want to do anything to hurt anyone. The world feels beautiful and perfect.

But then I remember how mean he's been to me, the lies about middle school, how he ruined the shirt Mom paid full price to get me.

I'm gonna do it.

He needs to learn he can't get everything he wants.

Plus it's on the list. And crossing things off a list feels really, really good.

I can't do this alone, though. I mean, it's on the list— it's required that we do it together.

"Ari," I whisper.

No response.

"Ari." I nudge her shoulder.

She groans, "I'm sleeeeping."

"I know. But it's time. The next thing on our list," I remind her. "We gotta do it."

She jolts up, and rubs her eyes. "Fine. But I'm only doing this because it's on the list. And I am loyal to the list." She fist-pounds me. "Got it?"

"Loyal to the list. Got it."

We tiptoe out of my room, careful not to wake anyone. We walk down the stairs as quietly as possible. The tiniest tap makes the loudest creak, like the entire staircase is going to collapse.

We make it to the bottom of the staircase without anyone waking up. I tiptoe into the den and find Ryan's guitar leaning against the wall. He was too lazy to even put it in the case. We're not supposed to just leave our stuff lying all around. Mom's told us that a billion times.

"What was that?" I gasp, looking in all directions when I feel like someone is watching us.

"What?" Ari whispers. "I burped. Sorry. Too much soda."

"Eww, Ari!" I whisper-yell. "Gross. And too risky! Hand me the scissors!"

"You sure about this?" she whispers.

I nod, and look around again.

"Now you have the hiccups! At a time like this." I put a finger to my lips as if that will get her to quiet down.

As quickly as I can, I clip a little off the edge of one of the strings. It's so subtle I doubt he'll notice. Not until it's too late—when he gets to the tryouts and it won't tune and his whole audition is messed up.

Perfect.

"Come on, let's go back up, *quietly!*"

She shakes her head at me as we tiptoe up the stairs. "I'm being as quiet as possible." A little laugh bursts out of her mouth, and then a little laugh pops out of mine, and soon we're almost full-on laughing.

"Stop!" I roll my lips together.

My heart is racing faster than it has ever raced before, and every second I think I hear something—my mom's door opening, Ryan's video games. We are totally going to get caught.

We walk into my room and collapse on the bed. Just in time, because a second later Ryan's door opens and he goes into the bathroom.

We're cracking up completely when we get back into my room. We cover our faces with pillows to tone it down.

When we catch our breath, Ari says, "We should have some kind of ritual. I mean, for after we've checked something off the list."

"Yeah?" I look at her.

"I know we didn't do it with the highlights, but I was just thinking. . . . Wouldn't that be cool?"

I sit down on the bed and rub my eyes. I feel like I could sleep for a billion years, but this is an important thing, and I want to think of something good. "What should it be?"

"I got it," she says, lying down. "It's an expanded version of what we already do. So, jump in the air, high-five, and then hug."

"Let's try it," I whisper. "But quietly."

We stand up and jump, softly high-five, and then quickly pull in for a hug.

"Amazing!" I whisper.

Ari shakes her head. "No. Beyond amazing!"

We're finally back in bed, all cozy under the covers. But I can't fall asleep. I'm psyched about our new ritual. And I'm in love with my highlights. But I have an aching pit in my stomach. It's like a combination of a stomach flu, cramps, and extreme agita. It's terrible. So terrible that even my perfect highlights aren't making me happy.

What have I done?

TWELVE

POOL AT NOON? I TEXT Ari. She's been gone for five days on this Hebrew School camping trip. Five whole days, and now we only have ten days before school starts.

It wasn't like camping in tents, she said. It was just, like, at a camp. A bonding experience, and maybe some of the kids will go there next summer.

I prayed the whole time she was gone that she hated it, and that she'll never go back, because these five days without her have been the longest five days of my life. The most boring, too.

Lunch, swim, work on the list? I text again, when I don't hear back from her.

Deal, she finally writes back.

I grab a clean towel out of the dryer on the way out and stuff it in my backpack.

"Be careful you don't blind everyone at the pool with that hideous bathing suit," Ryan says to me when I'm almost at the door.

"Well, your BO could kill an entire country, so I think that's the more important thing to focus on." I turn around and stare at him. "No wonder you didn't make the jam band. Your smell killed everyone!"

I get a niggling feeling that I do my best to squelch. It's his own fault he didn't make it, since he didn't even think he needed to practice. If he'd at least tried to practice, he'd have noticed the broken string. And he would have made sure he had the extras.

"You're evil," he says. "And ugly!"

I slam the door in his face.

On the walk over, I put Ryan's cruel behavior out of my head in order to do a little soul-searching. We have a little less than two weeks until school starts, and I focus on what's really most important on the list. I mean, I wonder what's going to make the biggest impact when we start school? We want to make a splash. We want to have stories to tell. Saying we hung out at the neighborhood pool all summer isn't very exciting. Highlights are cool and everything, but we need more.

We have a once-in-a-lifetime opportunity to make this first impression at middle school. We need to figure out who we want to be, what impact we want to leave on the world.

That's why this Whole Me Makeover is so important.

I look over the list again. And then right as I walk through the gate to the pool, tacked up on the bulletin board is an advertisement. It's new—I've never noticed it before, and I look at this bulletin board every single day.

TWEEN YOGA CLASS. BEGINNERS WELCOME.
7 p.m. at the Community Center on September 4

Clearly, the universe has an opinion here. This is the "thing we might hate" that we need to try! And it's something that will help us—well, me—calm down at the same time.

An essential part of the Whole Me Makeover.

Perfect.

And if there's a guy there who can become my new guy friend, or maybe even my first kiss, even better.

I think I'd call that a terrific trio—when one event fulfills three items on the list!

I show Ari the sign as soon as she gets to the pool, and we discuss it over burgers at the snack bar.

Ari thinks about it for a second and then says, "Ya know, they always say 'beginners welcome,' but the thing is, I bet the people in this class are going to be, like, professional yoga people, or yogis, or whatever they're called." Ari takes a bite and continues, "Maybe we should hire a private teacher for our first class, just to help get us started. Or watch YouTube videos or something. So we go in knowing at least a little bit about yoga."

"Come on, Ar." I roll my eyes. "We're gonna be fine. Since when are you afraid of not being as good as other people at anything? What's the worst that happens? We leave the class and never do it again. I mean, it's not like everyone at our new school is going to know we went to yoga and totally stunk at it."

"I know, but I'm scared. I've literally never done yoga before!" Ari deep-sighs. "And what if people laugh at us the way the boobage girls laughed at Freeze Dance?"

I think about that for a second. "Well, I feel like yoga is generally a kind sport . . . or practice. Is it a sport?" I shrug.

She stares at me. "See! This is going to be awful!"

"I know, that's why it's the thing we think we might hate!" I put some more ketchup on my fries.

"I don't know, maybe." She slumps over to the trash can to throw away the remnants from her burger.

After lunch, we go back to the lounge chairs for some sunshine and relaxation. We've pretty much gotten our pool days down to perfection. It's going to be hard to leave this amazing routine and go back to the early-rising, homework-filled, exhausting school routine.

This yoga is essential for our survival.

"Look at it this way: this yoga class is just for kids our age. We could make our new friends there, too. The friends we'll invite to the birthday bash. This yoga class could be a terrific trio."

Ari laughs. "What?"

"When one event fulfills three things!" I explain.

Ari laughs at me, passing me the bottle of sunblock. "I know you're excited, but we can't assume yoga is going to change our entire lives. And I'm not sure it's worth risking, like, mega-embarrassment."

I nod and turn onto my side. Something's going on in Ari's mind, and she's not telling me what it is. She's anxious. Nervous. This is not the Ari I know. I wonder if something happened on the Hebrew School trip?

I want to ask her what's up, but I feel like I should let it go for now. Maybe she'll come around and tell me herself. Maybe she's waiting for the right moment, when there aren't other people around.

I close my eyes, all set to take a perfect afternoon lounge-chair nap. Lounge-chair naps are the best kind of naps. Except for maybe hammock naps. But since there aren't any hammocks at the pool, lounge chairs really get the job done.

I'm drifting off to sleep, in the state of half awake/half asleep, when I feel someone standing over us. I turn to see if Ari's awake, but her mouth is hanging open, the way it always does when she's in a deep sleep.

I squint one eye open to see who it is.

Jason.

He's taller than I'd originally thought, or maybe it's just because he's standing over me. He's wearing a bright-orange bathing suit and a Mets T-shirt.

"Hi?"

"Oh, um, hi." I laugh.

He laughs, too, and then eyes me suspiciously. I feel like we're communicating through weird eye movements and it's kind of fun, but also feels a little creepy.

"You're Keely, um, no, that's not it. Kay—?"

"Kaylan," I say.

"I haven't seen you in a while," he says, like we're long-lost friends.

"Um." I look over at Ari, who's still sound asleep. God, what happened on that Hebrew School trip? She may sleep forever. "Well, I haven't been to the pool in a few days because it's no fun without Ari, and she's been away, and . . ." I have no idea why I'm telling Jason all of this.

I can't tell if he's cute or not. He's nerdy, but his smile shows confidence. And he has straight teeth. Like, naturally straight teeth. No need for braces.

He's looking at me, smiling like he knows something I don't know. Something I should know. "The pool can be fun without Ari. I'm always here!"

I crinkle my eyes to avoid the sun. "Yeah, you do seem really lively, joining the water volleyball game when you just moved here!"

He sits down on the edge of my lounge chair, since all

the other chairs are taken. I guess he was tired of stand-ing. "Well, more like moved back. You probably don't remember me, but I went to school with you in second grade."

I look at him out of the corner of my eye, trying to remember. Ari never mentioned he used to live here, but then again, she wasn't here in second grade, so maybe it didn't matter to her.

"Oh yeah! Mr. Greenstein's class!" I shriek and look over at Ari, almost trying to wake her up this time. "You did your country project on Italy, right?"

He stands up and claps. "I did! How did you remember that?"

"I remember you brought in pasta for the whole class," I say, trying to play it cool, not freak out that a boy is talk-ing to me and that I remembered something about him. "Are you ready for school?"

I stare off into space, like it's nothing, but inside I'm bursting a little bit.

Jason is new; he's Ari's neighbor. He's cuter than I first thought he was, but like, manageable cute. Not intimi-dating cute.

There is no doubt about it—he is definitely the guy friend we need for the list! The guy friend we need for life!

He can give us tips on guy stuff, tell us about what went on at his old school, and help me figure out what's going on with my brother.

"My old elementary school only went up to fourth grade," Jason says, "so I technically already started middle school, but now it's kinda sorta like I'm starting middle school again." He shrugs like it's no big deal. "Well, I mean, I guess I am just starting middle school, because, like, it's a new—"

"I get it." I laugh a little, as an apology for cutting him off. He talks a lot. But that's not such a bad thing, either. I run out of things to say, so I reach into my backpack for an orange, just to have something to do.

He moves to sit on the lounge chair next to me that a mom and baby just left. "Whoa, you are the fastest orange peeler I have ever seen!"

I crack up. "What?"

"No, seriously." He looks at me. "You just peeled that in, like, ten seconds, and the peel stayed all in one piece!"

Um. This is the strangest thing anyone has ever noticed about me. I mean, I've noticed it about myself because Ryan and I used to have clementine-peeling contests when I was in third grade, and he was in fourth. But for Jason to notice—wow. Kind of a big deal.

"It's a talent," I say, and start laughing. "I'm awesome at it. You should see me peel clementines." I pause. "That's really my best skill. Guinness Book of World Records worthy."

"You're probably the fastest peeler in the world." He

stares at the peel. "Like, you could enter a competition!"

Our laughing wakes Ari up. A few seconds later, she sits up, all frantic and confused like she doesn't know where she is.

"Arianna!" Jason says. "Hey!"

"Hey," she mumbles, still sleepy-groggy.

"How was your sister's sleepover?" he asks.

She looks at him, confused.

"Remember last night, you were walking your sister to a sleepover? I was throwing lawn darts. . . ."

"Oh yeah!" She sits up straighter and rubs her eyes.

"You told me you'd be hanging out here today," he says. "And, um, you are!"

He laughs at himself, so I laugh along, too. Sometimes you have to humor your friends. It's just the way the world works. He was trying to be funny.

"Ari, um, I mean, Arianna." I look over at her. "You didn't tell me Jason went to school with me in second grade. We used to play four square together!"

"Oh, um." She looks at Jason and then back at me. "It slipped my mind, I guess. Do you guys remember each other?"

"I kind of do," Jason says. "I remember you brought a bagel with cream cheese every day for lunch for the whole entire year."

"I wasn't so culinarily, um, sophisticated back then," I say.

"Back then?" Ari guffaws. "You're not that sophisticated now."

"I eat sushi!" I smack her on the knee. "And you're the one who's afraid of doing yoga!"

She hits me right back. "Shhh."

"All right, y'all," he says, getting up. "I'm gonna grab some food."

"Y'all?" I laugh.

"My mom's from Atlanta, so sometimes I talk like a Southerner."

"Southerners are cool," I say, because I can't think of anything else to say. I don't want him to get the feeling that I'm making fun of him.

"Yeah, they are." He nods. "Need anything from the snack bar?"

We shake our heads.

"Catch you later, then." He walks away and Ari and I sit there, looking at each other, talking with our eyes, until Jason's out of earshot and we're sure he won't be able to hear us.

"First kiss?" Ari asks.

"I was thinking more guy friend."

"He could be both," she suggests.

"How?"

She hesitates for a second. "My first kiss. Your guy friend."

"You said he wasn't cute enough for first kiss! Now he

99

is? And we need to have the same guy friend," I remind her. "For the list. And to help us figure out guy stuff. It's part of our whole new sophisticated personas. Ya know?"

She thinks about it for a second. "Yeah, but some people end up having crushes on their guy friends, and then they kiss them, and so . . ." She smiles. "Could be both!"

"A dynamic duo: when one thing fulfills two items on the list," I tell her.

"Exactly." Ari smiles.

THIRTEEN

"YOU DIDN'T NEED TO BE so rude before," Ari says as we're eating our ice cream later that afternoon. "In front of Jason, about the yoga . . ."

I pause to think about it. Was I rude? "You made fun of my culinary lameness!"

"I was joking." She licks around the side of her chocolate cone to even it out.

"I was, too!" I sneer. "Anyway, you still haven't told me about the Hebrew School trip." Something crazy must have happened. I never trusted that Tamar girl. "And we have to go over schedules! We have tons to do. We can't waste time in a fight."

"We're not in a fight, Kaylan. Sheesh!" She slurps some dripping ice cream out the bottom of her cone.

"Well, can you just tell me about the trip, already?" I

ask, picking a sprinkle off my cone.

"Okay . . . the trip. Well, Jules, Phoebe, Tamar, Cara—those girls over there." She nudges her head toward the lounges by the diving board. "They were all there. Plus some of the bikini boobage girls! I never realized they went to my temple. But the trip was kids going into sixth through eighth grades, so . . ."

"And?" I take a sip of water. Ice cream always makes me thirsty.

"It was kind of fun. Jules introduced me to all these girls who went to her elementary school but are randomly zoned for our middle school." My stomach starts to sink thinking about it, but I force it away so I can focus on the rest of the story. "And we hung out with boys. It was, like, kind of normal."

"What?" I gasp. "You didn't call me right away and tell me you hung out with boys? You don't even need Jason as your guy friend anymore." I flop my head onto the table. I don't even know if I can finish this cone.

"Kaylan." She taps my head. "We're not, like, BFFs. I just hung out with them, and it was fun. That's it."

I glare at her; I feel like she's lying, like she's leaving stuff out. "So then why are you, like, freaking out about yoga? You're acting weird!"

Ari starts massaging her sinuses. "Ice cream headache. And I am not acting weird! I just don't want to be the most uncoordinated one in yoga. Okay?"

"Fine!" I yell, half-kidding, half-serious. "Let's go back to the lounges and compare schedules."

"Fine!"

We walk back to the lounges, and the bikini boobage girls are in their usual spot, in the sun, by the diving board.

"Arianna!" one of them calls. "Your song is rising. . . ."

"No!" Ari yells back, laughing. "*Your* song is rising."

I look back and forth from the girl to Ari and back again. "Huh?" I ask.

"Oh, just a private joke." Ari laughs. "From the trip. I could explain it but it's really long."

"Oh. Um. That's okay." My throat stings.

They think they're so funny because they have all these jokes from the trip. I mean, who cares? It was five days. They can't possibly have gotten that close in that short of a time.

It takes us forever to make it back to our lounges because that girl Jules stops us for a hundred years to ask when Ari has math. She thinks her friend Sydney is gonna be in her class. "Sydney's nice," she says. "And she's really smart. She can help you study!" Jules keeps talking, and Ari keeps listening, and it's like I'm not even standing there.

Thank God Jules is going to the other middle school.

"So," Ari says, when we're back on our lounge chairs, close together, comparing schedules. "This sheet is just our first day schedule. See how it says here that it rotates by a period every other day?"

"Uh-huh."

Ari crinkles up her nose. "But we don't have any of the same teachers, so I guess we don't have any classes together."

My heart sinks like I just lost my favorite ring, the one my grandma gave me for my first communion. "Wait, no. That can't be."

I look it over again. "Wait! We have lunch together!"

"Oh!" Ari claps. "You're right! That is awesome! That's the period that matters most!"

I reach over and hug her. I don't care about Jules, or the private jokes from the Hebrew trip, or that she forgot to tell me Jason used to live here, or that she thinks my culinary tastes are pathetic.

We have lunch together. That's all that matters!

"What's this lovefest about?" Tyler walks over to us, twirling his whistle around his fingers. "Lovefests aren't allowed at the pool."

We pull apart from the hug, and my cheeks feel like they're on fire. "Um . . . not a lovefest, just looking over class schedules."

"Let me see," he says, putting his hands out.

"It's okay, Tyler, you're not in our grade," Ari says.

"Gimme. I'll tell you what to expect."

Finally, we hand the papers to him. He looks at each

one for two seconds and then says, "Yup, you're screwed. All these classes are hard." He hands the sheets back. "Good luck."

Ari looks at me and shakes her head. "What is his deal?"

"No idea." I lie back and try not to worry about Tyler. *Ari and I have lunch together.* I repeat it to myself over and over again.

"That was kind of jerky," Ari says, but I ignore it.

"Jason!" Ari yells down the row of lounge chairs, zapping me out of my calming thoughts. "Who do you have for science?"

He holds up a finger, goes to get something from his bag, and then comes over to us.

He shows us his phone. Apparently he took a picture of his schedule and has been trying to memorize it.

We compare classes. Jason and Ari have science together, but that's it. And he's in our lunch, too.

"I think all sixth graders have lunch at the same time," he tells us. "That's what Jules said. She knows, like, tons of kids at West Brookside."

I throw my head back against the lounge chair.

Jules knows everything, apparently.

FOURTEEN

THE THING ABOUT MAKING A guy friend is that it's actually kind of confusing. I mean, it's not that hard to literally *meet* the friend. Like the way we met Jason—he lives next door to Ari; we talked at the pool.

But then after that, it's hard to know what to do.

When you first become friends with a girl, you can invite her to sleep over. It speeds up the friendship really fast. Or maybe even a manicure date. Some girls like that. Not all, but some, and it's a good plan to have. You just sit there, and you can talk about nail polish colors, and it's like an automatic conversation.

And some guys like manicures, too, but you don't really know that when you first meet them, so it's a hard thing to suggest.

Basically, having a guy friend is confusing at the

beginning. You don't know what plans to suggest, because you've never had a guy friend before.

So for the first few days of guy friendship with Jason, I pretty much just text him random things. Like funny pictures of cats on hammocks, even though I don't even like cats. But he does. Or pictures of the food my mom makes for dinner. He says he's always hungry. Or funny, interesting, and fancy watches. Jason loves watches.

But the truth is, texting is a good thing to do at the beginning of a friendship. And then when we see each other at the pool, we can talk about the texts.

"Do you think we can consider Jason a real true friend yet?" I ask Ari after our last pool day of the season. It's our last night before life as we know it ends and middle school begins.

We're in my backyard eating blueberries in our towels.

We're not saying it out loud, but we're trying to stay in our towels as long as we possibly can. It's a way to cling to summer. As soon as we get dressed, summer will really be over.

School starts tomorrow; lingering in our towels is all we can do.

"Um." She pops a blueberry in her mouth. "You mean, like, can we cross it off the list and do our ritual?"

I nod. "Well, yeah, I do like the ritual. But I'm also just, like, curious."

"Well, I'm not really sure," she says. "I mean, we're

definitely friends with him. We text. We've shared orders of fries at the pool. We haven't been to each other's houses yet, though. . . . But I've been in his front yard."

"I know!" I slump back in my chair. "It's hard to invite a guy friend over. I don't even know what we'd do. Why is this so hard?"

"Well, I mean, he is our friend, and I think we can cross it off the list, so try not to worry." Ari adjusts her towel over her body, sits back in the Adirondack chair, and closes her eyes.

What is she doing? Doesn't she know that she needs to be calming me down right now? She can't just sleep.

"Ari!" I shake her a little. "Come on! We have to discuss tons of stuff. Do you see I am freaking out?"

"You're always freaking out, Kay. You'll still be freaking out in ten minutes when I wake up from my power nap!"

"Thanks. You're soooo helpful." I roll my eyes even though she can't see me with her eyes closed.

I decide to power nap, too, but of course I can't sleep. I just lie there with my eyes closed and feel the sun fade from my face.

Summer, don't go!

I go back inside to get more snacks and find my mom sitting at the kitchen table, scrolling through my cell phone.

"Mom!" I shriek. "What are you doing?"

She stammers, pushing my phone across the table, like she's in a game of hot potato. "Um, I was just deciding what to make for dinner. . . ."

"Mom! You were clearly looking at my phone!" I grab it off the table, about to shove it in my pocket, when I realize I'm only in a towel, so I just keep it in my hand. "You're spying on me!"

"Kaylan, I just glanced at it," she says, closing her eyes. "Calm down. Anyway, I pay for it! I can look at it!"

"Don't be a snoop," I say, grabbing a bag of popcorn from the pantry. I look back at her, all side-eyes. "Promise?"

"Promise," she sighs.

I get back outside and rip open the bag of popcorn, seething that my mom was invading my privacy.

A few minutes later, Ari grabs my arm like she just remembered something super-important. She pops up from her lying-down position. "First-day outfits." She turns to me. "We need to finalize."

"Yes! I've been waiting for this!" I stand up and pull the towel tighter around my body. I debate telling her about the Mom Snooping. I decide to save it for later; she doesn't need another thing to worry about.

We run up the stairs as fast we can.

When we make it to the safety of my room, Ari sprawls out on my bed, face into my pillows. Normally I'd say no wet towels on the bed, but we've been out of the pool so long our bathing suits and towels are completely dry.

"Are you okay?" I ask Ari.

She sighs. I have no idea what that means.

"What is it?" I press.

"I'm nervous, Kay." She flops over. "So nervous. We don't know this school at all. I know we went on that tour last May, but I forgot what we saw. I don't know where the cafeteria is. And what if all those girls that Jules knows are actually really mean? She thinks they'll want to be friends with me, but who knows? They could hate me! And what if Jason forgets all about us when school starts? And—"

I don't know what to do about this, how to handle it. I'm the nervous one. Ari's the calm one. That's just how it is. I don't like this. And shouldn't Jules's friends be my friends, too? Not only Ari's. She can't make new friends without me.

"Okay!" I put my hand on her back. It's really rare for Ari to show anxiety like this. I'm getting nervous just watching it. "Let's breathe."

"You're not nervous?" She shoots up. "Suddenly Miss Agita Kaylan isn't nervous at all about middle school starting tomorrow?"

"Um." I start laughing, half from my nervousness and half because Ari sounds so completely ridiculous right now. "Of course I am! But weren't you the one who said we needed to calm down and make a plan?"

She sniffles and nods.

"So?" I zone out for a minute thinking about Jason and the whole can-we-consider-him-a-real-friend-yet thing. "I'll be back," I tell Ari. "I need to pee."

The truth is, I do need to pee, but I also need to text Jason. And I know it's gross to pee and text at the same time.

Ari is totes freaking out about 1st day of school tomw. Advice?

Jason responds in three seconds—definite sign of true friend.

Everyone freaks b4 1st day of school. It'll be fine. We're in it together. Later, Terrel. Going to get burritos.

Now I know for sure we're real, true friends. He called me by my last name. Done. Solved. In my head, I'm singing, *Kay has a boy friend. Not boyfriend. But boy friend!*

I leave the bathroom and head back to my room.

"It's settled," I tell Ari.

"Um." She lifts her head up just the tiniest bit. "You just left the bathroom, so I'm a little nervous about what you're about to say. . . ."

I crack up. "Okay, that's fair. But no—I texted with Jason, and don't be grossed out because I was in the bathroom. I washed my hands, whatever. But anyway, he responded right away. And get this—he called me by my last name!" I screech out the last part.

"Whoa," Ari says, pretty much the opposite of enthusiastic.

I wait for her to say more, but she doesn't. She just throws her face back into my pillow.

Her negativity and her agita is bothering me. Ari's not the one who gets agita—I am.

"Ari," I say, and rub her back. "It'll be fine. We'll figure everything out. You had fun on the Hebrew School trip, and you didn't know a lot of the kids there."

She sits up, finally. "I did, by the fourth day. But the first three days were hellish. I didn't know where to sit for meals. Most of the kids were, like, BFFs. I don't know how, but they were. Tamar barely talked to me! She was sitting with the bikini boobage girls because they were all on the same teen tour earlier in the summer! Jules was okay, but even she had good friends there! My bunkmate was this new girl, Eve, who ate seaweed for snacks and snored so loud!" She pauses, sniffling. "I felt so homesick. I hated it."

"You did?" I ask. "You didn't tell me that."

"I wasn't allowed to have my phone so I couldn't text you! By the fourth day, I was having fun," she admits. "But the beginning was terrible. And Tamar and I are definitely not friends anymore. I think she forgot we were ever friends."

I glance around the room, trying to find some inspiration or a way to cheer her up. "Sorry about Tamar." I pause, feeling the tiniest bit happy but also really guilty for feeling that way. "I guess the main takeaway here is that the beginnings of things are bad?" I offer. "And then they get better?"

She lies back down, face into the pillow. I think she may be crying for real now. I can't tell.

I should know how to calm someone down, since I'm nervous every second of the day. But I just don't know what to say.

"So, first-day outfits . . ." I start talking and wait for Ari to sit up, or at least acknowledge that she's listening. "They need to be something cool, unique, something that accentuates our features. But they can't be too memorable. They can't make it look like we've tried too hard. Ya know?"

"True," she mumbles.

"Perk up!" I yell. "Come on, Ari. We can't be like this on the night before the biggest day of our lives so far. We can't let our nerves control us!"

I grab her arms, and gently pull her off the bed. She flops onto the floor, and I scroll through my music and turn on some Katy Perry.

"Dance!"

It takes a few seconds, but soon Ari and I are dancing around my room in our bathing suits. I make sure my door is locked. My mom usually hates having locked doors, but this is a special circumstance. We need our privacy. We need to feel free to release our anxieties.

"'I got the eye of the tiger, a fighter,'" I sing. "'Dancing through the fire.'"

"'Cause I am the champion,'" Ari sings into my hairbrush.

"'And you're gonna hear me roar!'" we scream-sing together.

I start kicking my legs out to the side, and Ari joins me, and we put our arms around each other's shoulders like we're in a Rockettes routine. This song is powerful; it makes me feel like I can handle anything.

Out of breath, we flop back on the bed.

"I feel better," Ari says.

"Me too."

"Shoot!" Ari says. "I was supposed to be home twenty minutes ago. My mom has this whole thing about us all eating dinner together, ya know, and especially before the first day of school."

"Of course she does." I roll my eyes but then feel instantly guilty. It's a nice thing that Ari's mom tries to do. I don't know why I'm rude about it.

"But we didn't decide on outfits!" I yell as she sprints down the stairs.

"Well, here's a piece of advice," Ryan says, walking past my room. "Don't wear that."

"Ugh!" I scream. "I hate you!"

"Ryan, don't torment the girls," I hear my mom say.

"You're always blaming me!" He stomps down the stairs to the kitchen. "By the way, Mom, I did what you said. I asked Mr. Gracie if I could have a chance to audition again."

"And?" my mom asks. My heart perks up a little. I guess it's good we have such a small house—we can hear conversations taking place downstairs.

"He said, sure!" He pauses, and I feel a touch of relief. "In the winter! My chance for the fall semester is shot! He doesn't care that I'm the best guitarist in the whole freakin' school!"

"Ryan," she says, and I hear the kitchen chair screech across the floor. "Sit down. Let's talk."

Ari looks up at me from downstairs as she's getting her shoes on. "Ouch," she mouths.

My heart feels like it's dripping slowly to my feet.

FIFTEEN

"LOOKIN' GOOD, KAYLAN!" MRS. ETISOF yells from an Adirondack chair on her front porch. I'm on my way to the bus stop on the first day of school. "Love the outfit."

Mrs. Etisof isn't exactly the most fashionable person in the world, so I'm not sure if I should take her word on how good I look. But, I mean, she does have eyes. And she reads a lot, so maybe she knows what's in style.

"Thanks, Mrs. E." I look up. "I better go; don't want to miss the bus!"

"Have a great day."

Even though Ari and I FaceTimed our way through final first-day-outfit decisions, I still feel unsure about my choices as I wait for the bus on the corner where my street meets Ari's street.

I decided on my cuffed jean shorts with the gray V-neck

and a navy boyfriend cardigan in case some of the classrooms are air-conditioned. Pair that ensemble with my strappy brown sandals and I'm set. I think. I mean, my legs are pretty tan, so that's good, and so are my arms. And my highlights are really visible now because the sun has totally enhanced them. The stylist said that would happen.

I study myself in the reflection of a parked car as I wait for Ari to get here.

She's late.

I can't handle lateness on a morning as important as this one. I mean, what if she doesn't come by the time the bus arrives and I have to tell the bus driver to wait? He probably won't want to, and then I'll feel weird, and have to beg him, and I may even start to cry.

New kids are going to be on the bus, kids I don't know, and I need a guarantee that I'll have someone to sit with. I need Ari. I keep shifting my weight from foot to foot. My cheeks feel itchy, but I don't want to scratch them too much and end up with red blotches all over my face.

Ari. *Get here already.*

Finally, after I smooth the left side of my hair for the millionth time, Ari arrives, strolling to the bus, with her new paisley tote over her shoulder. She's wearing what we decided on yesterday—a jean skirt and the polka-dot shirt she got last week. She wanted to go a little dressier than I did, which is totally fine.

"You look great," I say. Truthfully, I'd say that even if she didn't look great (which she does) because you need to feel good about yourself on the first day of middle school. There's no debating that.

"Thanks." She smiles and bounces on her toes a bit. "You do, too."

Ari admires herself in the window of the same parked car, and that's when Ryan and Tyler walk right up to us. Then they start fake-primping themselves, stroking their hair, and posing in hands-on-hips positions, trying to mock us, completely over the top.

"How do I look, Ryan?" Tyler asks.

"Oh, wonderful, Tyler," my doofus brother replies. "I'm so glad we spent all those hours picking out our outfits."

I burst out laughing. "Um, yeah. Your T-shirt has a ketchup stain and we haven't had hot dogs in weeks. Your shorts have holes in them. And you're wearing two different socks. Should I go on?"

"I think they're kidding," Ari whispers to me.

"I know that," I sneer. "Go with it."

"Your left sneaker lace is untied," she tells Ryan. He bends down awkwardly to tie it.

A wave of guilt about the jam-band thing washes over me. Ryan doesn't know I had anything to do with it. I guess that's a good thing. And he can try out next semester, so it's not a totally lost cause.

"Losers," Ryan says under his breath and walks to the

other end of the bus stop. Tyler shrugs and walks away with him.

And yeah, Ryan may look like he just rolled out of bed and into a vat of ketchup—but Tyler, he looks like he tried. But just the perfect level of trying. Not like he tried too hard at all.

He's wearing khaki cargos and they're wrinkled, but the right amount of wrinkled. And he's wearing a green polo. The collar is half-up and half-down, but it's okay for some reason. His hair is just the right amount of gelled.

"Tyler looks so good today," I whisper to Ari.

She glares at me. "What?"

"Tyler looks so good," I repeat.

She pulls my arm and leads me off to the side. "I heard what you said. Now can you finally just admit what's happening here?"

I nod. I kind of don't want to, but I also kind of do. Admitting it means we can talk about it. Really talk about it.

"Kaylan." She looks right into my eyes.

I nod again.

"You're totally into Tyler. Just admit it."

"Shhhhhh! He'll hear you!" I need to accept this right now and embrace it and tell the entire world: I have a crush on Tyler.

My heart expands like an inflated balloon.

I have a big crush on Tyler Beasley.

It was always there, sort of lingering in my brain. Like the way your adult teeth are there, waiting to come out after you lose your baby teeth.

He just looks so cute. So painfully cute. And he's a lifeguard—he knows how to save people's lives!

Ari shakes her head. "The bus is here. Can we just get through the day and then sort out this crazy crush on Tyler later?"

I nod yes, but the thing is—I'm not sure it can wait. Now that it's out in the open, it's like I have to talk about it. Like it will burn a hole in my brain or something or just grow bigger and bigger unless I fully discuss it. Right now.

But I hold it in. I get on the bus, and Ari and I share a seat and I force myself to think about anything other than Tyler. I focus on the dried-up gum on the bus seat in front of us. I focus on how Ari's hair smells like peaches. I focus on the fact that my pedicure is still perfect even though I got it done last week.

I text Jason: **on the bus**

And he writes back: **C U SOON! 1st DAY! YAHOO!**

I show Ari the text. "He's really perky."

"You guys text way more than we do," she says. And then she launches into some lecture about text etiquette that I can't focus on. "Plus we live across the street, so we kind of just say hey from the front yards and stuff."

I didn't think it was a competition.

Jason. Tyler. Jason. Tyler. First day of school. My thoughts are like a pinball, bouncing back and forth in the machine.

"Are you in there?" I hear Ari ask, and then realize I've missed most of what she just said.

"Oh yeah." I laugh. "I'm here."

"I just asked you what you have first period. I know we've gone over the schedules a billion times, but I forgot. I'm sorry."

"Don't be sorry." I take my schedule out of my backpack and show it to Ari. "Bixhorn. Math."

"Math first period?" Ari shrieks.

"I know. Brutal. But at least I get it over with." I put my schedule away, take a sip from my water bottle, and start to wonder how often I tell myself that I'll just get things over with. Seems like I think that kind of a lot. "You have history, right?"

She nods. "I can't pay attention to history first thing in the morning."

"But you love history," I remind her.

"I guess," she mumbles.

I think Ari's on the verge of tears. The only time I ever saw her like this was when she didn't make the volleyball team last year. Crying on the school bus on the first day of middle school is absolutely not acceptable; it's practically illegal, according to some middle school code of law. So I put an arm around her. "Ari, if you start crying, I'll tell everyone that you were cutting onions for an omelet before school . . . and you're having a delayed reaction."

"Huh?" Ari cracks up. "That's dumb."

"It'll distract people from your tears."

"I'm not crying," she says, laughing.

"After orientation, we'll make a plan of where to meet for lunch?" I suggest. "Okay?"

She nods. "But we don't know where anything is!"

"I know," I say. "But we will probably get another tour."

Thankfully, we're at school within the next few minutes.

"This is it," Ari whispers. "Good luck."

"Thanks. I need it." I clench my teeth. "Same to you."

I grab her hand for a second but then drop it because no normal person walks into middle school for the first time holding their best friend's hand. But then again, I'm not normal. I'm not even sure I want to be normal, so I should probably stop trying so hard.

"Welcome, sixth graders," a tall man with a mustache says as we walk through the double doors.

"I think he's the principal," I whisper to Ari. "But I'm not one hundred percent sure."

Ari nudges her head toward me. "Are mustaches still a thing?" she talks through her teeth. "They kind of creep me out."

"Yeah, me too," I say as we walk.

The tiles in the hallway are a dull peach, almost beige, and the air smells like flowery air freshener. It's so strong it makes my eyes sting.

"We're meeting in the auditorium before first period." Mustache Man moves his hands to the right like he's an air traffic controller at the airport. "Keep walking. Keep walking."

Ari and I look at each other as we walk and I'm pretty sure we're thinking the same thing: *Please please please do not let us get separated.*

The hallway fills up with students like we're vacuum-packed olives in a jar, and then the auditorium doors open, and we all spill in.

I stay close to Ari. So close our sides are touching. I cannot, cannot, *cannot* sit alone during this first assembly of sixth grade. This is like the agita I had over our fourth grade trip to the planetarium times a million. Ari was totally cool with sitting with whomever on the bus, and I was freaking out that I'd have no one to sit with and everyone would see that and think of me as the biggest loser in the grade.

Unfortunately, when Ari turns to go down a row, other kids get in between us, and then a group goes into that row from the other side. She gets the last seat there, and I raise my eyebrows and reach out my hand to try to grab her to get out and come with me, but the Mustache Man principal starts talking again, and she sits down. Without me.

The principal is on the stage, standing in front of a

microphone, urging everyone to quiet down and take seats, and I'm still standing there, in the aisle, looking for a seat. He's going to call me out and tell me to sit down, and everyone in this whole auditorium will stare at me.

That cannot happen.

I scan each row, and finally, I find a seat near the back.

I sit next to a girl with the silkiest black hair I've ever seen. My highlights could never compare to the beauty that is her natural hair.

"Hey," I mumble, and sniffle back tears.

"Hey," she mumbles back.

"I'm Kaylan," I say. Maybe if I keep talking I'll be able to hold myself back from crying.

"I'm June," she replies. "I went to—"

She doesn't get to finish what she was saying because the principal starts talking, for real this time, like he's making a speech he prepared. He's saying something about the importance of middle school and about how what we do matters. Our schoolwork matters. Our extra-curricular activities matter. The way we treat our peers matters. I half pay attention and half zone out.

My mind flops all around from thoughts of Tyler, to wondering where Jason is, to this girl June. Potential friend? Maybe. She's nice and she has shiny hair.

I go to take my phone out of the front pocket of my bag so I can text Ari, and we can make a plan about where to meet for lunch, in case we don't see each other again.

"Put your phone away," June hisses. "They are superstrict about phones! Teachers are watching."

My stomach drops, and I shove it back in my bag. I'm already in trouble.

And then, before I even realize what's happening, everyone starts getting up and shuffling out of the seats and into the aisles.

"What did he say?" I whisper to June, who then gives me a cross-eyed look like she's disappointed and a little shocked I wasn't paying attention.

"I heard most of it," I defend, and then June tells me she has to go because she's really nervous about finding her locker.

At least I'm not the only nervous one. That's something.

But then I'm alone again.

I look at my watch. It's not even eight thirty yet and I already wish the day was over.

SIXTEEN

AFTER MATH, ENGLISH, STUDY HALL, and art, it's finally time for lunch. I haven't had any classes with Ari, but we knew that, so it's not shocking. I came prepared, knowing I'd be flying solo most of the day. And it's been mostly okay. I'm surviving.

So I walk into the cafeteria, all calm and cool with my head held as high as possible. Ari and I didn't get to make our meet-up plan since we lost each other after assembly, and I was too scared to try and text her, but I tell myself to stay calm.

I'm sure Ari will find her way to the cafeteria, and I'll see her, and we'll get seats together.

I pretend I'm an actress playing the part of a confident student, and it helps. Truthfully, I feel like a tiny ant that could be stepped on at any minute. But if I pretend

I've got it all under control, the whole situation just feels better.

I scan the room for Ari. I search for her red highlights and her high ponytail and her paisley tote. Nothing. Just a giant sea of heads and green cafeteria trays. And it smells like disinfectant and tomato soup.

My stomach hurts.

I pretend to study the salad bar offerings. Being in such a visible spot will make it easier for Ari to find me. I'm sure my blond highlights look extra-amazing against the mustard-yellow cafeteria tile.

Should I stay here by the salad bar until she finds me? Or should I walk around and search for Ari? But then I risk looking like the loser who's walking around alone. Red flashing sign on my forehead that says: **THIS GIRL IS BY HERSELF. SHE DOESN'T KNOW WHERE TO SIT. SHE DOESN'T HAVE ANYONE TO EAT WITH.**

I can't keep doing this. I can't keep walking around alone. I'm like the sad middle school version of Where's Waldo? but I don't have that cute striped outfit. And I'm not sure anyone is even looking for me. Also, Where's Kaylan? just doesn't sound as good.

I look at my watch. I feel like I've been waiting three hundred years, but it's only been ten minutes. Still, Ari's late. Where is she? I need her. We need to decide where to sit together. Where we sit the first day determines where we sit the whole year. Everyone knows that. I can't figure this out on my own.

I do one more quick glance around; she's still not here. She's on her way, I guess. Maybe she stayed after class to talk with a teacher or maybe she's in the bathroom.

This is the worst day of the entire year to be late to lunch.

I take my bagged lunch of a turkey wrap, chips, a clementine, and a bottle of water, and I walk toward the back row of tables. I'll save Ari a seat. I'll guard it with my life, and I'll stare at the door so I can see her as soon as she comes in.

"Oh hey, June," I say, noticing an empty seat next to the girl from the auditorium.

She looks up from her sandwich, and I think I see relief on her face.

"Oh hey, um . . ." I can tell she's forgotten my name but I don't know if I should tell her or wait for her to remember or just ignore the whole thing. I wait for her to offer me the seat, but so far she just stares at me.

"It's Kaylan," I say, as I sit down. She nods and smiles.

As I'm unwrapping my sandwich, more girls come to the table. June seems to know most of them. But she doesn't seem to be best friends with them or anything. Just saying-hi kind of friends, not meet-at-your-locker-first-thing-in-the-morning kind of friends.

They half smile at me, and I half smile at them. They're talking about their schedules and how they already have homework. "Oh, Mr. Simms is the worst," one girl says. "Everyone knows that."

"My friend Jules, who knows everyone in the world, told me some of her friends from Hebrew were gonna be in our grade," another one says. "I forgot their names, though."

Of course Jules has already come up. But at least it gives me something to talk about.

"Oh, you know Jules?" I ask. "I met her at the pool this summer."

She looks at me, confused, even though she's the one who just brought Jules up. Then she turns away and goes back to talking to the other girls. My stomach burns like I've just sipped acid instead of water.

I'm sitting here, not talking, but I don't know what to say. I look around for Ari. I still don't see her!

Maybe I should say my name and introduce myself. But it feels like too much. Like it would be too hard to get the words to bubble up out of my throat.

I'll just sit here and eat and get lunch over with.

At least I'm not sitting alone.

At least I'm not walking around the cafeteria alone.

Between bites, I scan the cafeteria for Ari. Still no sign of her, and I'm getting worried. I wonder if I should leave and search the hallways. But we only have a half hour for lunch and I'm hungry and—okay I'll be honest—I'm scared of losing my seat.

She probably found another place to sit. Free-spirited Ari, or I guess Arianna, doesn't really worry about where she eats lunch. She just finds a spot and goes with it, and makes the best of wherever she is, the way she did after the first few days of her Hebrew School trip.

"We all went to Stratfield Elementary," one of the girls explains, and I immediately relax, like, okay, people are actually talking to me now.

"Oh yeah, I know where that is," I say, peeling the clementine on my lap. "My mom works over there. Did you guys get subs at Harvey Deli like every single day?" I ask them, trying as hard as I can to make conversation. I feel like I finally have something interesting to add.

"Um, yes," one of the girls says. I think her name is Cami. "The Harvey Supreme is literally my favorite sandwich in the entire world!"

"Mine too!" I yell, and then cover my mouth because I'm so loud the table in front of us turns around.

"We have to go together one day!" Cami says, and I know we're only discussing the fact that we have the same favorite sandwich, but it feels like a big deal. A big moment.

Maybe middle school won't be so bad after all.

Cami and I keep talking about the sandwich—how the mozzarella cheese is a little bit melted, and how it's weird that the cucumbers are on there, but how they really do add the perfect level of crunch. We're deep in

130

conversation when I feel Ari standing over me.

She's out of breath, and she's holding a brown lunch bag with grease seeping through the paper.

"I've been looking for you," she says.

"I've been looking for you, too!" I say, because it's the truth. I was looking for her for so long! It feels kind of like a lie, though, because I've already finished my sandwich and I've clearly been involved in a conversation for a while.

Ari scopes out the table and I do, too, and then I realize all the seats on the bench are taken. So I do what any best friend would do. I squish over.

"Sit," I say.

Ari shakes her head a little like she doesn't want to, and like sitting this close together is weird. Even though it was never weird before. We've shared chairs a million times.

"It's ok." I nudge over a little more, so she can see that there's clearly room for her.

She sits down eventually. I have half a butt cheek off the bench and our thighs are touching. It's hard for her to unwrap her sandwich because she can barely move her arms. We only have ten minutes of lunch left.

And Cami keeps talking. "I actually know the owner of the Harvey Deli," she says, excited still, like she's been waiting to start up the conversation again.

"Oh yeah?" I ask. I want to end this so I can ask Ari

how her morning has been and if she's seen Tyler and if I can come over after school so we can decide on the next item on our 11 Before 12 List. But I also want to keep talking to Cami because she's nice, and it seems like she likes me, and we have the same favorite sandwich! I kind of feel like I was meant to be friends with her, like the universe wanted us to sit together and discover all the stuff we have in common.

"Yeah," Cami says all matter-of-fact. "He lives across the street from me. So sometimes he brings over extra stuff. And he always caters our Super Bowl party, and yeah, he's just great."

"Cool." I smile and turn just the slightest bit away from Cami, not in a mean way, but in a way that says I need to check in with my best friend. She makes a noise like she's about to say something else, but then she stops. I feel a tiny pinchy feeling in my chest, like maybe I should have let her continue. But I guess it's too late. And I do need to focus on Ari, too.

"How was your morning?" I whisper to Ari.

"Fine." She bites into her sandwich.

"What's wrong?" I ask.

"Nothing. Stop." She talks through her teeth and doesn't look at me.

I turn back to face the table. Cami's still talking. Something about a vacation she took where they got stranded somewhere. I don't know. She seems to talk a lot, like maybe she's one of those know-it-all types. But everyone looks like they're listening to her.

I start to wonder—is Cami one of those girls? The kind that everyone wants to be friends with? And I don't even know it? I just had a conversation with her where we totally bonded and I didn't even realize it was so important, so valuable.

I mean, having a friend like that, maybe even a few friends like that, would completely change middle school for me. Like it could actually be fun, and not just something to get through.

The first step of the Whole Me Makeover, in a way. Maybe new friends are the makeover. But I never thought I needed new friends before.

"Can you at least introduce me?" Ari says through her teeth. And I realize I'm a terrible best friend. I should have thought of that on my own. But Ari's usually so friendly and easygoing. I guess I expected she'd introduce herself. This whole nervous Arianna person is confusing.

"Um, hey, I'm such a dimwit," I laugh, and announce to the table. A few girls give me looks, but I continue. "This is my best friend, Ari, I mean, Arianna." I giggle and feel completely stupid.

"Ari?" one of the girls asks. "My brother's name is Ari."

"Well, that's why I'm going by Arianna now," she

defends. "Ari was just a nickname my dad gave me when I was born. I think he secretly wanted a son and so he just started saying it and . . ."

I zone out and hope Ari stops talking. I can't believe I already messed up on the Ari/Arianna thing. What is wrong with me?

"So, anyway," I jump in, to try and fix things. "Anyone have Mr. Paino for science next period?"

"I do," Cami says. "Let's walk together." She hops up from the table and collects her trash. While she's throwing it away, Ari and I exchange looks.

Mine says, *We will meet outside the school doors at exactly 3:01 to discuss every single detail of this lunch and the entire day.*

Ari's says, *I am so mad at you, and this is the worst lunch of my life.*

I shrug it off, but I'm secretly happy. Cami seems fun. And she wants to walk to class with me. And we have the same favorite sandwich. No big deal.

"I have English now," Ari says, mournfully.

"You can walk with us, too," I suggest. "I think it's in the same direction, or at least on the same floor."

"Someone said something about meeting in the library for English, but I'm not sure."

But when Cami comes back and I'm standing up, she links arms with me, and soon we're off, walking out of the cafeteria and down the hall. I turn around a little, and I see Ari behind me and I know I've done something wrong.

I'm just not exactly sure what it is.

SEVENTEEN

THE THING ABOUT THE FIRST day of school is that you feel so great when you finish it. It's this complete feeling of relief, like you survived. You made it. But then you realize that was just one day. You have so many more to go.

When you realize that, the amazing relief fades.

And then you actually feel terrible and overwhelmed.

Maximum-high levels of agita.

I walk through the door and up the stairs, ready to collapse on my bed. As I pass Ryan's room, I stop ever so slightly. I hear beeping and crashing and the normal video game sounds, but no talking.

Once you realize you have a crush, you can't get away from it and you can't ignore it. It's, like, always there at the front of your brain. A hole in your jeans that keeps getting bigger and bigger every time you wear them.

My mom has a late meeting so she's not making dinner. I'm ordering pizza, want to come over? I text Ari, but she doesn't respond.

I can't wait forever—first days of school make a girl really hungry.

I try to tell myself that it's not a big deal. She's probably doing her homework and practicing piano. Maybe she's talking to her mom—she always likes to hear every detail about the day. And then they'll all have dinner—they're big on the whole family eating together. And Gemma talks so much; I'm sure they're still at the table listening to everything that happened on the first day of third grade.

I just feel extra-weird because Ari and I didn't ride the bus home together today. Ari had a doctor's appointment after school and her mom picked her up. I mean, who schedules a doctor's appointment on the first day of school?

That just seems cruel, but I didn't say anything.

After I finish my homework, I check my email, and then do some more eavesdropping. Ryan and Tyler never say anything.

I wonder if boys ever talk to each other at all, and I make a mental note to ask Jason about it once I've gotten to know him better.

My crush is in the next room and I'm not even getting

any good information. And my best friend is around the corner and we're not even rehashing our first day of middle school. Or working on our 11 Before 12 List.

Something is wrong here. Something is very wrong.

Finally, I can't take it anymore. I throw on my flip-flops, and I knock on Ryan's door and tell him I'm going to Ari's for a few minutes. He doesn't respond. He never responds.

I wait a minute for Tyler to say something, but he's quiet, too. So I take my house key and run downstairs before I have time to second-guess my decision.

"How was the first day of school?" Mrs. Etisof asks.

"It was, um, good!" I yell back. I really don't have time to talk right now, and I hope she gets that. I don't want to seem rude. It's great that she's outside so much, but sometimes I just don't have time to talk.

I glance over at Jason's house, hoping to see him outside, but he's not there.

When I get to Ari's, I walk around the side of her house to see if she's in her room, and then I realize that's super-creepy, so I run back around to the front and ring the doorbell.

Her mom answers a few seconds later. "Oh hi, Kaylan."

"Hi!" I smile. "Is Ari home?"

"Um, yes, she's home." Something seems off, but I'm not sure what. Usually, she's cheerier when she sees me. Maybe she had a bad day. Maybe the first day of school is hard on moms, too.

She holds the door open for me. "I think she's in her room."

I knock gently on Ari's door and then say, "Housekeeping! Do you need any towels?" I don't get any response. I wait a few seconds and then say, "Hey, Ar, it's me. I figured I'd surprise you." I laugh a little because I suddenly feel stupid saying all of this when I'm not even sure she's listening. "Can I come in?"

She opens the door. "Um, what are you doing here?" she asks.

"Well, I figured I'd surprise you, pop in, and we can rehash the day."

Ari sighs, walks back into her room, and I take that as a sign that it's okay to follow her.

The 11 Before 12 List is sitting out on her desk. I brought my copy, too, because I carry it pretty much everywhere I go.

"What do you want to rehash, exactly?" Ari asks me. "The fact that you didn't save me a seat at lunch? The fact that you and that Cami girl are BFFs now?"

"Ari, come on."

"Don't *come on* me, Kaylan." She pulls her hair back into a ponytail, and sits up straighter on her bed. "You know it's true."

"Well, it's not what I planned," I say quietly, and sit down on the edge of her bed. "I was looking all over for you in the cafeteria. And truthfully, I kind of thought you sat somewhere else."

"Kaylan," she snaps. "I would never do that. Not in a million years. On our first day of middle school! Never!"

"Okay." I look down at my worn-out flip-flops on the floor of Ari's room. They're visible proof in shoe form that summer is over, and we can't go back to it. "But why were you late?"

"I got lost!" She sniffles and rubs her eyes. "I was in the B wing, and I forgot that I needed to cross over to the A wing to get to the cafeteria. Somehow I ended up by the gym! I had to ask a teacher where to go! I don't even know what happened."

"Okay, well, we need to make a plan," I say, "so this never happens again."

Ari listens. "Go on."

"A meeting spot. A code word," I explain. "If we ever need to talk privately, we say the word *photo* and we meet by the darkroom on the third floor."

"But how will you know if I'm lost? Or how will I know you need to talk?" she asks. "And I didn't even know there was a darkroom!"

"I saw it today; I have astronomy up there. So, just know that's our meeting spot," I tell her. "Remember our code word. And we'll fine-tune it. And I'm sor—"

Right as I'm about to apologize for what happened

today, Ari's phone rings. She looks at it, smiles, and then answers.

"Hey, Jason," she says.

Jason?

They're at the talk-on-the-phone level of friendship now? Jason and I are just texting friends, and not even every day.

And she's mad at me that I talked to Cami at lunch?

"Yeah, it was good," she says, turning away from me. "I mean, the science teacher I have seems really strict. She grades homework! So crazy. How was your day?"

Seriously?

Then I realize I didn't even see Jason at lunch. I was too stressed about Ari. I wonder who he sat with. I'll text him later.

I stare at Ari, hoping she'll turn around and look at me and give me some kind of sign about what's going on. But she keeps her back to me. And I start to feel worse and worse. Maybe I should give them privacy. But I wouldn't know where to go.

Get off the phone. Get off the phone. Get off the phone.

I don't know what to do, where to look. I feel around in my pocket for my phone, but it's not there. I guess I left it at home. My throat burns like I'm about to cry. I feel like I should leave, but I can't leave right now, not with the way things are between us.

"Really? That's so weird," Ari says, and then bursts into laughter. "Just come over. I'll show you my schedule again."

Ari has been on the phone for three centuries.

Finally, after what feels like a million more questions and a million more minutes of laughing, she gets off the phone.

"That was Jason," she says, like I couldn't have figured it out. "He's coming over."

"I guessed that. Because you said 'hey Jason.' And also 'come over.'"

"Don't be rude, Kaylan." She hops off her bed and grabs her laptop off the shelf, opens it up, and starts typing. Like I'm not even here.

"Can we discuss what's going on?" I ask. All my good feelings about the first day start to fade away like marker on a dry-erase board.

"What do you want to discuss?" She closes her laptop and folds her hands on top of it.

"Um, first, why you're mad at me. Second, Jason. Third, what you're wearing tomorrow. Fourth, the list."

Second-day outfits are almost as important as first-day outfits, but nobody realizes it. I mean, everyone's still looking at you on the second day of school the way they are on the first. So it's just as big of a deal to choose carefully.

"I'm mad at you because you pretty much forgot about

142

me. I was wandering around alone, looking for you, after I was completely lost, and I was panicking that you were panicking. But then I found you, sitting without me, and you were totally fine!" she yells. "Jason is my friend and neighbor. He calls me. I call him. Remember our guy friend thing? I'm wearing my ripped black jean shorts and that hot-pink uneven-bottomed T-shirt we got at the mall a few weeks ago. And we have to decide on our next thing on the list."

"Okay. Thanks for responding to all my items." I smile. "I'm sorry you think I forgot about you. I totally didn't."

"Okay." She stays quiet for a minute and then, smiling, she says, "Listen, Kay, I gotta finish some homework." She puts her hand out. "Truce?"

I take her hand. "Truce." I pull my hand away and decide I'll stay and hang a few more minutes, until Jason comes over.

But Ari starts doing her homework, and I realize I'm just sitting here staring at her old class pictures on the wall. I stand up to leave.

"Hey hey hey," Jason says.

"Hey!" I say, and decide to sit back down.

Ari launches straight into schedule talk. "So you switched math with history? And you changed electives?" she asks. "That means we will have history together. . . ." They get into such an in-depth conversation about this that my head starts to spin.

"Guys, I know this conversation is important, but we also need to discuss something even more important," I start. "Do we think the hot lunches at school are made from real food? Or is it some kind of weird science experiment?"

I crack up, thinking they'll join in, but Ari just stares at me, and Jason only lets out a tiny giggle.

Finally Jason says, "I must admit, I, um, ate the burrito today."

"You ate a school cafeteria lunch burrito on the first day?" I shriek. "That's, like, the most daring lunch option you could've picked."

"It is." He stands up and bows. "And I lived to tell the tale. I am literally superhuman."

I clap for him and wait for Ari to join in, but she doesn't.

"Ari! Show some excitement—you and I have a superhuman friend!" I stand up and smile. "I better get home."

"See you at the bus in the morning?" Ari asks.

I nod. "And we'll decide on the next list item on the ride to school?"

"Sounds good."

"You two and your list." Jason laughs. "Should we take bets on if you'll actually complete it?"

"No, of course not," I say. "Obviously, we'll complete it."

"Yeah," Ari adds. "Kaylan thinks something really bad will happen to us if we don't finish the list." She looks at Jason and rolls her eyes.

"Ari!" I yell.

"Like, what'll happen?" Jason asks, sitting down on Ari's bed. "You'll have to finish sixth grade on Mars?"

Ari cracks up.

"Yeah, exactly." I glare at them. "Or everyone we know, ahem, our superhuman friend, will turn into frogs!"

Thankfully they laugh at that, and I leave Ari's room and her house. For a few seconds I feel better, like we worked things out and didn't let awkwardness linger. That's what happened with my BFFs in fourth grade, and then the lingering went on so long that by the time any of us dealt with it, we weren't even really friends anymore.

That can't happen with Ari and me. I won't let it.

But on the walk home, I start to feel the agita again. The Jason thing is bugging me. I mean, that didn't seem like the first time he'd called her. And then he came over—and it was sort of fun, but also a little awkward. I felt left out of their neighborly friendship.

When I get home, I find my mom sitting at the kitchen table, staring at her phone.

"Kaylan!" she screams.

"What?" I startle.

"I had no idea where you were! I've been calling your phone over and over again. I checked your computer. I searched your room. I have been—"

"Mom." I put my hands on her shoulders. "Calm down. Please calm down. I was at Ari's. I told Ryan."

"He said you disappeared." She starts wiping her eyes, and I see tears dribbling down.

"Mom." I step back and fold my arms across my chest, fired up and angry.

I take a deep breath, and I put an arm around her. I guide her over to the couch in the den.

Once we're seated and she's stopped crying, I say, "I told Ryan. It's not my fault he's a complete imbecile. I'm sorry you were worried. I had a hard day, too."

I didn't plan to cry, but once I start talking, the tears well up in the corners of my eyes.

"Oh, Kaylan, shhh," she says. "It's going to be okay." She pulls me into a hug, and soon I'm soaking my mom's dressy blouse with my salty tears. I can smell her flowery perfume, and I want to cuddle against her forever and ever. I want her to magically make all my problems disappear. I want to be five again, watching cartoons with her on the couch after kindergarten, eating the snack buffet she put out for me, and not worrying about homework or boys or friends or anything.

She strokes my hair. "I'm sorry I got so worked up. I should relax. You're responsible."

"I am responsible." I sniffle.

We sit there for a little while longer, and she tells me some funny story about how one of her coworkers got a singing telegram for her birthday.

"He was dressed up like a giant rabbit, and he sang

'You Are My Sunshine.'"

We laugh a little about that, and she strokes my hair. "How was the rest of your day?" she asks.

"Well, my classes were okay, nothing crazy, but then everything went downhill at lunch," I start. "I was trying to find Ari so we could sit together but then she was late, and I couldn't walk around alone and then—"

I choke back tears but pretty soon I'm full-on sobbing again.

"First days are always hard. For everyone. It's okay," my mom says over and over.

I want to believe her, but I don't. It doesn't feel okay. I want everything to feel normal and safe and manageable. I just don't know how to make it that way.

EIGHTEEN

FOR THE NEXT WEEK, EVERY day at lunch, I make sure to save Ari a seat at the table with Cami and June and the other girls. They're not our friends yet. Not really. They're pretty much just lunch friends, but I'm okay with that. There are other girls who sit at the opposite end of the table, and I don't even know their names. Ari knows a few of them from some of her classes, and a few from Hebrew, but they're not BFF material. Not yet, anyway.

"Wait, so tell me about the kiss again," Cami says to June, leaning over the table.

My cheeks flash hot, and I look around. Have they all kissed someone already? And Ari and I are the only ones who haven't?

Saara looks down at her lap, and then goes up to refill her water bottle. I doubt she's kissed anyone.

"It was at this church family camp thing, at the end of the summer," June starts. "A million churches all together, like every Korean kid in Connecticut was there." She smiles. "And I met this kid Chris, and we just talked. I don't know." She starts giggling and we all stare at her, waiting for her to continue.

"And?" Cami asks, eyes wide.

"And that was it. We kissed on the last night." She shakes her head fast, all flushed. "I can't talk about it anymore, guys. It's too weird!" she squeals.

"Come on, June," one of the other girls from the end of the table says. I think her name is Amirah. "You have to give more details!"

She shakes her head again. "I can't! Lunch is over!" She stands up to throw away her trash. "Ta-ta!"

Everyone stares at her as she leaves the table, and then we all just look at each other. She just left us hanging. I want to know how the first kiss actually happened, the steps from beginning to end. I wonder if anyone else has a first kiss story to share, if they'll share them tomorrow.

Ari and I talk with our eyes as we're leaving the cafeteria.

My eyes say: *So glad we're walking together.*

Ari's eyes say: *Me too.*

"Bye, guys," Cami says to us.

"Bye," we reply at the same time.

Cami always stops in the bathroom after lunch to

triple check that there isn't any food in her teeth, so she doesn't walk with me to science. It's kind of good because Ari and I can walk together and make plans without anyone else feeling bad.

"So you're coming over after school, right?" I ask her, as we walk down the hall.

"Uh-huh."

"Let's try to do two things on our list this week," I suggest.

"I have one idea that'll work perfectly for us," Ari says. "My temple is having this major event this weekend to raise money for the local soup kitchen. And they need volunteers to pass out hors d'oeuvres and stuff."

"Yeah?"

We stop in front of the classroom where Ari has English and finish chatting. "So I thought it could be our help-humanity thing or at least help us get started with it. I know we attempted to clean up the toys in your basement, but that wasn't really helping humanity. Just your mom."

I think about it for a second. "Yeah, you're right. We can definitely do it," I say, careful not to shoot down her idea. Everyone's allowed to help out at Ari's synagogue, and I've gone to fun events there like the Purim carnival, but I always feel a little funny, since I'm not Jewish. "But we still need something bigger." I bulge out my eyes. "Like, major."

Ari looks around the hallway, like she's embarrassed people will hear us. "Um, okay, Kaylan." She laughs, walking into her classroom. "I guess we'll discuss it more later."

On the walk home from the bus stop, Ryan and Tyler are in front of us, and I can't focus. My heart is all pat-pat-flutter-flutter, and I can't calm it down.

Tyler's shorts are hanging low on his hips, and he keeps yanking them up as he walks.

Step. Yank. Step. Yank.

I keep thinking that Tyler walked right here, just moments ago. He's right in front of me. My shoes are touching the same sidewalk that his shoes touched.

I feel like a total crazy person. Why am I thinking about these things? This obsession with Tyler is in full force and I don't even know when it started or why.

It's like it just happened, out of nowhere, like when your feet grow and suddenly your shoes don't fit. You didn't see them grow, you don't even know when they grew. But you know your shoes don't fit anymore.

"Look at him," I whisper and nudge Ari with my elbow.

"What?" she whispers back. I clearly caught her in the middle of deep thought.

"Tyler." I nudge my head in his direction.

"What about him?"

I glare at her, but she doesn't notice. I stop walking,

pull her close, and whisper, "Look how his hair sticks up just the tiniest bit in the back, like that one little piece of hair at the base of his neck. And that little patch of sunburn on his neck, like he missed a spot. He's so cute."

Ari cracks up. "Kaylan, seriously? I mean, I get that he's cute. But is that the only reason you like him?"

I nod, wondering how many reasons you really need to like someone. We let them get a little farther ahead of us, so I'm sure they won't overhear. "He's not just cute. He's so cute. And look at the curls on the back of his head. They just stay there, like, perfectly. Like he curled them himself, but he didn't, they're natural. And they're so cute!"

"You've got to stop saying cute!" Ari hits me on the arm.

I squeal, and probably too loud because a few seconds later Ryan and Tyler turn around to look at us.

"Why are you guys following us?" Ryan asks.

"Um, duh!" I yell. "We live in the same house, flea brain."

"Um, duh, but there are other ways to go. We take the long way so we can pass the skateboard park. *Duh*."

Tyler doesn't say anything, but he laughs when Ryan says that. Probably because he feels that he has to. I mean, they are best friends.

Ari rolls her eyes in their direction. "Don't listen to them," she says under her breath.

Ari and I get to my house and make a whole buffet of snacks on the kitchen table, the way my mom used to do when she was home in the afternoons. Chips and chocolate-chip cookies, pink lemonade, and every snack we can find in the pantry.

"I'm going to get my copy of the list!" I tell Ari, running upstairs.

But by the time I get back downstairs, Tyler and Ryan are feasting on our buffet. And Ari is sitting at the table, looking at her phone. Probably texting Jason.

All those snacks that I was so excited to eat suddenly make my stomach feel all rumbly, like I swallowed too much water.

With Tyler in the room, even picking up a single chip feels impossible. And if I managed to pick it up, it would take me forty-five minutes to eat it.

I go to tuck the list into my backpack, but Ryan snatches it away before I have the chance.

"What's this?" he asks.

"Oh, nothing." I try to grab it back, but he holds it above his head and I can't reach it.

"Ryan! Come on! Why do you even care what I'm doing, anyway? Your life is so lame that all you have to focus on is your little sister's stuff?"

Tyler puts his hand into the chips bowl, not even paying attention.

"Ryan, come on," Ari says. "Just give it back."

But he ignores her, too.

"Whole Me Makeover!" Ryan bursts into laughter and attempts to show Tyler the list. My cheeks are on fire. My heartbeat is in my ears.

I stand up on a kitchen chair and snatch it away from him. Thank God he didn't see the *Sabotage Ryan* part!

"Get out of here," I say, to Ryan of course but also to Tyler, because the truth is I can't think clearly when he's around. Words come out jumbly, and I start to itch all over.

Ryan takes the whole bowl of chips and leaves the kitchen with it. Dummy. He doesn't know there's a whole other bag in the pantry.

"I don't know why he's become literally the biggest jerk in the world," I tell Ari. "I mean, he wasn't always like this."

"You've been asking me this for a month already," Ari reminds me and bites into her apple. "He's become a jerk. What can I say?"

She's suddenly cold and patronizing. Like she's the smartest person in the world and I don't know anything at all.

Everyone is changing around me. I feel like I'm at the airport, standing on the regular floor, while everyone I know is on one of those conveyer belt people-mover things.

"Anyway, back to the list," I tell her, trying to refocus.

"I say we tackle the *Do something we think we'll hate* thing next."

"Yeah, I wonder if there's a yoga club at school. We're still gonna do yoga, right?" She looks at me. "Maybe we could even use it for gym credit."

"Hmm, maybe." I finish my cookie, hoping the instructor from the class at the pool was okay. She got into some water skiing accident. "I need to exercise and calm down, and this solves both."

Ari's about to respond when her phone vibrates.

Oh no. Is this another Jason call?

She starts typing back a text reply, and I can't help but ask who it is. I'm nosy.

"This girl Marie. She sits at the other end of our lunch table."

I nod, eager for her to get to the point.

"She's in my math class, and we exchanged numbers so we could go over the homework, but it turns out she's really cool. She's always texting me about new bands and stuff."

I try to seem impressed and happy about this Marie person, but inside I'm singeing. Ari gets mad at me for talking to other girls at lunch, and yet she has a new texting BFF.

Not cool. Not cool at all.

"She lives around the corner from that cool coffee place. Where they have all those crazy muffins," Ari tells me like it's the most interesting thing she's ever talked about. She's talking about muffins. Snooze. "Ya know what I mean?"

I nod. "Yeah. I've been there a hundred times."

"I'll ask Marie where she does yoga," Ari says, all excited like she's come up with an amazing plan. "I totally forgot, but she goes to a yoga class every Wednesday after school."

"Great," I say, pretending as hard as I can to be into this idea. "Do you think Tyler, like, only thinks of me as Ryan's sister, or does he think of me as a real person?"

Ari laughs and takes another sip of lemonade. "Ummm. I have no clue. Both, I guess."

"Hey, flea brain," Ryan calls from the hallway. Oh God. Did he just hear that? He just heard that whole entire thing, I bet.

"Don't answer, pretend we're not here," I say to Ari through my teeth.

"He's staring right at us, Kay." She nudges her head in his direction.

"Ari, I know my sister is the most annoying person in the world. All she does is talk about *Tyler*," he sings. "You're probably sick to death of hearing about him!"

"Ryan!" I scream, and run over to start pounding on his back with my fists. "Get out of here! You don't even know what we were talking about!"

"Right." He runs away, letting the screen door slam behind him.

Ari looks down at her lap. "Um. That wasn't great."

"Yeah, not at all." I stare out the window and ignore my throat-stinging-about-to-cry feeling. "Wanna do homework together?"

"Actually, I think I have to go. My mom said something about my grandma coming over. Don't worry about Ryan," Ari says, grabbing an apple out of the bowl. "Can I take this for the walk home?"

"Sure," I grumble. "Text me later?" I ask, but what I'm really thinking is, *If you're not texting Marie . . . or calling Jason.*

My brother just completely harassed me, and she couldn't even stay.

Ari nods and leaves my house and I'm left at the kitchen table all alone with a million snacks in front of me. They're all my favorite stuff, too—chocolate-chip cookies, Cheetos, those little cheese slices wrapped in wax, mini Snickers—and I don't want to eat any of it.

This is not how I envisioned this afternoon going. Not at all.

To be honest, I'm not sure anything is going according to how I envisioned it. Not this afternoon, not the list, not middle school.

I wonder if anyone's plans ever go the way they think

they will go or if life is basically one big question mark.

I finish the whole bowl of strawberries and try to come up with an answer, but by the time I'm done, I feel just as clueless as when I started.

I decide to text Jason: **What's up?**

Nada.

What r u up to?

At this kid Andre's house. Peace.

So Jason has new friends, too. I mean, I expected that. Just because he was our new guy friend didn't mean we were going to be the only friends he had.

I walk up the stairs, all ready to start my homework, when I hear, "What's your sister's deal?"

It's Tyler.

My deal?

"Um, her deal. I don't think she has a deal. But she's a pain in the butt, I can tell you that," Ryan replies. "See, if you want to get to the next level on this game, you need to make sure all the mines are covered. It's the only way."

"Yeah, man. I know," Tyler says, and then pauses for a second. "But your sister is way less of a pain than mine."

My heart bubbles up a little when he says that—like water for spaghetti right as it's about to boil.

It's not even that nice of a thing, that major of a compliment.

But Tyler was talking about me. Really and truly he was.

Maybe Tyler doesn't just think of me as Ryan's sister. I mean, if that's the only way he thought of me, he wouldn't wonder what *my deal* was.

I'm a real person to him.

NINETEEN

FOR THE NEXT FEW DAYS, I live on Tyler's words. I mean, really live on them. I think about them all the time.

But your sister is way less of a pain than mine.

"So what do you think he meant by that?" I ask Jason. We're sitting in the entryway of the school, waiting for our moms to pick us up. I feel a little weird talking to him about this stuff, because it's kinda personal, but he doesn't seem to mind. And isn't that part of the point of having a guy friend? Guys have to know what other guys are thinking way better than girls know what they're thinking.

I'm kind of glad it's just Jason and me for a change. Ari stayed for extra help, too, but I guess her session didn't get out yet.

"Um." Jason makes an over-the-top-perplexed sort of

face. "He means—wait for it—that you're less of a pain than his sister."

"Jason!" I yelp. "Be serious. Please. For once."

"Well, he probably means what he says. But what he's not saying is that he's thinking about you enough to bring you up. So I'd say that's something."

"Something? What do you mean?"

"No clue." He stands up when he sees his mom's car pull into the school lot. "Later, Kaylan. See ya *mañana*."

My mom is always late. She's late so often that I barely even expect her to be on time anymore. She's so late that all the after school clubs are letting out now, and the parking lot is filling up with more cars. I stare at my phone, like someone really important is texting, and I'm so busy that her lateness doesn't even get to me.

I'm still waiting for her when Ari and Marie come down the hall from their math extra-help session.

"Hey, Kay," Ari says to me, making a sad face. She knows all about my mom's lateness.

"Oh, hey, Kaylan," Marie says, like she's known me her whole life. She's fake-chummy and I hate that. At least be real. That's my motto. I mean, I made it up just now, but it's still my motto. My new motto.

"Hey," I reply. Marie and Ari aren't alone, though. Soon three other girls from the end of our lunch table come traipsing behind them.

They sit down on the bench, all five smooshed

together, and another girl says, "That was soo hilarious. I can't believe Ms. Dashner had, like, no idea he was chewing gum!" And then another girl says, "I bet he does that in every class and gets away with it."

"Totally," Ari adds.

Seriously? They're talking about someone chewing gum like it's just *sooo* fascinating.

"Arianna is so going to be the first one of all of us to have her first kiss," Marie declares, like that's what they went over in extra help, and it's a fact that everyone needs to know.

First one of all of us? Ari's part of an "all of us"?

"Stop." Ari hits her on the arm, and then looks at me like she's making sure that I heard.

Oh, I heard. I heard loud and clear.

"Yeah, Arianna, I agree," another girl says.

Things are shifting and I feel it. But I don't know what it is exactly and I don't know why it's happening. And the scariest thing of all: I don't know how to stop it.

"Oh, guys, my mom's here," one of the girls says. "Come on."

They all get up at the same time and walk toward the double doors. Ari stops right in front of me and says, "I'll call you later, Kaylan. Okay?" And she blows me a kiss.

I guess that one mom is driving all of them home, but they didn't think to offer me a ride. My best friend didn't even offer me a ride home! I feel like my head is on fire.

After that, I sit on the curb and wait forever for my mom. And people give me these pity looks while I'm waiting. They ask things like, "Are you okay? Are you sure you don't need a ride? Can we call someone for you?" I just smile and say I'm fine, but what I really want to do is find some secret bunker and hide away from all these people. If I have to be waiting here forever, I'd at least like to be invisible.

When my mom finally arrives to pick me up, she says through the open window, "So sorry, Kaylan. Everything ran late today, and then there was traffic."

I get in the car and slam the door.

I don't say anything; I just sit there and stare out the window as she drives out of the school parking lot.

"Are you okay?" she asks.

"No! You're late. I mean, really, really late. People thought I'd been abandoned! And I'm starving. They don't have snacks at extra help, ya know."

"Kaylan," she says, driving through the yellow light. "I came as fast as I could. There were a few last-minute patients I had to see. My phone was out of battery and I didn't want to waste time charging it to text that I was going to be late."

"Fine."

"You know I'm doing my best, right?"

"I'm doing my best, too," I say, even though I wonder if that's really true. Maybe we all think that we're doing our best, but we could actually do a lot better. I mean, how does anyone know what their best really is? Maybe it's something we feel. Or maybe it's how exhausted we are at the end of the day.

I don't think my mom's doing her best, even though she says she is. Her best would be arriving on time. It's like a basic part of motherhood. And life.

"We'll order in Chinese food," my mom says, like it's a remedy that's going to make everything better. It won't make everything better—but it's a start. My mom and I have a thing with food—we like eating together. It comforts us.

"Can we both get egg rolls?" I ask. Usually we share an egg roll and an order of scallion pancakes, but I'm feeling extra-hungry tonight.

"Sure," she says, pausing, like she's about to tell me bad news. "Can we discuss social media for a second?"

"Um . . . what about it?"

"How much you do it, I guess? The principal sent an email that we need to be vigilant about social cruelty, what our children are doing online, and I just want to be aware."

I roll my eyes. "Really, Mom? You think I'm cruel on social media? Don't start this, okay?"

"Kaylan, I'm your mother, and frankly, this social media business scares me. People can really get hurt. And do not speak to me like that!"

"Fine. Sorry. Honestly, I don't even go on that much. Maybe an Instagram pic every now and then . . ."

"Okay, well, maybe we can look at it together sometime soon," she says, pulling into the driveway. "Go upstairs and do all your homework. We'll eat at seven."

I put an arm around her as we walk inside. "Mom, you don't need to worry so much about social media. But the lateness thing—try to work on it, okay?"

She laughs and drops her bag on the entryway table. "I'll worry about what I want to worry about. That's my right, as a mother."

"Mothers are the only ones with rights, I guess!"

I traipse up the stairs.

TWENTY

MY PHONE RINGS AN HOUR into my homework. It's Ari FaceTiming me. A tiny little corner of my brain calms down when I see her number. Like, okay, we're still friends. She still cares about me. She hasn't totally moved on to Marie and the other lunch table girls.

I click the green button, and I see her sitting on her bed, her hair tied up in a bun.

"What's up?" she asks, not looking at the camera in the right way, so I see mostly the top of her head.

"Ugh." I lean back in my desk chair. "My mom is suddenly obsessed with social media."

"Huh? Like she's on it?"

"No." I laugh. "Like she wants to know what I'm doing on it."

"Oh, whatever, moms being moms," she says, popping

some gum in her mouth. "What else is up?"

"Ryan's being a pain again. He keeps saying he's gonna tell Tyler I like him. It's gonna be so embarrassing."

"I don't even get why you like Tyler," she says. "I mean, he never even says anything. And he laughs like a weird cartoon boy."

When she says it like that, my cheeks get hot, and I feel like I have to defend him—like he's running for president and I'm voting for him, and I need everyone else to vote for him, too.

"Well, he's supercute, which you know, and he's, like, cool, and he never gets flustered and stuff. . . ."

Ari looks away for a second, like her mind is wandering and she's thinking about something else. "Uh, okay. You didn't really say much. But whatever."

"Well, I'll make a list of all the reasons he's awesome." I pause. "Is Ryan right? That you're sick to death of hearing me talk about Tyler? I mean, I haven't even been talking about him for that long."

Ari looks away from the screen and stays quiet for a few seconds. "Well, you do kind of fixate on things."

"What?" I recoil.

She looks back at the screen and says, "You asked."

"Fine," I say, swallowing hard. I feel like I was just slapped in the face with her honesty. Sometimes it's okay to lie a little, I think. "So what else is going on, then?"

She takes her hair out of the bun and shakes it around

a little; the red highlights still look so good. "Well, did I tell you that Jason is actually going to this watch convention next week? With his grandpa and his dad. Where they just look at watches!"

"No." It stings that Jason didn't tell me either. Especially since I text him a picture of a different watch every day. I am trying so hard to show interest in his interests! I'm really trying to be a good friend to him.

"Isn't that so weird?" she asks.

I nod. "Well, we know he really likes watches." And then a tiny little flicker goes off in my brain—does Ari like Jason?

Thankfully, I hear my mom calling me to come down and set the table so I can end this FaceTime call.

But then all through dinner, the only thing I'm thinking about is Ari and that awkward comment about Tyler. She thinks I fixate on things. I guess she's right. But I thought she sort of accepted that about me. Maybe even embraced it. I'm her best friend. "What's wrong with her?" Ryan asks my mom, waving his spoon in my direction.

"Ryan," my mom whispers. "Leave her be. Leave her be."

"Sheesh. I'm just asking. She hasn't said a single word this whole meal. Not even asking for another dumpling."

"Pass the dumplings, please," I say.

But instead of doing that, Ryan pops the last one in

his mouth. "Should've spoken up sooner," he says, and laughs.

I don't respond. He's looking for a fight.

And I won't give it to him.

TWENTY-ONE

IT TAKES ABOUT A WEEK to coordinate it, but Ari and I finally go to the yoga class at the studio where Marie goes. Marie was supposed to go with us, but she got stomach flu at the last minute. I know this is the meanest thing in the world to say, but I'm happy about it. I'm happy that Marie is hovering over her toilet, puking her guts out while we are on our way to yoga. I'm horrible. I know I am.

But the thing is, Ari and I need some time together, just the two of us. We can get things back to the way they used to be. I know we can. We need to be just us, 100 percent in it and focused on our friendship, with no distractions.

"This doesn't seem like a beginner's class," I whisper to Ari when we're in downward dog.

"It's actually mixed levels," she whispers back. "Sorry."

I thought that yoga was one of those things where you only have to do what you're comfortable with and what you're, like, physically able to do. But my wrists hurt, and having my butt high in the air like this is making me dizzy for some reason, like it's making my equilibrium (is that even a thing?) all unbalanced.

It's ten minutes into the class and I already feel worse about myself than I was feeling before.

I wasn't sure that was possible, but this is definitely something I thought I'd hate, that I am actually hating.

"Just try," Ari says, when she sees me hanging out in child's pose for way too long.

"I am," I defend. I try to do that pose where one leg is high in the air and you're supposed to lean all of your weight on one arm. I slip and fall flat on my face, literally ripping a piece of the yoga mat off with my fingernail.

I burst out laughing, unable to control it. And that's when Ari starts laughing, too. Soon, we're both flat on our stomachs, laughing hysterically.

"Okay, so I think you're still as uncoordinated as you were when we had to learn those African dance moves in gym last year," Ari says, trying hard to get the words out through her laughter.

I laugh. "Yeah, my coordination has not improved. Sorry," I say, when the teacher comes over to us.

"Girls," she says. "I'm glad you're enjoying yourselves.

But please do try and focus."

"Focusing," Ari says.

For the rest of the class, I really try and do everything and follow the teacher's instructions. At least I think I mastered happy baby, so that's something.

And I'm grateful that we put this on our list. Maybe we won't become amazing at yoga or anything, but at least Ari and I laughed together. For that moment, it felt like things were the way they used to be.

Back to BFF. During yoga, at least.

After class, Ari's mom drives us back to her house.

"I don't think we're masters at yoga yet," I announce when we're comfy on the beanbag chairs in Ari's room. "But it's a start. Can we check it off our list and move on to the next thing?"

"I guess."

"Victory ritual!" I say. I stand up and grab her hand, so she does, too.

Jump in the air. High-five. Hug.

Sometimes we shorten it and call it the JHH. It helps us remember it.

Ari sits back down and stays quiet for a minute. "I know we just did the JHH, but now I'm thinking—we only did yoga once. Does that count? Should we have checked it off already?"

"I think so. We never said we had to be yogis."

She rolls her eyes. "Okay, that's true, but the point was

that we did one thing we didn't like, and maybe we didn't give it enough of a chance."

"I guess we could always go to one other class," I say, resigned.

Ari leans back in her chair. "Marie really likes her class."

"You're obsessed with Marie's yoga class!" I laugh, mostly kidding, but a tiny bit serious.

"I'm obsessed? Yeah, right!" She rolls her eyes again. Did she always roll her eyes this much and I'm just noticing it now? "What should we move on to, then?"

"I'm kind of hoping for the first kiss thing," I announce. "They talk about it at lunch a lot. Ya know?"

"Well, I'm, like, in the exact middle of the table lately, so I usually end up in conversations with Marie and the girls on her end," Ari reminds me. "And they don't talk about it every day. So I don't really know. Why are you guys so obsessed with it anyway? Because of June and Cami?"

Her question stings even though she probably didn't mean it to come out the way it did. Also, wasn't Ari the one discussing first kisses with Marie just the other day?

The thing is, Ari's pretty much part of Marie's group now. Sydney, Kira, Lizzie, and the one they just call M.W.—I don't even know what it stands for. And June and Cami and the quiet girl, Saara, are really the only new friends I've made.

She doesn't need to insult them.

But maybe she's jealous. June's probably the prettiest girl in the grade, and she does like to tell people how she had her first kiss this past summer at camp. So I guess that might get annoying to hear over and over again.

And Cami's bubbly and chatty and pretty much friends with everyone in the grade already. I see how that can be intimidating.

"I guess," I say. "But I'm hoping I can kiss someone, too, pretty soon, anyway. It is on our list. And we don't have tons of time left. We have, like, a month and a half."

Ari doesn't say anything.

"Why? You don't want to?"

"No, I do." She leans forward. "I'm just not obsessed with it."

I pretend to scratch an itch on the side of my eye, but what I'm really doing is forcing the tears to stay where they are. This works sometimes. I do it when my dad calls. I always cry when I talk to him. Every single time. I should be used to the fact that he moved out, that he lives in Arizona for work now, and that he doesn't want to be married to my mom anymore.

But I'm not used to it. I don't think I'll ever be used to it.

"So our birthday party," Ari says, changing the subject. "I feel like we need to send out invitations soon. Paper or online?"

"Def online," I say, stretching out my legs. "We shouldn't waste paper, and I think people will respond quicker if they get an email."

Ari nods. "Yeah, you're right. And you still think we should have it here?"

"Definitely," I say. "Easy peasy, we'll order pizzas, and get soda and stuff, and we can have it in your backyard if it's nice, or in the basement—"

"Okay, but the guest list." Ari stands up, and turns on her ceiling fan. "That's gonna be tricky. Ya know?"

"Yeah," I reply, after a deep breath. I adjust my legs on the beanbag chair so they don't fall asleep. "You make a list of who you think we should invite, and I will, too, and then we'll compare and finalize. But—we still have tons to do before the party. So what should our next list item be?"

I pick the list up off of Ari's desk, and we look it over together.

Eleven Fabulous Things to Make Us Even More AMAZING Before We Turn Twelve

1. Make a guy friend. ✓
2. Do a Whole Me Makeover.
3. Get on TV for something cool we've done (not because we got hit by a bus).

4. Help humanity.
5. Highlight our hair. ✓
6. Do something we think we'll hate. ✓
7. Fulfill lifelong dream to kayak at night to the little island across the lake. (First step, find a kayak.)
8. Kiss a boy.
9. Get detention.
10. Have a mature discussion with our moms about their flaws.
11. Sabotage Ryan. ✓

"Well, here's the thing," Ari starts, leaning forward on her beanbag chair, and I get the sense that something bad is coming. "The help-humanity thing. We haven't really decided on what that's going to be."

"Yeah, I feel like the temple thing will be too awkward," I explain. "I don't want to be around Jules and all those girls. And it needs to be something really important. Like cleaning up an abandoned park, or collecting donations for moms who can't afford diapers, or starting a new food pantry."

My heart starts beating faster and faster. I'm more heated up about this than I expected to be.

"I want to invite Marie to do the list with us," Ari says like it's no big deal.

"What?" I can't believe what I'm hearing.

"I want to invite Marie to do the list with us," she repeats.

"Why?" I stumble to get the word out.

"To help humanity," she explains, talking with her hands like she's making a speech. "She doesn't have any friends. I know it seems like she's part of that group that sits at the end of the lunch table. She's not. She tries so hard. Too hard. They all find her annoying. No one likes her. She just sits there because her mom and Sydney's mom are first cousins."

She pauses for a moment. My throat stings.

Helping Marie doesn't feel big and important.

"This could help her," she goes on. "We could help her become less annoying to other people."

"Um, I don't think we can really do that."

Ari shakes her head. "I just feel like we can help her with social skills, and that could have a ripple effect. I mean, it's like a major personality makeover for her. Did you know that before me, she had never talked on the phone to anyone? I mean—"

"Okay. Stop." I can't hear any more about Miss Sob Story Marie. "I feel bad about that," I mumble. "But the list was our thing."

"Don't be so exclusive," Ari says, looking at the mini figurines on her windowsill instead of looking at me. "You need to think of other people besides yourself sometimes, Kaylan!"

I get up to go to the bathroom, but I don't really need to pee. When I'm in there, with the door closed, I put my head against the cool tiled wall and sob. I sob quietly so Ari can't hear me. And when I stop, I rub my eyes with cold water to remove the redness.

Maybe helping Marie is helping humanity, but in a very, very loose way. In such a loose way that I'm not even sure it counts. And if helping humanity is hurting your BFF in the process, then is it really even helping humanity at all?

There's one thing I know for sure, though: Ari and I are not back to being BFF.

Not at all.

Ari and I started this list together. It was our thing. She was my BFF. I know people say you can have more than one best friend, but you can't. It just doesn't work. Marie is snatching Ari away from me, and Ari's just going along with it. I don't care that she's annoying and she's never talked to anyone on the phone. It's not our job to fix her.

"Ya know what?" I say, as I leave the bathroom. "Do the list with Marie. Go to yoga with Marie. Eat lunch with Marie. Do everything with her. Be Marie's BFF. I'm done."

"Fine," Ari screams. "At least she doesn't spend every second talking about a dumb boy!"

I storm down the stairs and out of Ari's house and I

run all the way home. I glance behind me a few times to see if Ari follows me. She doesn't. Not that I wanted her to. Okay, maybe I did a little bit.

But just a little bit.

TWENTY-TWO

IT'S BEEN A WEEK WITHOUT Ari and life without her is pretty boring.

I sit at the end of the lunch table with June, Cami, Saara, and the straggler girls who sometimes sit there when they're not at extra help. They're June's friends, and I know they're not my friends. Not yet, anyway. But I'm okay with that.

The Whatevers, is how I think of them. They're nice and all. But since I'm not really part of the group, they're just *whatever* to me.

After the friend drama I had in fourth grade and now this Ari drama, I think I'm okay with being a loner for a little while. My plan is to be that cool, aloof girl. The one everyone wonders about.

I guess I've been trying to figure out for a while what

kind of middle school girl I was going to be. That was the point of the Whole Me Makeover, so I might as well lean into it.

I'll try the loner thing for a while and see how it works.

I'm walking to science when I see Mrs. Bellinsky hanging up the audition sheet for the fall talent show. I look closely and see that the date of the show is my twelfth birthday.

November 1.

It's a sign. A sign that I have to sign up. This talent show was basically made for me. Maybe it's part of the Whole Me Makeover, and maybe it's going to be recorded for the local news and will help me get on TV!

It's on my birthday. My twelfth birthday. The culmination of the entire list!

Okay, and I'll be honest—after Mrs. Bellinsky hung it up, I also saw that Tyler was signing up. That was also a sign. I mean, here I am: without a best friend, lonely, and hopelessly in love with Tyler. Then there's a fall talent show that just so happens to take place on my twelfth birthday, and the boy I'm obsessed with is signing up for it.

Of course I need to participate.

I make a mental note that if we still have our joint birthday party, it has to be on Ari's birthday. It can't be the same night as the talent show—no one would come!

There's just one problem—I'm not sure what my talent

is. Luckily I have a few weeks to figure that out. This is just the sign-up sheet. It's still a while away.

I may have sabotaged Ryan's chances for making the jam band, but he still plays guitar. Maybe he can help me learn? Doubtful. He hates me. I used to be able to juggle. And now that I have all this time, I can really practice.

I'm just not sure if juggling is seen as dorky or cool. Or is it dorky-cool? I'll have to take a survey at lunch.

As soon as I get to science, I sit down and turn toward Lizzie. "Are you doing the talent show?" I ask her.

She raises a corner of her mouth. "Nah," she replies. "I'm not really a talent show kind of gal."

I laugh. "Lizzie Lab Partner! Of course you are!"

"You're still calling me that?" She taps her pencil against my forehead. "No, really. I'm not a talent show person. I'll come cheer people on, though."

I sit back in my seat and face forward as soon as we see Mr. Paino coming in. "Should I try out?" I whisper to her, even though I already know my decision.

"Totally!" she whispers. "Please do it!"

"Any ideas for my act?" I ask her, as Mr. Paino writes on the dry-erase board.

"Not a clue," she replies, scribbling down the notes.

After school, I call Jason and hope that he can help me decide on an act. He's my trusty resource for all things creative.

"I heard about you and Arianna," he says as soon as he answers.

"You did?" I wasn't going to tell him. I figured he didn't want to hear about our girl drama. And I didn't want him to feel like he had to pick sides.

He sighs into the phone. "Yeah. Well, okay. I *overheard* Arianna talking about it to that girl Marie. They were on Ari's front porch after school today."

"And?"

"That's it."

"That can't be it, Jason." Sometimes I think this guy friend thing isn't all it's cracked up to be. He seems so dense. Like he doesn't understand that he needs to give all the information, not just a sliver. It's like eating the icing and forgetting about the rest of the cupcake.

"I don't really remember. . . ."

"Well, was Ari crying?"

He laughs a little. "Sorry. Um . . ."

"Did she seem really upset?"

"I guess? Maybe. I mean, she wasn't like screaming or anything. I'll listen better next time," he says, resigned. "Sorry."

"I'm sorry. I didn't mean to make you feel bad." I sink back into the couch. "I'm just going through a rough time right now. That's all."

"I hear you," he says. "Want me to come over?"

"Really?"

"Yeah, why not? We can do homework together."

As much as I'd love some company, my stomach flips when he suggests it. We've never hung out just the two of us before.

Ryan will definitely make fun of me for having a boy over. Also, I'm not even sure I'm allowed to, even though Jason is a friend. And third of all, what if Tyler sees? He might think I have a boyfriend and then I'll have zero chance of kissing him. Not that I really have a chance anyway. At least I don't think I do.

"Kaylan?" Jason says, and I realize I've been quiet for a really long time.

"Hi. Um, yeah, I'd love to do homework, but I can't because my mom is on her way home and we're, um, going shopping." I say it all so fast that I'm not even totally sure what I said.

"Oh. Okay. No biggie." He stops talking and I can hear him crunching potato chips or maybe pretzels. "I gotta go, though. This science lab seems hard."

"Okay. Good luck. Bye."

When we're off the phone I feel as if I've let something go, like a balloon that I didn't care about, lazily tied to a beach chair. But as soon as it's floating in the air, I really miss it.

It would have been nice to have Jason here doing homework with me. Because the truth is, my mom has a staff meeting and she won't be home for dinner. And Tyler and

Ryan picked up tacos and they're eating in Ryan's room.

I'm also sure it would have been awkward. What if Jason came up to my room and sat on my bed, and then I had to think about that when I went to sleep tonight?

And I bet his socks smell bad, because boys always have smelly socks. I'd have to use Febreze. And what would we have talked about? I mean, I guess the watch convention . . . but it would be weird to be one-on-one, in my room and stuff.

I'm too lazy to head upstairs to do homework. It's been that kind of week. So instead, I decide to stay downstairs, snack on honey-mustard pretzels, and use my mom's laptop.

It's slower than mine, but it'll do. I sign into my email and check for any sales going on at Perry Boutique downtown, and then I log into Instagram. My phone's out of battery and I'm too lazy to charge it. This is a new level of lazy and I'm not proud of it.

Okay, so for some reason my mom's computer is already signed into my Instagram account. But I've only been out of phone battery for, like, a day. This can only mean one thing.

MY MOTHER HAS BEEN LOGGING INTO MY INSTAGRAM ACCOUNT!

She's spying on me again!

My first instinct is to call Ari, but then I realize I can't do that. So I do what any sensible girl would do—I change the password. Immediately.

It's now *notformoms12*, and I'll change it again if I have to.

I feel surprisingly good after this, like I've accomplished enough for the day. Unfortunately, I have about three hours of homework to do, and I haven't even started it.

Then I get another idea.

I run up the stairs and knock on Ryan's door. When he doesn't answer, I start talking. "Ryan, you're never gonna believe what Mom did."

Silence.

"It's seriously crazy," I say.

He pops his head out. His cheeks are red and splotchy and there's a big tear droplet under his left eye. I peek my head around to see where Tyler is, but he's not in there. Unless he's hiding under the bed, which I seriously doubt.

"What is it, Kaylan?" Ryan asks. But instead of sounding mean, the way he usually does lately, he sounds exasperated.

"Um, nothing." My voice turns quiet. "I was just gonna tell you something Mom did. But, um, it can wait."

I peek around again, really confused because Tyler is always here.

"I'll be down soon," he replies. "Mom left me money, so we can order in those subs you like."

"Oh. Okay." I half smile, happy about the subs, but wondering what happened with Tyler. They talked about him coming over and eating tacos together on the bus this morning. "Sounds good."

I traipse back downstairs to get my backpack and start my homework, but that Ryan interaction pulls at my brain like a loose thread in a sweater.

He was crying, I think. But Ryan doesn't cry. Never. I swear, I've maybe seen him cry like twice in my whole life. Once, when he was in second grade, when his Little League team lost the championship game, and once when our grandpa Frankie died. He was ten.

Ryan didn't even cry when our dad left. I think he was too angry to cry. Especially because they were supposed to go shoot hoops at the YMCA that weekend and go out for burgers and shakes after.

I feel like now that I saw that tear, I'll never unsee it. It makes my throat hurt.

I try to focus on my homework, but there are too many distractions. My mind jumps back and forth from Ryan, to the list with Ari and how I'll finish it, to the talent show, to Jason. And of course to Tyler. I'm always thinking about Tyler. Even when I'm thinking about other things, thoughts of Tyler and his perfectly curly hair are there.

I keep putting my hair up, but it gives me a headache, so I take it down again. My neck feels itchy.

My mind won't slow down and my whole body is freaking out because of it.

Middle school students shouldn't have homework. Just making it through life these days feels like more than enough to handle.

TWENTY-THREE

I'M IN MRS. BELLINSKY'S ASTRONOMY elective, and Jason and I are passing notes.

Why aren't you trying out for the talent show? I pass the first note discreetly when Mrs. Bellinksy's back is to us.

I'm more of a behind-the-scenes guy. Maybe next year . . .

So behind-the-scenes guy—help me with my act!

We're paying attention, but Mrs. Bellinsky always puts the lesson online, so it's not as important for us to take notes in class. And also, it's an elective, so no one takes it super-seriously.

Then Jason writes: *What about competitive clementine peeling?* And I burst out laughing. I can't contain myself.

And then, in the middle of my laughing, Mrs. Bellinsky

comes over, grabs the note off the desk, and tells us we have detention. No warning. Nothing. Just detention.

And then I remember the list.

9. Get detention.

I'm accomplishing something on the list without even really trying! But then I remember Ari, and how we are supposed to do the list together. And I feel bummed again. How will we do our JHH ritual together? We won't be able to.

I guess this is one of those times when you really don't want something to happen, but then you realize you kind of do want it to happen, even though it's a bad thing.

Jason and I arrange to meet outside of the detention classroom as soon as school ends. Neither of us want to walk in alone. Every day I grow more and more grateful for Jason. It may be because I don't have Ari anymore, but I don't tell him that. And truthfully, I'm not even sure that's the reason.

Jason's a good person. He focuses on everything I say, like he's really listening. He cares about people. Sometimes kindness is the only important thing in a friend. Probably all the time.

By the time I get to detention, I'm exhausted from worrying. Worrying can make you really tired. I'm not sure if everyone knows that, but it's true.

"Thank God you're here," I say to Jason. He's finishing a bag of pretzels.

"You want the last one?"

He's giving me his last pretzel!

I nod and take the bag. There is literally only one pretzel left, but I'm grateful for the sustenance.

"I'm nervous," I say.

"Don't be." He shrugs. "We'll say we're sorry, do what they tell us, smile, say thank you, and go home."

I nod, unsure if that's the right approach. I guess it is.

"That's all you need to do in life," he tells me before we go in.

"Really?"

"Yup." He nods. "My dad says the secret to being successful at work is going in, saying good morning, doing your work, and going home."

I'm not sure how that advice applies here, and I'm also not sure why Jason's dad tells him this since he's only in sixth grade. I decide to store it away in my brain for a later time. Maybe when I get my first job.

We walk into the classroom, and there's a teacher I don't know or even recognize standing up in front and writing on the board.

He writes the word DETENTION in big black letters. I guess in case we forgot where we were, or in case someone stumbled into the wrong classroom. Then he writes:

1. Do homework
2. Write apology letter to teacher
3. Sit quietly
4. No talking

I'm not sure why he needed both number 3 and number 4. But one thing's for sure: he likes lists as much as I do!

Detention teacher sits back down at his desk, opens a paperback book with yellowing pages, and starts reading. He doesn't even tell us his name.

Jason and I look at each other and express our confusion with our eyes. Then I get to work. And when I'm sitting there, all still and quiet with my thoughts, that's when the agita sets in. Super-extreme agita.

It always starts with my thoughts spinning around and around like the roller ball thing on my computer. And my eyes don't know what to focus on. Then my scalp tingles, and my whole body gets hot—even my earlobes, which are extra-hot. My throat itches like I'm sitting with seven cats on my lap.

Putting detention on our list was a terrible idea. Everyone in here looks miserable, angry, exhausted. One kid is breaking pencils in half in his lap. Every time I hear the snap—my whole body jerks and my heart pounds a little faster.

The detention teacher doesn't even notice.

I try to tune it all out and focus on my homework. I have an English essay and a history worksheet, some pages to complete in my math textbook, and I have to finish a science lab we started in class.

I don't understand it at all; maybe I'll text Lizzie Lab Partner when I get home to see if she can help me with it.

I'm knee-deep in my English essay on *The Watsons Go to Birmingham* when I see Ari walking in out of the corner of my eye. At first I think it's a mirage. But then I look up, and then I realize that it is in fact her.

Ari is here.

In detention.

With me.

We could JHH! Right now!

I'm consumed with the most insatiable need to find out what she did that got her here, but of course I can't ask. I need to abide by the no-talking rule. God only knows what happens if you get in trouble while in detention. Then where do they send you—to the principal's office for a whole week?

Every few seconds, I feel the tiniest sense of relief that everything is going to be okay, and I'm almost done with this dreadful afternoon. Then I remember the saddest part of it: my mom.

Every kid that gets detention gets a call home.

The worst punishment of all lies in front of me, and I have no idea what it will be.

Ari takes a seat in the row in front of me, but we don't make eye contact. I'm not even sure she notices that Jason and I are here. She gets out her notebook and starts writing.

The clock above the door ticks and ticks; the loudest clock tick I've ever heard. It's the kind of sound that will stay in my brain even after I've left this room.

I need to know why Ari is here. I need to tell her that we're actually accomplishing something on the list together, and we didn't even plan it that way. I need to tell her that at the end of this, we can do the JHH.

The JHH works even when you're in a fight, I think.

Thinking about the list is magical. I went from super-extreme agita to dread about my mom's punishment to elation that Ari is here, too.

Detention is bringing us back together.

Finally, an hour passes, and the detention teacher who never even told us his name alerts us that we can go and that detention is over.

I wait for Jason and Ari outside the classroom.

"Ari!" I yell, because she's walking by, not even seeing me. "I mean, Arianna!"

Shoot. I already messed up. I know she wants to be Arianna here, and I really do try and remember that, but I've been calling her Ari for two years and three weeks. It's hard to change.

She turns around, and for a second I think she's going

194

to run over and hug me, and all will be okay.

"We gotta do the ritual," I tell her.

She doesn't even smile.

"The JHH," I remind her.

"I gotta run, Kaylan," she says and keeps walking, like she has super-important places to be. My heart is a crumpled-up piece of paper.

Thankfully Jason comes out, and we walk down the hallway together, to our lockers.

"We survived," I say.

"Oh yeah."

"Now I just have to deal with the wrath of my mother," I groan, getting some books from the top shelf.

"It happens to the best of us," he replies, trying to make me feel better.

"Why do you think Ari got detention?" I ask him as we're walking to the pickup circle.

"You didn't hear?" he asks me.

I shake my head, and my heart pounds. Did she do something really terrible? Like vandalize the principal's office? My mind starts spinning with crazy ideas.

"She skipped math yesterday," he tells me. "She was hanging out in the back section of the library, and Ms. Monte caught her."

"Really?" I shriek. "Ari loves math."

"Don't know what to tell you," he says. "That's what happened."

"Who was she hanging out with?" I ask.

He pauses, and squints like he's trying to remember. "I guess that girl Sydney? Is she the one that's BFF with Jules from the pool? Or is it Amirah? Or M.W.? What does that stand for?"

I laugh a little. He has no idea who any of the girls are. And *Jules from the pool* sounds like some kind of alternative folk singer. "No, but seriously, who was she in the library with? You really don't remember?"

Jason zips his coat. "I don't remember. Sorry." He over-the-top frowns at me. "I gotta go, Kay. My mom is waiting." He peers out the glass doors. "Your mom is out here, too. On time today!"

"Yippee," I reply.

"Seriously, don't discount the clementine thing. You're kind of amazing at it, and I think it could be really funny," he says as we walk outside. The cold air slaps our faces.

"I'm not sure I can do funny."

"Oh, Kaylan! Are you kidding? You are so funny, and you don't even realize it! Perk up, Terrel!"

I laugh a little. The way he says it—*Terrel*—it just feels cool and relaxed, like we get each other.

TWENTY-FOUR

I WALK AS SLOWLY AS I possibly can to my mom's car, and I rehearse the speech over and over again. I'm just going to tell her that I totally messed up, and I don't have any excuse for it.

But when I get in the car, she has the windows rolled down (even though it's forty degrees) and she's listening to my music. Taylor Swift.

She says, "Hey, sweetie," which is definitely not the way she greets me when she's mad. And then she says, "We're going out for dinner tonight, just the two of us. Hibino?"

Mom's suggesting sushi? This is rare. We used to eat it all the time when my dad was still, ya know, living with us, but since he left, money's been really tight, and I always feel bad asking to go out for sushi.

"Sure," I say. "Where's Ryan?"

"He's eating at Tyler's tonight. They're finishing a history project."

"Oh."

"He seems off lately, doesn't he?" Mom asks, making a right turn and not looking at me. "Just not himself. Ya know?"

I nod. "Yeah. He's such a jerk most of the time."

"I agree. I'm worried about him." My mom clenches her face tight, the way she does when she's trying to hold back tears. She probably doesn't know that I know this. And if she knew I knew, she'd only try harder to stop doing it. So I won't tell her.

We get to Hibino and sit at the table right by the window, my favorite.

We order our usual stuff—spicy tuna rolls and salmon avocado rolls and chicken pot stickers and edamame to start.

My mind flops back and forth between calmness and anxiety. I keep remembering about the detention and then fretting about discussing it with my mom, and then forgetting about the detention and feeling okay, and then I go back to remembering again.

I wish my brain could just settle on one thing.

"Kaylan, I need to talk to you," my mom says after she finishes a pot sticker.

Uh-oh. The worst is yet to come. She was trying to

soften the pain with sushi. I'm in trouble.

I nod. "Okay . . ."

"I'm worried about you, too," she continues. "Not just Ryan. You don't seem like yourself. And I wish you'd talk to me more. Open up. Tell me what's going on."

This feels like a trap. Moms do that sometimes. They try to act all calm and kind and sweet and stuff, and then you open up and bam, you're in trouble.

"Oh, ya know," I reply, dipping a pot sticker in the soy sauce. "Just middle school stuff. A lot of homework."

My mom sets down her chopsticks and glares. "Kay, come on."

"What?" My cheeks flash red. I can feel them burning.

"You're not going to tell me what happened after school today?"

And there you have it. Classic mom trap.

"I was going to tell you," I defend. "But then we were having this wonderful dinner that you suggested, and I didn't want to ruin it." I half smile.

"Kaylan "

"Mom."

"Come on," she says, and I realize I don't have much choice in the matter. I don't even know how to explain this. I don't really want to get into everything about Jason. She may think I like him or decide he's a bad influence. And I don't even know if I want to tell her about the talent show yet. I tell her one thing, and she asks a million questions. It happens every time.

Our sushi arrives and we put wasabi in our soy sauce and separate our ginger.

I'm stressing about telling her the detention saga when I have a literal epiphany. An amazing moment where even a bad thing turns into a good, helpful thing, and it makes me feel like life will actually make sense one day: this is the perfect opportunity to check another item off the list.

Mom pops a piece of spicy tuna roll in her mouth, finishes chewing, and then says, "I'm waiting."

"Okay," I say, resigned. "I'll tell you what happened. I decided to sign up for the talent show."

"That's so great," she says between bites. "Amazing!"

"That's not the main point of the story," I say. "Jason and I were passing notes to discuss my act for the show, and that's when we got in trouble. Because of course I can't ask Ari, because we're not talking . . . but I don't want to get into that. I mean, she said such mean things, like how I fixate on things."

"I'm sorry you're not talking. We can discuss that if you'd like." My mom dips another dumpling. "But what exactly do you fixate on?"

I look away, pretending to be uber-focused on a waiter bringing over a sushi boat. "Oh, I don't even know . . . like fashion trends, I guess." I can't believe I almost slipped about the Tyler crush and the 11 Before 12 List.

Thankfully, I caught myself.

Moms don't need to know everything. A little bit here and there, but not everything.

"I see," my mom says, and sips her water.

A tiny little twitchy guilt feeling settles into my stomach. Maybe I should've told her. Maybe it's mean to keep stuff from her. I mean, she is my mom. And she's going through a lot, not having my dad around to talk to.

But no. I can't tell her. Not yet.

"Detention was terrible. I can tell you that much, so I will be doing all that I can to behave myself so that I never have to go back there again," I explain.

My mom rubs her eyes in her I'm-tired-and-frustrated way and I feel bad that I've caused her to feel this way. I should be doing all I can to make things easier for her, and I seem to be creating more problems. But the thing is, I'm pretty sure that's what kids do. And parents are just supposed to be okay with it.

I add an "I'm sorry" for good measure and take another piece of salmon avocado roll.

"I wish you had told me," she says. "I want to ask you something." She pauses for a million years. "Is there something I'm doing that makes you and Ryan not want to talk to me?"

Oh my God. How easy is this? She is literally handing me the opportunity to check *Have a mature discussion with our moms about their flaws* off the list.

I can JHH by myself when we're on our way to the car.

I slowly sip my water and plan out what I'm going to say. "I guess I just feel a lot of pressure," I start and realize I have no plan for how to continue. "You're so great and stuff." Okay, buttering someone up can help. "And I want to do great and I want you to be proud of me. And so that's a lot of pressure. And it's, like, hard to be a kid with all the schoolwork, and social media makes it seem like everyone is living the perfect life all the time."

"Go on," my mom encourages.

"And, like, the thing is, I'm not sure you really get it," I add. "You don't know what it's like. You didn't grow up with a cell phone! And also, stop snooping on my Instagram! I thought I warned you—"

"You left me no choice," she says. "We get emails from school all the time about cyberbullying and inappropriate pictures posted online, and you don't talk to me, and you've been acting so . . . off. And I worry so much about your friendships since Brooke and Lily. And now that you're not talking to Ari, I really worry. So . . . I had to."

"Not cool."

"You and Ryan don't talk to me," she says. "So I'm not able to understand what's going on with you."

I look down at my empty plate and wish I had more sushi to eat. I always wish I had more sushi to eat.

"I'll try to share more," I say. "But do you promise to listen and not just tell me what to do? Can you promise

202

to try and put yourself in my shoes?"

She sniffles and says, "I promise."

"And also, there's one other thing," I add, and realize I'm not done with this talk. "Sometimes I feel like you just want me to be a baby forever. And you're so worried and overprotective. You don't want me to walk around the neighborhood alone. You still think I should be in bed by nine thirty."

I stop talking when I see little puddles in the corners of her eyes.

"I know," she says. "I know you're not a baby anymore."

"Okay." I deep-sigh and look down at my plate. I pray that my mom's stopped crying.

"Sometimes I just really miss the old days," she says. "When we'd walk home from preschool holding hands, and I'd put out snack buffets. And we'd cuddle in bed after your bath, and I was able to fix every little thing with a Band-Aid or an ice cream."

She sits there, crying quietly at the table for a minute. She's crying in a restaurant, and everyone is looking at us. The waiter comes over but then stops when he sees her crying and backs away.

I make a scrunched-up, awkward *sorry* face, and he mouths that he'll come back.

Moms aren't supposed to be sad in front of their kids. It's not fair. Moms are supposed to smile and pretend that everything is fine and deal with their sadness about kids growing up and marriages falling apart later.

"I'll try," she says. "Really, I'll try."

We order mango sorbet for dessert, and we stop this conversation and move into my mom telling me how her friend Nancy is planning a family trip and maybe we'll go with them, and don't I like Nancy's daughter? And on and on.

Nancy's daughter is okay, kind of boring. Her name is Becky and they live in New Jersey and we see them once a year. But a vacation would be nice, I guess.

I doubt it'll happen, but it's put an end to the conversation we were having before, so that's a good thing. Everything feels lighter after that, more manageable.

We drive home and pick Ryan up on the way. I half hope my mom will tell me to go ring the bell and then Tyler will answer, and we'll talk and smile at each other for a second. But then I half hope that my mom will just honk and Ryan will come out. Maybe I'll catch a glimpse of Tyler in the entryway.

But neither of those things happen.

We pull into Tyler's driveway, and Ryan and Tyler are out front playing basketball. I want to sink through an imaginary hole in my seat. Now I have to see Tyler in front of Ryan and my mom when I'm already feeling awkward from dinner. Or maybe he won't notice me. He'll just say good-bye to Ryan and go inside.

The seconds that take place between when Ryan sees

that it's us and puts the basketball down, and when he gets into the car feel like three million years.

Ryan gets in the backseat and mumbles out a tired "Hey."

I think I'm in the clear, but a second later, Tyler appears at my window.

"Hey, Kaylan," he says.

Okay. Does he not realize that my mom is sitting right here? And my brother is in the backseat? What is he doing?

"Hey." I freeze. I can't think of anything to say. I don't know how to act right now.

His breathing sounds loud, like really loud, and even though there's a window and a car door separating us, I feel like it's the closest we've ever been. It feels too close. His breathing feels like it's directly in my ear. I can't look at him.

Instead, I stare at the dried-up mud on the toe of my left sneaker. Must clean that.

"Just wanted to let you know that we need to finalize our acts for the talent show pretty soon," he says. "I, um, wasn't sure if you knew."

"Oh, um, okay." I run my words together. "Thanks."

"Cool. Later."

He walks away from the car and I keep staring at my muddy sneaker and pray that my mom and Ryan stay quiet. *Please don't say anything. Please don't say anything.*

For a few minutes, it's totally silent in the car, and I'm nervous about what's to come. And then my mom starts asking Ryan about his homework and why his science teacher called and said he's failed the last two quizzes.

I feel like the meanest person in the world, but I'm actually grateful for the distraction. The attention's not on me. And no one said anything about Tyler.

Phew.

TWENTY-FIVE

A FEW DAYS LATER AT lunch, I try to get the Whatevers to help me come up with an act for the talent show. They don't seem interested. At all.

June says, "Kaylan, I told you a hundred times you should play the flute. You're good at the flute."

I'm not sure why she doesn't realize that would be really lame and boring, and why she doesn't realize that I'm not good at the flute. She's never even heard me play.

And then Cami says, "What about some kind of dramatic reading of celebrity tweets?"

Her mom is a high-powered agent or lawyer or something, so Cami sometimes acts like she's twenty-five and she knows about all sorts of stuff that doesn't make any sense to me.

"I'm not on Twitter. I don't know how it even works,"

I say, and then I start to realize that I may be shooting down everyone's ideas. "But thanks for all the suggestions."

"So join it," she says. "I'll show you during study hall. But honestly, you don't need to be on Twitter to read tweets."

I really don't even know what she's talking about, so I tell her I will give it some thought and I go back to finishing my lunch.

"You're never going to believe this convo I had with my mom last night," I overhear Ari say from the end of the table.

Saara starts asking me about the English essay, but I try to avoid conversation so I can eavesdrop.

"What happened?" Sydney asks.

"Oh yeah, you texted me about that," Marie adds. "How did it go?"

My throat stings, so I take a sip of water and keep listening.

Ari raises her eyebrows and says, "She was like, I want to be close with you, and I want us to make a time each week that we spend together, just the two of us."

"And?" Sydney asks.

"And I was like, okay . . . but it seems weird, right?"

"I dunno," Kira says. "It's kinda nice. My mom works all the time."

They're quiet after that, but I get the sense there was

more to that conversation than what Ari's saying. How her mom probably made her biscuits for breakfast this morning with fresh raspberry jam from the farmer's market to make her feel better.

I bet she fulfilled the *mature discussion with our moms about their flaws* thing.

I feel the strongest urge to run over to her and tell her that we need to do the JHH right now. But maybe she did it on her own, in the mirror.

Even if we're not talking, we're doing the same things at the same time. We're on the same wavelength, like BFFs should be.

I'm by the garbage, throwing away my lunch bag, when I see Ari walk right by me. She's with Marie and Kira.

They look at me, and I half smile, about to bring up the mom talks and the JHH, but then they look away.

Thankfully Jason comes up to throw away his trash and I relax a little. I take a deep breath and force myself to put the Ari drama away for a minute. "What's up?"

"Nada," he says. "Want to study for that history test after school? All the teachers are giving the same test this time."

I think about it for a second. I wonder why he's not studying with Ari. Or maybe this is a trap to get us to be friends again. Either way, Jason's smart; I bet he'd be a good study partner.

He continues, "My mom went grocery shopping

yesterday and our snack inventory is at an all-time high."

I can't help but laugh. Jason just has this way of making the most mundane things feel great. Sometimes in life you need that. Actually, you probably need that at all times.

"Sure," I say, and my stomach turns bubbly. Not that there's any reason to be nervous. Jason's just a friend. A good friend.

"Awesome," he says, after finishing the last sips of his water. "And we can work on your act, too. Seriously, I know I've said it a hundred times, but I think the competitive clementine peeling is really going to put you above and beyond your competition."

"Okay, Jason." I pat his shoulder, and then jerk my hand away like I've just touched a hot burner on the stove. Why did I touch his shoulder? I didn't plan to touch his shoulder. It just happened. Like, my arm reached out without my realizing it, and then extended from my body, and my hand landed on his shoulder.

"See ya, Kay."

Kay? He's calling me Kay.

My heart pounds as I walk to math.

This is Jason. I need to calm down.

The rest of the day seems to go in slow motion. One minute I'm excited about the Jason study session, and the next minute I'm coming up with excuses like food poisoning so that I can bail.

Finally, after my last-period pop quiz in Spanish, I'm at my locker packing up when I feel a tap on my shoulder, and I jolt.

"Are you coming straight to my house or going to your house first and then walking over?" Jason asks. Everyone else around us at the lockers overhears and makes *ooh* faces at each other, like *what's up with Kaylan and Jason, and why haven't we heard?*

I ignore it, but my face burns.

"Um, I'll go to my house and drop most of my stuff, change into something more comfy, and then meet you at your house," I say quietly. The truth is I'm already wearing a zip-up hoodie and my most comfy jeans, but I think I need a few minutes alone in my room to prepare for my first-ever study session with a boy.

This is a big moment. I need to pump myself up in the mirror, talk to myself, stuff like that.

Plus, if I walk to his house with him, our hangout will start that much earlier, and what if we run out of stuff to talk about by the time we even get to his house?

That would be terrible.

"Sounds good," he says. "Later, Terrel."

I'm walking home from the bus stop, the way I do every single day. I look for Mrs. Etisof. I know I need to get to Jason's, but I really feel like chatting today. I kinda want to bring up the talk I had with my mom. And maybe the Ari stuff, too.

Oddly enough, I don't see her on the porch or hear her.

"Mrs. Etisof?" I call out. I wonder if I should ring her bell. This is so strange. She's always outside. "Mrs. Etisof?"

"Kaylan?" I hear her call, unsure of where it's coming from.

I look around, walk up the path to her front door, and peek around the side.

"Kaylan, over here," she says. "In the back."

I walk around her house, and find her on the back deck, staring into a slightly cracked-open window.

"What's going on?" I ask.

"I got locked out. I knew it would happen sooner or later. I've been so forgetful lately. My daughter has an extra key, but she's in Japan for work. . . ."

"Um." I look at her for a second. "You're never inside. Are you sure you want to go in now?" I laugh, hoping that will make her feel better.

She smiles. "Do you think I can dive in through this window? Is it open enough? I can't tell. I'm not good at depth perception."

Is she serious right now? She's seventy years old and she wants to dive into her living room through an open window. Aren't her bones brittle? I always see commercials about osteoporosis.

"I don't think so, Mrs. E." I fold my arms across my chest, and survey the situation. "Maybe a locksmith?"

"Eh, I hate to bother. People are busy." She pauses. "But I need to take my afternoon pills."

"I have an idea," I say. "I can crawl in."

"Oh, Kaylan! Your mother will have my head if you get hurt," she says.

"It'll be fine!" I assure her.

"Are you sure?"

"Totally!" I clap and get a surge of excitement about this. "I used to do gymnastics. Remember? I'd cartwheel all the way from my lawn to yours."

"I do remember!" She pauses and thinks for a second. "Okay, I'll be here to spot you. Thankfully, the carpet in there is very padded."

I stretch a little, and then curve my arms forward like I'm about to dive into a pool. I bend my knees a little and turn onto my side. I make it halfway through the window, and then Mrs. Etisof boosts me the rest of the way holding my legs, like we're in some kind of wheelbarrow race, and both of us start to laugh.

"We're a good team, Mrs. E," I laugh. "We should enter some kind of contest!"

But then I'm in. I unlock her back door and grab her keys off the kitchen table. It's covered with newspapers and art supplies and half-filled glasses of water. Mrs. E seems disorganized, kind of like I feel about life right now.

Maybe we're all a little disorganized.

"Voilà!" I hand them to her, as soon as I make it back outside.

"You're a hero, Kaylan Terrel!" She hugs me.

"I don't know about that." I smile. "But I'm happy to help!"

My heart sinks a little, thinking about Mrs. Etisof all alone, locked out. I'm not even sure how long.

I walk home and reassure myself that I'm not alone— I have my mom, and Ryan when he's not being a jerk. And I guess I have my dad, even though he barely comes home to visit us now that he lives in Arizona. I miss him, though. I miss the way he'd leave the Sunday comics for me on my seat at the kitchen table every week. And I have Jason, even though he makes my stomach hurt sometimes. And Tyler—well, I don't really have Tyler. But I wish I had him. And he makes my stomach hurt, too.

I *am* alone. Kind of.

I'm alone without Ari. I wonder if I took it for granted that I'd always have her with me. How we planned that we'd go to college together, and be roommates, and then eventually we'd live in the same neighborhood, in houses next door to one another.

I don't have her now. And I don't know if I'll ever have her back.

And that's what really hurts.

TWENTY-SIX

BY THE TIME I MAKE it to Jason's I'm so pumped about my rescue mission that I can barely focus on the studying. I'm so good at crawling through windows—I should probably be better at yoga. Maybe I do need to give it another chance. . . . I wonder if there is a way to make diving through a window my talent show act.

The inside of Jason's house is all colorful, and the walls are covered in family photos and little artistic prints, but there are still some moving boxes in the corners.

We go up to Jason's room, and there's a pile of folded laundry on the dresser. His boxers are on the top of the pile and they're plaid and colorful and it freaks me out that I'm sitting so close to his underwear.

"You okay, Kay?" Jason asks, and then cracks up. "Get it—'kay Kay?"

I groan. "I get it. I just crawled through a window to unlock Mrs. Etisof's house," I tell him. "I'm, like, so proud of myself."

"You're a rock star."

"Thanks." I laugh.

He makes a fist and holds it under his mouth like he's a reporter with a microphone. "Did you ever think you'd be able to squeeze through such a small space?"

"Well," I start, doing the same thing with my hand. "To be honest, I kind of knew I had it in me. Like some deep hidden skill, waiting to be unearthed, but I wasn't sure I'd ever have the opportunity to try it out. . . ."

He cracks up, falling back onto his bed.

I sit down and swivel around in the desk chair, and try to think of something to say. Silence still feels a little weird between us. "Do you think schoolwork is getting really hard?" I ask.

He sits back up. "Yes! It is way harder than it was in Atlanta."

I nod. "Well, at least I'm not the only one who thinks it's impossible." I don't mean to do it, but I catch a glimpse of Ari's house out of the corner of my eye. I wonder if she knows I'm over here. I wonder if she'll show up. I wonder if she misses me as much as I miss her.

"Don't stress too much," he suggests, sitting on the edge of his bed. "Come in for a hug. It'll help."

I stand up, and he does, too. We do that thing where

our hands are on each other's shoulders, and I'm not sure which direction to move my head. But then we're hugging and he smells like the barbecue-chicken pizza they served for lunch, but it's not completely grossing me out.

"There," he says, pulling away. "Feel better?"

I nod, even though I'm not really sure I do.

"What should I do about Ari?" I ask, sitting back down on his desk chair.

He shrugs and sits on his bed. "I don't know. Also I'm not sure if I should bring this up, but did you hear about her and that girl Sydney getting on TV?"

"What? No! Tell me!"

He throws a Nerf ball against the wall, and it bounces back to him. "Sheesh! Okay! Well, there was some kind of, like, community service day at Ari's temple, and Sydney's dad is, like, in charge of the board. Ya know, he's the CEO or something of, like, a big important company—"

"Who cares about her dad? Just tell me!"

He throws the ball directly at my head this time. "I'm getting there. Whatever, they went to it, and there were news cameras there doing a story on community service events making the world better, or something like that . . . and they interviewed Arianna and Sydney."

"Oh." I stare at Jason's framed diplomas, and avoid eye contact with him. My throat gets tight. Sydney did that event with Ari when it should have been me.

Don't cry. Don't cry. Don't cry.

"So, Louisiana Purchase?" he asks. "It always cheers me up."

"Sure." My voice comes out scratchy.

We study and Jason quizzes me and I only get half the answers right. All I can think about is how Ari did two things on the list without me. Two things at the same time—help humanity and get on TV. Did she even realize it? She must have, knowing Ari. Did she JHH without me twice or only once? Did she do a double JHH with Sydney?

My phone buzzes as we're working on practice questions; it's my mom.

"Kaylan, where are you?" she asks.

I look around Jason's room, wondering what to say, my stomach sinking to my toes. "At a friend's, studying for the history test."

I hold the phone away from my head and mouth to Jason, "I'm in trouble; I forgot to leave a note."

He nods, all understanding.

"Get home now, Kaylan. I've told you a million times that I need to know where you are, and you keep violating our rules."

"Sorry. I'm leaving now." I hang up.

Jason's eyebrows curve inward. "We didn't do the practice test yet."

"I gotta go," I say, stuffing my review sheets in my backpack. "My mom's freaking out."

"Moms seem to do that. Don't they?"

"Definitely. I mean, she has reason to freak. But whatever. Okay. See you tomorrow."

I grab my bag, run down the stairs, and sprint all the way home. I don't even look toward Ari's house. I don't want to see her hanging out with someone else.

I think about that study session the whole way home—how Jason's confident that he knows stuff, how he was impressed with the stuff I knew, how he took time to explain things to me. He always seems to get what I'm feeling—he even tells me about Ari.

It's weird that I can't get Jason out of my head. Maybe because of all the new people I've met this year, he's the only one I want to hang out with.

I take my phone out of my pocket when I'm almost at my house. Ari would get it. Maybe I should just text her, call a truce, and end this battle.

Ari, I miss you. We need to talk.

I stare at the text, but I don't hit send.

TWENTY-SEVEN

ON SATURDAY, I'M SITTING AT the kitchen table eating a bowl of Cheerios with cut-up banana when my mom hands me the phone.

"Who is it?" I mouth.

"A man named Barry Wallach, from Channel Eight."

"What?" I mouth again. My mom doesn't understand the mute button.

"He wants to talk to you."

A little more information would be helpful, but okay. I'll deal with it.

"Hello," I say.

"Hi, Kaylan?" he asks, tentative. "My name is Barry. I'm a producer at Channel 8."

The way he says it, it sounds like he expects me to know who he is, so I respond with an excited "Oh, hi!" It seems like the least I can do. People on TV always want everyone to know who they are, I think.

"We heard what you did."

"Um?"

"You helped get Mrs. Etisof back into her house by climbing through her window." He says it all dramatic, like he's the voiceover on some kind of intense documentary. He laughs and I do, too, because this whole thing is just so silly and bizarre. "And we'd love to offer you and a guest tickets to our nightly talk show. We always have fun guests and giveaways!"

"Um. What?" I didn't even think Mrs. Etisof watched TV at all . . . but my mom watches that show every night!

"Mrs. Etisof's nephew is a producer here." He pauses. "She wanted to do something nice to thank you for that heroic effort."

"For real?" I ask, and then try to rephrase my words to sound more professional. "Yes, um, I'd love to."

He goes over all the logistics—what to wear, what time to be there, what door to go in, where our seats will be.

I hang up the phone and tell my mom the whole story.

"Wow. That's so exciting!" She yells way too loud for this early in the morning and then pulls me into a hug.

"Um, Mom." I gently squiggle away from her. "Do you want to be my guest?" I figure it's the least I can do since she's been through so much. And I mean, the only other person I could ask to go with me would be Jason. And I'm just not sure we're at that level of friendship yet.

Ryan comes pounding down the stairs and into the kitchen. "What's happening? I heard Mom scream."

So my mom tells him the whole story as he's grabbing all the cereal boxes out of the pantry and then mixing them all together in the giant bowl usually used for serving salad at a dinner party.

"That's really bizarre, but cool, I guess," he says after a bite of cereal. "Hope you don't do anything embarrassing on TV."

"I'm not actually going to be on TV, dimwit." I leave the kitchen and run upstairs. Actually, it would be great if I was going to be on TV. I'd be able to check that off the list. And prove to Ari and Sydney that I can get on TV, too. In an even cooler way!

I already helped humanity by helping Mrs. Etisof. And if you help one person, you help the world. At least, I think so.

I've been trying to do the JHH by myself. But I just can't.

It's kind of impossible to hug yourself and high-five yourself. And it also feels like the most pathetic thing in the world.

I can't take this situation with Ari anymore. I need to call her. This is a super-exciting thing. Ari's dad loves this show; he says it's the best way to calm down after a stressful day. And they do pan the audience, so maybe I will get on TV. . . .

I stare at my phone for about three minutes before I decide to call. It rings. And rings. And rings.

And then voicemail.

So I don't know what to do. Should I hang up and Ari will see a missed call? Should I leave a message?

"Um, hey, Ari." The words come out of my mouth after the beep. "Just wanted to, um, give you some kinda exciting news. So, yeah. Call me back if you can. Okay. Bye."

I hang up and exhale and my heart pounds even harder than it was pounding before I made the call.

I sit and wait for a few minutes to see if Ari will call back. I sign in online and see if she's there. I check her Instagram and see if there are any new posts.

Nothing. She's probably out with Marie or Sydney or one of those girls. They're probably on their way to the movies, and they're going to share popcorn and Goobers and get giant sodas and have the best day ever.

I wonder if I should text June or Cami. I have their numbers, but we're not really at the texting level yet. I don't know exactly what we are. Just lunch-table friends, I guess.

It's weird, though, because Jason and I were texting friends pretty much right away. But he won't get it. He hasn't lived here long enough to get the excitement of the Channel 8 nightly talk show.

I continue searching through my closet for an outfit in case I get on camera. Before I realize how much time has passed, my mom yells up the stairs that it's time to go.

I settle on a jean skirt with gray tights and a dark purple button-down sweater. It looks cute but also sensible and mature.

My mom decides to dress up for the occasion—but not in an over-the-top, cheesy way. She's wearing a flare-y black dress, patent leather platforms. And the perfect shade of red lipstick.

On the drive over to the station, my mom is mostly quiet. I can tell she's thinking about saying something but isn't sure she should say it. She'll look at me, and then back at the road, and then open her mouth, and then look back at me again. But no words seem to come out.

It's making me nervous.

Finally she mumbles out a "Listen, Kaylan," and I know nothing good is going to come after that.

"Yeah?"

"I'm so glad you invited me to come tonight. I've been feeling so out of touch with your life," she says, and I force myself not to grumble. Didn't we just talk about this? Maybe my mom just can't stand the silence.

"Mom. You're not. Nothing is going on. I mean, nothing except that we're going to this amazing show tonight, and I climbed through a window." I laugh. "That's pretty much it."

"I know—but you and Ari? Still nothing?"

I shake my head side to side.

"Have you tried calling?"

I shift in my seat and roll down the window. I don't want to admit that I have. That I pray every night for her to be my friend again. It feels so pathetic. So desperate. "Please, let's stop talking about this," I say.

"Okay," she says, resigned.

Finally, we get to the station, and my mom parks the car and we walk in together.

I tell the receptionist my name and she replies, "Oh, so you're Kaylan! And this is your guest?"

"My mom." I nod and smile.

More and more people start to arrive, and then a young guy with a headset and an iPad comes out. "Are you all ready for the show?" he yells to the crowd. "Come on back!"

We follow him down a long hallway and then into a room with rows and rows of seats and a stage with two armchairs and a mini table between them. The lighting is super-bright and it feels like it's two degrees in here.

But none of that bothers me because we're going to see a live show!

Another lady meets us at the door and shows us to our seats. "Front row," she whispers to my mom and me. She curves her fingers to pull me in closer. "There's something under your seat. We only tell certain people about it."

My mom and I make eyes at each other. What could it be? Did we just win a car or something? A vacation home in the South of France? My mind swirls with the possibilities.

We finally make it to our seats, and I glance around to make sure no one is looking. I feel like this is a secret I need to keep, at least for now. Everyone's busy settling themselves, so I sit down and look underneath my chair.

A piece of paper.

I flip it over and read:

You have been selected to participate in the show! Come up with answers to the next three questions, and be prepared to share them with Petey G. Please give your sheet to one of the pages once you've signed the release. Have fun with it!

1. *What's on your mind right now?*
2. *Invent your own ice cream flavor (we have connections to Ben & Jerry's).*
3. *What's the craziest thing you've ever done?*

I turn to my mom. "I can't do this. Let's get out of here." I wanted to be on TV but not by myself and not in this awkward way meant for adults.

"Kaylan," she says softly. "This is so much fun! What's wrong?"

I show her the sheet. "You do it. You'll be better."

She shakes her head. "She picked you. I think they like

to have different ages." She smiles. "You'll be great."

I slump back in my seat and hesitate before I sign the release form. My mom needs to sign it, too, since I'm a minor. I regret agreeing to this. I regret everything. If Mrs. Etisof hadn't gotten locked out, I wouldn't have had to crawl through her window, and she wouldn't have given me these tickets as a token of appreciation.

"Welcome to the showwwwwww," a tall, skinny guy says, jumping up and down with a microphone. He moves his hands, guiding us all to get out of our seats. "Put your hands together for Petey G!"

Petey G runs out doing some kind of aerobic dance move where he raises his knees in the air like he's training for a race or something. He puts his hands to his heart, like he's so grateful for all of our applause, and waits for us to stop clapping.

"Thank you. Thank you. Take your seats," he instructs. "No, please, really, take your seats. You're making me nervous."

Everyone laughs.

"So, we have a crazy show for you all tonight. A man who can stand on his head and drink a milkshake at the same time, a woman who can take apart a phone and put it back together right in front of your very eyes, and the mother whose video of her six-month-old baby dancing went viral . . . but." He pauses. "Before all of that. We must start with . . ." He holds his arms out and everyone shouts, "Audience participation!"

"Oh no. Mom. Come on! Run!" I try to stand up, but my mom taps my knee and gets me to sit back down. "Mom! This is too much."

Petey G launches into a discussion about audience participation and how it was always his favorite thing as a kid—and that's when it hits me.

I have a really good chance of actually getting on TV. I've been so nervous this whole time that I didn't realize I was so close to accomplishing something on the list.

Loyal to the list! Loyal to the list! I repeat over and over in my head to calm myself down.

I must face my fears of potential complete humiliation for saying the dumbest things in the world on live TV, if only for the list's sake.

Petey G comes out into the audience to talk to a guy named Curt who's not very funny at all. It's like he didn't even try not to be bland and boring, like he wasn't impressed with being on the show. His made-up ice cream flavor was hummus. I mean, come on. Ew.

"Okay, well, Curt—thanks for playing!" Petey G walks back up onto the stage and says, "Our next guest is . . . Kaylan Terrel! All of eleven years old."

I'm frozen in my seat, waiting for Petey G to come over to me.

"We're gonna have her come on to the stage, folks: her answers were just that unique." Petey G laughs. "Eleven years old, folks. Come on up, Kaylan!"

My mom gently pushes me to stand up, and my heart is pounding so loud I'm sure the whole audience can hear it. I walk slowly down my row and up the few steps to the stage.

"In all fairness, I'm almost twelve," I say into Petey G's microphone, and everyone laughs. It feels like a veil of confidence just appears over me. Like I'm wearing a costume, and no one sees the real me right now. I don't even see the real me.

"Okay, Almost-Twelve Kaylan." He points to the other armchair. "Take a seat."

I sit down and he says, "So, have you ever been on TV before?"

I shake my head. "Not that I know of." I look out into the audience. "Mom, have I?"

Laughter again! Uproarious laughter, not just giggles! My mom shakes her head; she's cracking up, too.

"Good to know." He smiles. "What's on your mind right now?"

I want to say something funny but all I can think of is the Ari stuff, and the Jason stuff, and the Tyler stuff, and the list. I can't say any of that on live TV! "Well, to be honest, I'm gonna be in a school talent show soon. And I don't know what to do for my act," I say. "So . . . any ideas?"

The audience completely cracks up then, and I wasn't

even trying to be funny.

"Email me," I say. "Or meet me after the show! I'll be by the side door."

Petey G is fully laughing now, shaking his head. "Well, you've come to the right place," he says. "Ice cream flavor?"

"That's easy." I sit on the edge of my chair. I'm freezing and sweating at the same time; it feels like my body can't decide which direction to freak out. "Strawberry ice cream, marshmallow, and crushed-up pink Starbursts."

"Did you know about these questions in advance?" he asks. "That's a very specific flavor."

"I didn't. But dream ice cream flavor is something I've been pondering for years." I look out into the audience. "So Ben and Jerry, if you're listening—you can have my idea, free of charge. Ready for the name?"

The audience nods.

"Katy Berry!"

They all applaud and laugh, and Petey G says, "It does sound delicious." He pauses. "Okay, ready for the final question?" he asks me, and I nod. "Craziest thing you've ever done?" He looks out into the audience. "She's only eleven, almost twelve, folks."

I pause to think a second, putting a finger on my chin, all dramatic, and everyone cracks up again. "I started middle school." I pause, for emphasis. "And let me tell you—it is pretty darn crazy!"

Right then, the entire audience bursts into laughter.

"I did also crawl through my neighbor's window to get her keys because she was locked out," I continue. I feel like I'm on a roll and I can't stop talking. I've never felt this way before, but I love it. "And that's how I got here!"

Petey G says, "Standing O for Kaylan Terrel. KT. Does anyone ever call you that?"

"They do now!" I yell out. "Thanks, everyone!"

"Best guest we've ever had," Petey G says. "I kind of feel bad for our other guests tonight." He looks toward the back, all jokey like he's worried they were listening.

I go back to my seat with red cheeks and a pounding heart. My jaw kind of hurts from smiling so much.

"You were amazing, Kaylan!" my mom whispers, pulling me into her as soon as I've sat down.

"I was, right?" I smile.

"Definitely. No doubt about it."

I sit there for the rest of the show, not paying attention because I feel so empowered. Under the bright, hot lights, with an entire audience out there and all the people watching in their homes, too, I felt different. Like a new and improved Kaylan. A funny Kaylan who could say stuff and not worry it would come out wrong.

On that stage, everything came out right.

No agita whatsoever.

TWENTY-EIGHT

I SLOW DOWN AS I pass Mrs. Etisof's house on my walk to the bus on Monday morning, and I'm so grateful when I see her on her front porch.

She was away on an all-day painting retreat on Sunday so I didn't get to see her and tell her all about the show.

"Kaylan! TV star!" she calls out to me. She's bundled up in a parka, sipping a mug of tea.

"Thank you, Mrs. Etisof." I walk up there for a second. "It's all because of you, though! Thanks for getting me the tickets."

"All because of you, Kaylan Terrel. The most considerate, thoughtful neighbor!" She raises her mug like we're toasting each other. "Have a good day at school!"

I run down her steps and toward the bus, and I kind of feel like I'm floating, like the wind just carries me wherever I need to go.

When I get to school, I realize that people are actually talking about the show. I had no idea so many kids my age watched it. Or maybe their parents do, and so they heard about it.

I waited all weekend for Ari to text me or call or email or something. I don't even know if she saw me. Or if she thought about me doing the JHH by myself when I got home. If she did, she didn't care to get in touch.

We both got on TV.

I accomplished what I wanted to accomplish.

Take that, Ari. But I was funny! I made people laugh. That should count for something extra, I think.

I am totally winning this competition!

At lunch, the Whatevers are saying how I was so funny, even their parents cracked up. "Even my grandpa laughed," Saara says. "And he never laughs."

Kind of sad for Saara's grandpa. Maybe I'll ask her about him one day.

They compliment my outfit and my hair and go on and on about how great I did.

I'm not gonna lie—I enjoy the compliments.

"Do you want to go to Harvey Deli to celebrate your celebrity status?" Cami asks, laughing through her words.

"Yeah! That's such a great idea," June adds. "Maybe Friday after school?"

Saara nods. "I'm free."

"I'll ask my mom if she can drive us," Cami continues. "I mean, she's usually around, but she may have to drive my brother . . . and I don't know if he'll have a playdate. . . ."

I shift in my seat. Maybe I can't really be a loner now, after I've been on TV. I'm kind of a local celebrity. I mean, I'll need friends. An entourage, even.

"Um, maybe . . ." I say. "I'll check with my mom."

"Come on, Kaylan! We haven't gone yet and we both have the same favorite sandwich!" Cami says, going on and on about it.

I keep listening to her, but out of the corner of my other ear, I'm eavesdropping on Ari and Marie at the other end of the table. Are they talking about me being on TV? Did they hear all my compliments? Does Ari know the Whatevers invited me to hang out?

"He's so cute," Ari says. But I don't know who she's talking about. This is torture! I need to know.

I keep listening, while I "uh-huh" Cami about the Harvey Deli plans.

"I feel like he has major first kiss potential," Ari goes on.

"Noah is a definite cutie name," Sydney says. "Every Noah I know is really cute!"

What? Who is Noah?

I ever so gently turn my head in that direction so I can listen a little more, but then Marie and I make eye contact, and I look away and pretend to be super-interested in Cami's plans.

After lunch, Jason comes up behind me at my locker. He puts his hands on my shoulders and then quickly moves them away.

"Kaylan, you rocked it," he says.

I turn around. "I did?" I don't know why I play dumb; I know I rocked it.

"I'm sorry I didn't text you; my phone got lost in the washing machine. I mean, it got washed, so . . ." He smiles in a crooked kind of way, one side of his mouth higher than the other. Did he always smile like this, and look so cute? And I never noticed? "But you totally rocked it."

"Thanks, Jason." I lean in to hug him and then pull back. Jason and I are not hug-in-the-middle-of-the-hallway friends. "And sorry about your phone."

"I'm coming over after school today," he announces. "We're practicing your clementine peeling. Okay?"

"I haven't totally settled on that yet. I mean, what if someone from the show writes to me with an amazing idea? But no one at the show gave me any ideas, so I'm not going to count on it."

"Well, we can always add more in," he declares. "But this is going to be hilarious. Really, really hilarious."

"Okay. I gotta go. I'm gonna be late."

I'm walking to class, thinking about Jason's crooked smile, when I see Tyler at the end of the hallway, by himself. This is rare. He's one of those people who's always surrounded by a group.

"Hey, Kaylan," he yells, way too loud for the hallway, and Mr. Bernard, who is on hallway duty, scolds him.

"Shhhhh." I am not getting detention again. Never again. When I get closer, I whisper, "Hey."

"I saw you on TV."

"Yeah." I don't know what to say. When I'm around Tyler, words don't come out of my mouth the way they normally do.

"It was cool." He smiles. "It's like a big thing for kids to be on that show. My parents watch it every night. They never have kids on."

"Uh," I stammer. I can barely mutter out a "thanks" before he tells me he has to turn to go to science.

"I'll be at your house later," he says, nudging his head in my direction. "Maybe we can hang."

"Um, yeah. Sure."

"Later, Kaylan."

I think I'm about to hyperventilate. My head feels all cloudy and hazy, like I don't know if this is really happening or if it's a dream.

Tyler and I just touched arms, he told me he's coming over later, he wants to hang.

This is huge. This is huger than huge.

I replay the whole thing in my head over and over on my walk to history and then as I sit down, and Mrs.

Clarke passes out the worksheet, and I'm working on it, the problem hits me: Jason will be at my house, too.

Jason and Tyler. Jason and Tyler. Jason and Tyler.

My cheeks prickle, and I have to take my hoodie off because I'm sweating so much.

I want to hang out with Jason because he's my friend and he's helping me with the talent show and because sometimes I have this insatiable urge to hug him. But I always want to hang out with Tyler, because, well, he's Tyler and he has first-kiss potential written all over him.

Should I tell June and Cami about this conundrum? Maybe they'll have advice.

"Kaylan," Mrs. Clarke says. "You don't look like you're working."

"Oh, um, sorry." I smile. "I am."

I stare down at the worksheet and force myself to concentrate, or to at least make it look to Mrs. Clarke like I'm concentrating.

It doesn't work as well as I think it does.

"Kaylan, can you come talk to me for a second?" she asks as I'm packing up my books. I nod and smile, and try to look calm. I doubt that's working either.

"You seem very distracted," Mrs. Clarke says when I'm at her desk. "I'm concerned."

"Oh no. I'm okay, Mrs. Clarke." I pause, unsure of what to say, and then something comes to me. "I'm not sure if you know this, actually, but I was recently on TV." I bulge out my eyes for extra emphasis.

"I'd heard that, Kaylan." She smiles and then it falls flat. "And that's terrific. Really. But you need to focus on your studies as well." She starts collecting some papers on her desk and looks away, and I think this is a sign that it's time for me to leave.

"Okay, Mrs. Clarke. I will."

Sheesh. You'd think I'd get a little pass being a TV star?

If only I could channel the awesomeness that came over me on the Petey G show and put that into my history worksheet.

TWENTY-NINE

I SPEND THE REST OF the day fretting about the Tyler-and-Jason combination at my house later this afternoon.

I have so many things I wish I could talk to Ari about that I decide to write them down. That way if we ever do start talking again, I can catch her up on everything.

I'm waiting for the bus, looking around for June and any of the Whatevers. I don't see anyone and I hate this. I hate to be standing around, alone, while everyone else around me is chatting.

I take out my notebook and start making a list of all the stuff that has happened since Ari and I stopped talking.

I hung out with Jason one-on-one. I sometimes wanted to hug him.

I climbed through Mrs. E's window.

I got on TV.

Tyler asked me to hang out.

Even though I'm trying to look busy keeping this list, the bus line at the end of the day is still probably the loneliest place in my world. I don't know where Jason is—maybe he got a ride home with someone—and Ari always pretends she doesn't see me.

When I had Ari, life was the opposite. Always someone to sit with on the bus, to talk to, to rehash the day with. Now no matter how well my day went, the bus line reminds me of what I've lost.

I don't know how many more days I can get through like this.

By the time I get home, I've filled three journal pages with stuff to tell Ari and potential talent show acts, but I'm nauseous from writing all of that on a moving bus.

I walk in the door, expecting to have a few minutes to relax and change and have a snack before everyone shows up, but no.

Ryan and Tyler are already at the kitchen table, eating popcorn.

"Hey," I say, as I walk by.

They don't even acknowledge that I'm there.

I start to wonder if that interaction in the hall with Tyler even happened. Maybe I dreamed it.

So I go up to my room and stare at myself in the mirror for a few minutes, deciding if I should change clothes or not. I mean, it's just Jason. Tyler seems to have forgotten about me, anyway.

A few minutes later, there's a knock on my door.

I daydream for a second that it's Ari. And she's changing her mind about being mad at me. I'm still a little mad at her, but I'd give in. I'd forgive. I miss her. I want her back.

But no—it's Tyler.

He's alone.

"Um, hey," I say.

"Hey, Kaylan." He leans against the doorframe. "Cool room."

He's been in here before, so why is he looking around like he's in some kind of museum? Also, I still have my babyish pink wallpaper. There's nothing cool about it.

"Uh, thanks."

I peer around the corner to see if Ryan's behind him and they're going to do something dumb, like spray me with Silly String. But I don't see him.

"Later," Tyler says.

"Later."

I don't get him. He stops by my room and then it's like he has nothing to say. Does he think things and not say them? Or is his mind just mostly empty?

Then, a few minutes later, there's another knock on my door.

"Terrel, it's me, Jason. The front door was open."

"Come in," I say.

He plops down on my bed, and his shirt rides up a little, and then I see a sliver of his boxer shorts, the same ones I saw in the laundry that day, and it freaks me out so I have to look away. I sit down at my desk, and pretend I forgot to write something down.

"I have an idea."

"Yeah?" I ask, sliding around on my wheelie desk chair to face him.

"Fast clementine peeling isn't going to be enough," he says.

"Um?"

He stands up. "You're going to sing while doing it."

"I can't sing, Jason." I shake my head. "I mean really. I'm tone-deaf."

"That's what's going to make it even funnier, Kaylan!" he yells. "You're not like singing in an opera. You're singing in a funny way!"

"I really don't know about this." I get up and open the door to my room, just a crack. "Let's go downstairs and get a snack, and keep discussing it."

Ryan and Tyler are in Ryan's room playing some game that's so loud I can hear it through the walls, so I figure it's safe to go into the kitchen with Jason.

We get downstairs and I take out a bag of chips and two cans of Cherry Coke. We sit across from each other at the kitchen table, a bowl of clementines between us.

Jason finds a pen and paper in the drawer and starts writing down songs for me to sing. He suggests some current ones like Lady Gaga and Katy Perry, and then classics like "Girls Just Wanna Have Fun" and "The Shoop Shoop Song."

"'It's in His Kiss'?" I ask. "I can't sing that onstage."

He slurps his soda and says, "Yes! Yes, you can!"

We go back and forth on this a billion times and crack up while we're snacking.

"Kaylan," he says in his reassuring tone. "You are going to rock this. You have to think of it as total, over-the-top, wacky humor. Ya know?"

I laugh again. Jason puts an orange peel in his mouth, covering his teeth, and tries to talk. "Something like this? Add this to it?"

I do it, too. "How do I look?" I crack up so hard that I need to put my face on the table to take a break.

We're laughing so much that it totally catches me off guard when Tyler says, "Yo. Ryan. You didn't tell me Baby Kaylan has a boyfriend?"

Baby Kaylan?

"Is her boyfriend a one-eyed alien? Because that's the only creature that would go out with her!" Ryan bursts out laughing. I turn around and Tyler high-fives him.

"Yeah, well, only a blind alien would go out with you!" I yell, but they're already back upstairs.

I turn back around and see that Jason's cheeks are

bright red. "Um, yeah," he says. "So we have a good list. Don't you think?"

"Oh, for sure."

We sit there quietly for a few more minutes, and the only sounds I can hear are the crunching of potato chips and the slurping of soda.

"Hey, Kaylan," Jason says like he's starting a difficult conversation.

"Hey, Jason," I reply.

"Like, we're friends, right?"

I nod, swallowing hard like I have a brick lodged between my tonsils. "What are you talking about?"

"What Tyler said before," he continues. "About a boyfriend? We're not . . . ?"

"Jason. Come on!"

"Okay." He laughs. "You know Arianna is like obsessed with boyfriend stuff, right?" I think he realizes what he's said when he says it, and then looks down at his feet. "I mean, everyone is. . . ."

"You know I don't talk to Ari," I remind him, sounding snippier than I'd meant to. "So how would I know?"

"Right. I don't even know why I brought that up."

I shrug.

We go back to our list and keep adding songs, and my heart feels heavy.

I didn't want Jason to be my boyfriend. At least, I don't think I did. But then why do I feel so deflated? Like a pool toy that didn't last the summer.

And then his Ari comment? What was that all about?

I make a mental note to add this to the Things I Need to Talk to Ari About list.

Wow. I have a lot of lists going on right now.

Maybe this is a sign that all of the loose ends are going to fall into place pretty soon—all of my lists coming together and everything starting to make sense.

For a list maker like me, a lot of lists has to mean something.

It has to mean something good is about to happen.

I can't fall asleep that night. Jason's comment about Ari being boy crazy just swirls around and around in my head, and I can't get it to stop.

So I focus on the thing that was supposed to calm me down: the 11 Before 12 List. I snuggle up under my covers and read it over. It feels like a million years ago that Ari and I made this list together. I've accomplished so many things since we wrote it.

But I'm not done yet.

Eleven Fabulous Things to Make Us Even More AMAZING Before We Turn Twelve

1. Make a guy friend. ✓
2. Do a Whole Me Makeover.

3. Get on TV for something cool we've done (not because we got hit by a bus). ✓

4. Help humanity. ✓

5. Highlight our hair. ✓

6. Do something we think we'll hate. ✓

7. Fulfill lifelong dream to kayak at night to the little island across the lake. (First step, find a kayak.)

8. Kiss a boy.

9. Get detention. ✓

10. Have a mature discussion with our moms about their flaws. ✓

11. Sabotage Ryan. ✓

I wonder how many of the things Ari has done without me, and how she did them. If she made her own ritual to do after she's completed them, or maybe she even made a ritual to do before she starts them. Ari's thoughtful and careful, and I bet everything's working out perfectly.

I overheard some of them—the TV thing, maybe even the first kiss with Noah.

I'm a good eavesdropper, but maybe I need to step up my game.

Or maybe I just need to get Ari back once and for all.

THIRTY

ALMOST A WHOLE WEEK PASSES, and I don't make any progress winning Ari back. I don't even really come up with a plan that make sense. All I've got is: sneak out of school, get Ari a strawberry milkshake, put it in her locker.

I try to sit more toward Ari's side of the table at lunch, but it's pointless. There isn't always good eavesdropping material. No Noah mentions this week. But I did find out the day Marie's getting her braces off. January 27.

Our birthdays are only three weeks away and we have the hugest stuff left to do. And my superstition is still in full effect—what will happen if we don't complete the list?

Maybe, like, I won't have my first kiss until I'm

twenty-five, or I'll develop a freaky mole on my arm . . . some kind of weird curse.

By the time I get to the talent show meeting after school, I have a million knots in my stomach. All the Tyler interactions I've ever had over the past few weeks are swirling around in my brain. I keep hearing his voice saying *Baby Kaylan*, and it makes my skin prickle.

It's the end of the day, so my hair is greasy and I have a yogurt splotch on my shirt from lunch. It's way too risky to be too close to Tyler, so I sit in the first row and take out my math homework. I figure this is good for two reasons: I'll get it done, and I'll look busy, so when people start to come in, I won't look like I was just sitting around waiting.

I'm in the middle of a complicated algebra equation when I hear Tyler's voice.

"Dude," he says. I don't know who he's talking to. "She's like, chill. Like, not like other girls. I don't know, man."

I have no idea who he is talking about, but my skin turns tingly. Oh, how I wish I had invisible powers. Please God, let me have invisible powers. Let me have invisible powers right now. I sink down into my seat so they don't see me.

"Yeah?" the other kid asks. All I know is that it's definitely not Ryan. Thank God.

"Yeah."

I don't know why I'm excited. He could be talking about

any girl in the world. They walk around to the other side of the auditorium, and I can't hear anything else they say to each other.

The best thing for me to do right now is to put that conversation out of my head entirely and focus on this talent show.

Mrs. Bellinsky, who's my astronomy teacher and the teacher who oversees the drama department, the talent show—basically all things theatrical in the school—comes on to the stage.

"Hello, everyone," she says.

A bunch of kids mumble back a tired hello and she says, "Oh, you can do better than that!" and then we yell out an exasperated hello, and everyone laughs.

"Okay, so I'm thrilled you're all here!" She claps. "By now I hope that you've secured your acts and you've been practicing. I'd like each of you to come onto the stage today, tell us what you'll be doing, maybe give us a brief preview."

Brief preview? The knots in my stomach twist around themselves a hundred times and it feels like they're reproducing and now there are billions and billions of knots.

I can't do a brief preview. I don't even have any clementines, and I haven't decided on what songs I'm singing. I never should have listened to Jason. He's not even here, he's not even participating. What does he know about

West Brookside Middle School's talent shows, anyway? He's new to the school, just like I am.

"We'll go in alphabetical order," Mrs. Bellinsky says, and then she starts calling people up.

I'm grateful to be a Terrel today. At least I have some time.

Tyler's last name is Beasley, so he doesn't have quite as long to wait. My knots turn into bubbles. I'm excited to see his act. Also, this is an occasion when it's okay to stare at him, and no one will think that's weird. It's literally allowed, required, expected.

The A kids go and their acts are pretty boring, to be honest. A few singers, all of them doing Taylor Swift. Mrs. Bellinsky says she's going to have to make some adjustments. "There's such a thing as too much Taylor Swift," she explains.

I'm not sure I agree with her.

There's a bongo drummer. His name is Clive and he's in eighth grade and he has long hair. His parents own the health food store near the train station. Then this girl Hara holds up her phone and takes duck-face selfies of herself while her friend Brianna gives commentary. It's supposed to be funny, but something isn't working. It just feels like they're trying to hard.

Then it's Tyler's turn.

He walks up the few steps to the stage, takes the

microphone, and says, "How many of you have heard of Weird Al?"

No one responds. The thing is, I know all about Weird Al because my dad was a huge fan. Come to think of it, Weird Al was probably the only thing my dad was a fan of. He learned about Weird Al when he went to summer camp. I guess he was happy then. He was always cranky as a dad—angry about work and bills and it always seemed like he wanted to be somewhere else.

"Okay, so none of you know who Weird Al is." He laughs. "Basically, he makes up his own versions of famous songs, and they're always funny. But I'm going to be better than Weird Al. I'm going to be funnier. I'm going to take what Weird Al did and make it my own. Weird Tyler. But Cool Weird. So think: Alternative Tyler."

Alternative Tyler? Is he really standing up there insulting Weird Al?

Mrs. Bellinsky looks confused, but everyone is laughing.

"Here's a brief preview: one of my songs will be called 'Uptown Junk.'" He pauses. "Get it. Like 'Uptown Funk'?"

Tyler tries to be funny. He is confident enough to go up there and do something completely different—something most people don't even know about. And he's not nervous at all. He just does it. Like he doesn't care what people think at all. The thing is, his cuteness makes whatever he does seem okay. And maybe that's not okay—cute people can't just get away with doing whatever they want. They have to care about what they do and say, too.

It feels like three hours pass before it's my turn, but then Mrs. Bellinsky says, "Kaylan Terrel," and I start to sweat.

So I walk up to the stage, and I say, "Okay, now, I decided to go the funny route." I wait for laughter or applause or anything, but the crowd is silent. Truthfully, they look half-asleep. We have been here a while, so I get it. "I'm the fastest clementine peeler in the world. Please time me as I peel. I won't let you down." I wait for laughter. A few chuckles here and there, but not as many as I'd hoped for. "But it's not only that. I can peel them while singing classic songs." I pause again. "I'll probably peel about five on the night of the performance in under forty seconds. I'm not a good singer, just keep that in mind, okay? That's part of the humor."

I don't know why I'm explaining my joke. I know that's, like, the big no-no of comedy.

"But just go with it—"

Mrs. Bellinsky interrupts me. "Kaylan, let's get started, okay?"

My throat prickles. I force myself to nod, and get started.

And then I remember I don't have any clementines.

"Anyone have a clementine? Sorry. I didn't come pre-pared. I didn't realize this was a run-through."

A kid in the back row finds one and throws it to me. Thankfully, I catch it. It feels slimy, like his hands were sweaty, and I gag a little bit but I try not to make it noticeable.

I'm not sure it's possible for this to go any worse than it's going. I kind of want to drop this sweaty clementine and run right out of the auditorium. Maybe transfer to another school.

I stand up straight and think about the night on the Petey G show. I try to find that Kaylan.

"Here comes the sun," I sing, and then start peeling. "Do-do-do-do." And then people start laughing. Really laughing. They're not even forcing it. "Here comes the sun." At least it doesn't seem like they're forcing it. "And that's it! Remember, I'll have more clementines the night of the show."

I hold up the peel. And take a bow.

"Eleven seconds," one kid calls out. I give him a thumbs-up.

I look around for Tyler and try to see his reaction. He's in the back, and he's sort of paying attention but sort of talking to his friends. Did he think this was funny? I have no idea.

I kind of thought Jason would show, or hang in the doorway, or just check in to see part of it. But I guess I didn't know we were doing the previews, so he couldn't have known either.

Still, I wish he was here.

"Thank you, Kaylan," Mrs. Bellinsky says. Her eyebrows are crinkly. "That was certainly unique."

She calls up the next person, Dylan Thursber, and I sit in my seat and cover my cheeks with my hands, trying to hide the insane level of redness.

The boy with the crew cut and glasses sitting next to me whispers, "That was awesome."

I smile. "Thanks. I think Mrs. Bellinsky was a little weirded out by it."

"Whatever." We both look over at her, and she notices us talking, so he whispers, "It was cool."

He's the last one to go, and his act is half breakdancing and half rapping, and I can't tell if it's supposed to be serious or funny.

"That was great," I whisper when he's done, because no matter what it was supposed to be, we can all use a compliment.

When the run-through is over, the boy says, "I'm Eric."

"Kaylan."

"Seventh grade kind of sucks," he tells me, out of the blue, like he's warning me about danger to come. As we're walking to the late bus, I keep turning my head in search of Tyler. I want to look for him, but I don't want it to seem like I'm looking for him. I hope to catch him in my peripheral vision, but so far, nothing. It's like he disappeared.

"Sixth isn't really the greatest time either," I reply, laughing.

Eric is so nice, but right now feels like the time to find Tyler. My awesome act will be fresh in his mind. I can't waste this moment. "I gotta go," I say. "I forgot something in my locker. See you at the next rehearsal!"

"Oh, uh, okay. Bye!"

I run off in the other direction and feel like the meanest person in the entire world. But a girl's gotta do what a girl's gotta do.

It should be, like, some kind of unspoken rule that people with crushes can be forgiven for doing sometimes mean, and mostly strange, bizarre stuff.

The crushes mess with our minds somehow. But it's not permanent.

At least I don't think it is.

THIRTY-ONE

AFTER THE TALENT SHOW RUN-THROUGH, my fame keeps rising. It feels like everyone in the entire school heard about my clementine peeling. I like that. I guess it's so unusual that it really stands out? But the thing is, it hasn't changed everything.

Ari's still not talking to me.

Tyler and I haven't even had a real conversation yet.

Aside from my newfound fame, things aren't that different.

I still haven't totally figured out my Whole Me Makeover. I don't know exactly who I want to be, or what difference I want to make. And the scariest part is—I don't know what else I should be doing to get there.

On the walk home from school, I see Mrs. Etisof out

on her front porch. She's all bundled up in a heavy coat, painting at her easel.

"Mrs. Etisof!"

"My girl!" She puts a dab of paint in the corner. "Want to see my latest painting? They've commissioned me for a piece to hang in the Boat House on Arch Island!"

"Are you serious?" I ask. "That's huge!"

"I know! Come see!" I move closer to her. She smells like flowery lotion and acrylic paint.

She's painted Brookside Lake and Green River and trees all around, and then Arch Island with the Boat House, and the gazebo and people, and picnic blankets spread out.

"Amazing." I sit down next to her on the floor. "I love it!"

"It's not done yet," she continues. "I want to add more color. . . ." She pauses and looks at me. "You always look like you're in such a hurry lately," she says. "Can you stay for a few minutes?"

I look at my phone even though I know what time it is. My first instinct is to say that I need to get home and do homework. But I really just want to get home and see if Tyler is there.

"I can stay for a few minutes," I reply. "What's new?"

"Wonderful," she says. "Well, hmmm. What's new? I think I can get out for one last paddle before it gets too cold. And the kayak racing competition we're planning for next summer is going to be huge! But tell me what's new in your world."

"Well, I'm doing the fall talent show," I start, and then I launch into a whole description of the clementine thing and realize halfway through that it sounds crazy. "And then of course, there's boy drama."

As I talk to Mrs. Etisof about all of this, I realize how starved I've been for a best friend. Without Ari, I don't have anyone to talk to—I mean, really talk to—about what's on my mind, and what I'm obsessing about. It's like I'm trapped in my own head, stuck there, with the thoughts revolving around and around, but never really getting anywhere. And I know my obsessing is how we got into the fight in the first place, but a girl needs a best friend. It's a fact of life.

I know Mrs. Etisof is seventy, but she's a good listener.

"Hmmm" is all she says, and then I wonder if she is really a good listener. Maybe she was totally spaced out this entire time. "I've seen you with Jason," she says, after a long pause. "He's a nice boy."

"He is, right?" I feel myself getting fired up.

She nods, and turns her painting every so slightly so I can see it again. "I love all the little boats on the river."

"I might do an evening scene, too, of the same spot," she says. "And add in lots of stars."

"Very romantic," I add.

I want to tell Jason about this painting and how good Mrs. Etisof is since his parents have so much art hanging around their house. I think he'd like it, and maybe they could commission Mrs. Etisof to paint something for them.

I'm really thinking about Jason a lot all of a sudden. I guess we are becoming real, true friends, not just texting friends.

"I better get home," I tell Mrs. Etisof.

"Bye, dear," she says. "I'm going to add some more magenta to the island part."

As I walk home, I half pray that Tyler will be there and half pray that he won't be. I guess it's okay—this way I won't be disappointed with either outcome.

I'm almost at the door when I look at my phone. A text from Jason and a text from Cami. I stop and sit down on my front steps.

Jason: **Everyone is talking about your act!**

Me: **I don't know why Mrs. B had us do the preview! It was supposed to be a surprise.**

Jason: **Bc last year some kids didn't prep at all, and they came on stage and just started wrestling and it got intense.**

Me: **Really? Wrestling onstage?**

Jason: **Yup. Andre told me about it. His sister was in it.**

Me: **Ohhhhh. I gotta go inside. Talk later.**

Jason: **Later.**

Cami: **Harvey Deli has a new sandwich. It's called the Blanche, named after a Golden Girls character. I'll tell you all about it in school.**

Me: **Oh yay! So exciting. They only have new sandwiches like every few months.**

Cami: **I KNOW!**

I get inside and my mom and Ryan are in the kitchen fighting about something.

This probably sounds mean, but I'm happy that Ryan's the one fighting with her for once. I can just sneak by and go upstairs and focus on my own troubles, without having to deal with my mom.

Of course I leave my door open, so I can hear what they're talking about.

"Mom, relax." Ryan sounds like he's forcing himself to speak calmly, like he has it all under control. "Everyone is going to this party. It's totally fine."

"I don't know the person throwing the party," my mom explains. "You need to tell me the person's name, address, and give me all the details."

"That's psycho, Mom!" he yells.

"Ryan," she warns. "I'm willing to work with you on this, but you're not meeting me halfway."

"I should've lied to you," he says with force. "I should've just said I was going out with Tyler or something. Forget it. I'm skipping the party."

He runs upstairs and slams the door to his room.

My mom huffs around the kitchen, taking out pans to cook dinner and making more noise than she usually does.

I'm tempted to knock on Ryan's door and come up with some elaborate plan to get him to this party to make up for the whole jam-band thing. But I don't think now's the right time. He's too angry.

I text Jason again and ask him if he knows anything about a party going on this weekend. A few minutes later, he replies. **No clue. Let's crash it.**

I'm trying to think of a witty thing to write back when he says, **Hang out tomorrow?**

My heart pounds with excitement. What is happening?

I write back, **Yes!** But then I realize I have the dress rehearsal for the talent show. **Actually talent show dress rehearsal tomorrow. Sorry! Hang this weekend?**

Then it feels like three million years pass before he replies. **Oh wait, I can't crash the party. I forgot my dad and I are going to a basketball game.**

"Kaylan! Ryan! Dinner!" My mom yells, and I run down the stairs because I'm hungry and because right now it's really easy to be the good one in my mom's eyes.

"Hi, Mom." I smile. "How was your day?"

"It was fine. And yours?"

"Good." I tell her about Mrs. Etisof's painting as she

puts a piece of chicken and some asparagus on my plate.

"Ryan!" She yells up the stairs again. "Dinner is happening. Come down now. Or don't eat!"

She shakes her head.

"What's up with him?" I ask.

"I wish I knew."

"Same."

We're almost done eating when Ryan finally shows up.

"There's some chicken left," my mom says. "Help yourself."

She gets up from the table and starts doing the dishes.

I glare at him. "Way to join us," I sneer.

"Way to be the most annoying person ever to live." He stabs a fork into his chicken cutlet.

"No, that would be you." I talk through my teeth. "You're really upsetting Mom, you know."

"Sorry it's taking away from you upsetting her. The way you do every day."

My mom turns around and throws a dishtowel on the counter. "I can hear you two, you know. I've had enough. I'm going upstairs. This kitchen better be cleaned up when I come down to make breakfast tomorrow."

We hear the door close to her room and then Ryan and I stare at each other. "Are you okay?" I ask.

"Yeah. I'm fine." His chair screeches against the floor as he goes to put his plate in the dishwasher. He stays there, his hands firmly placed on the kitchen counter, talking with his back to me. "Can everyone stop asking me if I'm okay? You guys are the ones that aren't okay."

"Ryan," I plead. "Seriously, you can talk to me. Remember, we used to be friends? We'd put on concerts on the back deck. You'd play the toy saxophone. And I'd sing. Remember our lemonade stand? Remember when you dressed me up in your wrestler costumes and taught me how to do a pile driver?" I know I sound pathetic right now, listing all the memories I have, but maybe sometimes you need to sound pathetic in order to get through to people.

"Stop, Kaylan." He turns around, finally. "Please."

He storms out of the kitchen and up the stairs and I'm left alone with my half-eaten dinner plate.

"Guess I'm loading the dishwasher by myself!" I scream up the stairs. "You're the worst brother in the world!"

I rinse the plates and stack them against each other between the dishwasher slats, and wonder if things between Ryan and me will ever get back to the way they were before all we did was yell at each other. I want to go back to our bike rides around the neighborhood, and searching the house for change to get an extra ice cream at the pool.

I feel like I've been abandoned by my brother. He won't talk to me. He won't even help clean up.

THIRTY-TWO

THE NEXT MORNING I LOOK for Ari at the bus stop like I do every day, even though I'm pretty sure she's not going to be there. I overheard her telling Marie and them that her mom has been driving her. It's not really that big of a hassle because she has to drive Gemma to Brookside Elementary School anyway. I know Gemma refuses to take the bus because she'd be the first stop and she'd be on the bus for a million years before actually getting to school and she doesn't have any neighborhood friends to sit with like Ari did.

Jason doesn't take the bus either since his dad literally drives by the school on his way to work. He's offered me a ride a few times, but I've turned him down. It seems too stressful to have to sit in a car with Jason and his dad that early in the morning. My brain isn't awake yet. I probably still have orange juice breath. I can't handle making conversation.

So I take the bus by myself and try not to stress too much about it. Ryan sits all the way in the back with some kids I don't know. Tyler's dad has been driving him lately since Tyler overslept so many times and missed the bus.

I spend today's ride to school thinking about the dress rehearsal for the talent show. I can't believe it's tonight. When I picture August 1—Agita Day—it seems like a million years ago.

My birthday will be here so soon, and I haven't planned for it at all. I've been so focused on all the other stuff. I guess we're not doing the party. Maybe I should just do something with Jason, Cami, June, and the Whatevers instead, but I don't even have the energy to think about it, really.

It's the saddest thing ever to think you're going to have a joint birthday party with your best friend and then when the time comes, you're not even talking and you don't even have a celebration.

I'm sure my birthday will be a Carvel cake with my mom. Ryan will try to spit on it. Maybe my dad will call and it'll be some awkward conversation, and my grandma will send me a gift card.

It won't even be as good as the awkward sleepover I had with Brooke and Lily for my ninth birthday, right before the breakup.

I make it to lunch, and June and the Whatevers are already at the table when I get there. I open up my lunch bag to find a soggy turkey sandwich, a bag of chips, and a clementine. My mom's lunches are really slacking lately, probably because she makes them so early in the morning and can't think clearly.

Normally, I'd worry about something like that. But right now my mind is too crowded with other stuff.

"I can't believe you bailed again on our Harvey Deli date," Cami says, spreading out her lunch. "What do you even do on the weekends?"

I shrug. "I'm sorry I bailed. I had a bad headache," I say, which is a total lie unless you count moping and getting ahead on my homework as a headache. "I don't really do anything. Sometimes I hang out with my next-door neighbor. She's painting something for the Boat House on Arch Island."

"Isn't she, like, seventy?" June laughs.

"Yeah, but old people are wise," I say, laughing too now. "Let's hang out this weekend. Okay? I'll text to make a plan."

They shrug like they don't believe I'll ever show up. "Can I please rehearse for the talent show right now?"

I'll admit that I said that pretty loud in hopes that I'd

get Ari's attention. She and her crew are at the other end of the table, laughing about the lunch aides, like always.

She looks up for a second and then back down at her gross cafeteria mac and cheese. It's kind of crazy that we've been at the same table for this whole fight. I've overheard little bits and pieces about her life—like random stories about Gemma (I miss her!) and juicy little tidbits about the kid Noah from Hebrew School—but I wish I could hear them from Ari.

I wish they were more than tidbits.

"You're gonna stand up in the cafeteria and perform? Right now?" June shrieks. The other girls shake their heads.

"I'll sing quietly." I glare. "I mean, I've already been on TV, so I'm okay in front of crowds."

Cami laughs. "You're so weird, Kaylan. You know that, right?" She pauses. "A good weird."

My cheeks redden but I don't dwell on her comment. I think she meant it as a compliment. "Someone time me."

June takes out her phone even though we're not supposed to have them in school. She gets the timer ready and points to me when it's time to start.

I peel and sing a snippet from "Here Comes the Sun" under my breath.

When I'm done, I hold up the peel.

"Ten seconds," June says. "Wow."

The other girls sound like a chorus of "that was

amazing" and "how do you do that?" And I glance down to the other side of the table, and I swear I see Ari smiling. Our eyes meet for a second. I smile. And then she looks back down at her food.

She's impressed. I know she is.

Finally, the last bell rings and it's time for the dress rehearsal. My whole body feels bubbly. If I'm this nervous now, I have no idea how I will feel when it's time for the actual thing. I might faint from anxiety. It's hard to know for sure.

Mrs. Bellinsky claps as she walks into the auditorium. That's her way to get our attention. She does it in every class she teaches.

"Okay, people. Quiet. Quiet now, please." She talks and claps. There's a rumor that she used to be a Rockette, but I'm not sure it was ever confirmed. "I need to see people in costume. Makeup on. Instruments ready. Clap three times if you can hear me."

We all clap halfheartedly and I keep looking at the door to see who's coming in. Tyler's not here yet. He's late. Or maybe he bailed.

"I'm so sorry to say that I need to leave town next week," she says once we're all quiet and listening. "I have an unexpected family emergency. So that is why we are having the dress rehearsal so early." She continues to go on and on, and I stop listening.

I have a more important thing on my mind: Where is Tyler?

Mrs. Bellinsky is still talking about decorum and behavior for the event when he walks in.

"Sorry I'm late, Mrs. B," he yells, interrupting her. He has a crew of three other boys with him, even though none of them are in the talent show. I don't think they're supposed to be here.

"Tyler, be seated at once." For some reason, when Mrs. Bellinsky is in the auditorium she thinks she's in a real theater and she starts talking in this very over-the-top, theatrical way.

I cover my mouth so I don't start laughing.

Tyler and his boys sit right behind me. All the hairs on my arms stand up, and it's like I can't get comfortable in this chair knowing he and his friends are so close. I don't know how to sit or where to put my hands. I feel like I need to fix my hair.

I'm forcing myself to listen to Mrs. Bellinsky and not eavesdrop on their whispering. And then I feel a tug at my ponytail.

"Kaylan," someone whispers.

I try not to turn around while Mrs. Bellinsky is talking, even though there is a boy in the row behind me calling my name. I'm a feminist. I don't jump whenever there's a boy involved.

At least I hope I don't.

269

But then there's another ponytail tug.

"What?" I hiss.

"Hey." Tyler smiles.

"Kaylan!" Mrs. Bellinsky says forcefully. "Are you listening to anything I'm saying? Decorum in a theater! Turn around this instant!"

"Sorry." I look down at the floor and mumble a "thanks for getting me in trouble" loud enough for Tyler and his boys to hear me.

When it's time to get up and go backstage and get ready, I make sure I'm not the first one up. I might have a wedgie; I'm not totally sure. And I don't want Tyler and the boys to notice. I want them to get up first, so I can follow behind. I keep turning my head, ever so slightly, to get a glimpse of what they're doing.

When they're shuffling down the row, I follow the group backstage.

My act doesn't require a costume, so I'm just lingering about, trying to look busy and also interested in whatever the other students are doing.

"Wanna help me with my costume?" Tyler asks me, smiling a wide, over-the-top smile. He literally just appeared out of nowhere. I had lost him in the group of kids for a few minutes.

"Wait. What?" I stammer.

THIRTY-THREE

"I FIGURED YOU'D BE GOOD at helping me get my wig to look just right," Tyler says.

"You did?" I don't have any wig experience. But I don't know why I am debating this right now. I should be thrilled, ecstatic, jumping up and down. But instead I'm freaking out. I don't know how to do makeup. Or put on a wig. I mean, I guess you just put it on, but . . . and I can't be that close to him, touching his face, his hair. I've never been that close to a boy before. It's like my limbs feel extralong and out of place, like I don't know what to do with them.

He nods. "And I need some makeup help, too."

"Wait, why do you need makeup?" I ask. "Aren't you just singing your own made-up songs?"

"Yes." He eyes me like I'm a complete buffoon. "But

I need a look. I can't just, like, go up there, looking like regular Tyler. And stage lights wash everyone out! Don't you know that?"

"Um."

"I need to look like Alternative Tyler." He points to his face. "That's why I have a Mohawk wig. And I'm going to wear KISS makeup."

"KISS?" I ask.

I take a step back because everything seems to be going really crazy right now. I didn't know boys thought about stuff like this—stage makeup. And wigs.

"It's a band!"

"I know," I shriek. "But are you singing KISS songs?"

"No! But it's part of my look."

He's not really making much sense. But he's just so cute that it almost doesn't matter.

"So. Uh." He stares at me, waiting for me to say something. "Will you be my stage assistant?"

Stage assistant?

This is literally the most awkward conversation I've had in my entire life and yet I don't want it to ever end. I am so close to Tyler right now. He's asking me to do his makeup. And help him with a wig. A shiver shoots down my back.

He owns a Mohawk wig.

I will be forced to touch him.

Me, Kaylan. Forced to touch him, Tyler.

"So where should I sit for my makeup?" he asks.

All around us people are buzzing about—getting on costumes, putting on makeup, all sorts of stuff.

"How about over here?" I lead him to a bench in the back corner of the stage. He sits down. "Did you bring makeup with you?"

He nods and hands me a pink makeup bag. "It's my mom's. I think I can use her eyeliner to do the black triangle parts."

Something about the way he says it is so sweet and funny at the same time that I completely burst out laughing and then Tyler looks embarrassed.

"I'm sorry," I say.

He shrugs.

I try to apply the makeup standing up but then it's just too weird, and I can't get a good angle, and it all comes out blotchy. I try to follow a picture I found by Googling on my phone. My hands are shaky. We are so close and I wish I'd popped some gum in my mouth before we started. I try to back up so he can't smell my breath, but then it gets even more messed up.

I have to start again.

"This is kind of a hard design to do," I tell him.

"Don't you know about makeup? Girls all wear makeup, right?"

"Um." I bite my lip. "I don't really wear makeup."

I sit down next to him and take the round sponge thing

(I have no idea if there's a technical name for it) and start rubbing the concealer on his face.

I try to focus, but all I can think is: *I am touching Tyler's face. I am touching Tyler's face.*

And then, midapplication, when I'm trying to finish the side of his nose, he puts his hand on my hand. It's not sweaty, thank God. But it's warm, like he'd had it in a glove this whole time.

"Thanks for doing this, Kaylan." He looks into my eyes.

This is it, I think. *I know it is.* Tyler Beasley is going to kiss me, right here, right now, on this stage.

I manage to mumble out a "no problem."

And then he says, "Listen, a friend of mine is having this party Saturday night. You should come."

Wait. So he's not going to kiss me?

But he is inviting me to a party.

That's something. That's a big something!

And then I remember—the party Ryan was talking about, actually fighting about, with my mom.

"Kaylan?"

I haven't said anything. I've been silent, I guess. Just dabbing his face with this weird sponge.

"Oh yeah." I stop dabbing for a second and then continue. "Party. Cool."

"Are you okay?" he asks.

"Yeah." I step back as if inspecting my work on his

face, but really I'm just stepping back from this situation a little bit.

"So you'll come?"

I nod. "Yup. Okay, you're all set. You look fab, Cool Tyler."

He cracks up and then high-fives me. "Just call me Tyler."

Mrs. Bellinsky yells out that it's time to start the rehearsal. I don't have makeup on. I'm not in a costume. I was just planning on wearing my regular clothes and maybe a cool scarf or something, and ya know, being myself.

At least I have my phone with some songs loaded on iTunes so I'm prepared with background music. And I brought more clementines this time.

"So." Mrs. Bellinsky talks into the microphone and it screeches. "Sorry. Sorry. So we know that getting ready for this dress rehearsal took us a long time. A verrrry long time. We'll need to do better before the main event. Or you'll all need to show up the night before."

She waits for laughter, but no one laughs.

"Anyway, let's get started." She calls everyone up in the order we'll be performing but tells us she's still fine-tuning the exact final order.

So the group of eighth graders that does some kind of fifties-style dancing medley goes first, and then there's seventh grader Stephen Board, who plays Mozart on the cello. After that I zone out for a little while, and when I zone back in, Tyler's making his way to the stage.

"I'd like to thank Kaylan Terrel for helping me with my makeup," Tyler says.

"Okay, Tyler." Mrs. Bellinsky interrupts. "Let's get started."

So he starts. His first song, "Uptown Junk," goes something like, "Uptown Junk. Throw it out. Throw it out." It's really bad. Like, really, really bad. And then he does a parody of Taylor Swift's "Bad Blood": "Mad Mud. We used to have mad mud. In our cleats. After soccer."

I look around, and it seems like people feel like they should laugh, so they're forcing it because honestly—this isn't funny. No one in the entire world could find this funny. These parodies are dumb, and the words don't line up with the music, and it all just feels like a mess. I'm cringing that this is happening, and that he thinks it's so great and so funny.

He thinks he's Alternative Tyler.

He thinks that everyone thinks he's Alternative Tyler.

But even through my cringing and his bad songs—I don't deny his cuteness. Even in his Mohawk wig. I mean, he's supposed to be my first kiss.

And I have to be loyal to the list.

THIRTY-FOUR

I KNOCK ON RYAN'S DOOR as soon as I get home from the dress rehearsal.

"What?" he says.

"Can I come in?" I ask. I wonder if he knows about Tyler and the talent show.

No response.

I continue, "I have sweets. Your favorite, too."

"No thanks."

"Ryan. Please." I know I sound so pathetic, begging to go into his room, but we need to strategize. If we work together, we can get to this party.

"Kaylan, seriously." He opens the door a tiny crack, just wide enough for me to see the corner of his nose. "Did you take some kind of weird lame potion? I swear. You're out-laming yourself every day."

Out-laming myself?

"Are you done?" I ask. "Because I know how you're going to get to that party on Saturday. I know how you're going to convince Mom that it's okay to go."

"Yeah. How?" He closes the door in my face. "Maybe if you just accept that you're the biggest loser in the world you will stop annoying me."

"Fine. I'm done." I walk away from the door. "I'll be at the party. And you won't be. I guess you didn't realize Tyler invited me."

He opens the door. "Yeah, right! In your dreams!"

Seriously, it's like my dad took Ryan's personality with him when he left and now Ryan has reverted to acting like a two-year-old.

My mom comes home a little later and yells up the stairs to tell us she picked up sandwiches from the Harvey Deli near the doctor's office where she works.

I text Cami.

Me: **Guess who's the luckiest girl in the world? I'm having Harvey Deli for dinner!**

Cami: **JEALOUS! You promise you're really gonna come on Sunday?**

Me: **PROMISE! ☺ WE GOTTA GET THE BLANCHE!**

Cami: **Yes!!!**

I sprint downstairs and put on my biggest smile. I'm about to have the best dinner ever, and I'm actually going to have plans with friends this weekend. I promise myself I won't bail this time. Cami isn't Ari, but if every-thing goes well at the party, I'll need someone to rehash with.

"I got you that eggplant sandwich you love," Mom says.

"Mom!" I wrap her in a hug. "Thank you so much. Why are you the best ever? Seriously, the best *ever*."

She steps back and puts the greasy white bags on the kitchen table.

"Okay, Kaylan." She looks at me with her hands on her hips. "What do you want?"

"Huh?" I crinkle my face and go to the cabinet to get plates and cups.

"Don't *huh* me," she says.

"I can't tell you I love you and thank you for bringing home the best sandwich on the planet?" I sit at the table and begin to unwrap all the food.

She shrugs. "You can. And I love you, too. Where's your brother?"

I yell to him to come down, and he shows up a few minutes later.

"Thanks for the meatball sub, but I'm still not talking to you," Ryan says to my mother, pouring a tall glass of lemonade.

"Well, hello to you, too," she says.

He doesn't respond. He's taking this way too far. Especially since he doesn't realize there's actually a very simple solution.

"This is still about the party?" my mom asks.

He still doesn't respond.

I can't handle the silence anymore. Well, it's not really silence since both my mom and brother are such loud chewers. But I can't stand hearing the chewing anymore.

"The party Saturday night?" I ask. I think it's good to play dumb at first and then slowly ease into the reveal.

"I think it's Saturday night," my mom says. "I don't even know anymore. All I said was that I needed to know if the parents were going to be home, and if I could have a phone number, and Ryan wasn't willing to go along with that."

"You completely freaked out. No one gives out home numbers anymore. Don't you know that, Mom? I have a cell phone."

I put down my sandwich and take a deep breath. "Okay, everyone. Let's calm down a minute."

"Shut it, Kaylan," Ryan says. "You don't know anything. I don't know why you pretend that you do."

I pause and exhale and control my temper. "I know who's throwing that party. I know that I'm invited. And I know that I can assure Mom that the parents will be home."

Ryan stares at me. It's clear that he doesn't know if I'm lying or telling the truth. But he's intrigued. His eyes soften. He looks at me, and then at my mom, and then back at me. He waits for me to continue.

Mom sips her seltzer and I think she's also confused. Maybe she thinks I'm lying.

"Tyler invited me to the party, by the way," I tell them. "But I know who's throwing it. It's that kid Craig in eighth grade. The one with the purple hair. Don't freak out, Mom." I look at her, and she smiles. "His sister Lizzie is in my grade. She's my lab partner. So anyway, I asked her what's up with the party. She said her parents are letting Craig throw it because he got all As."

Okay. Now I am embellishing a little because I have no idea if that's the reason. I think Craig just wanted to have a party. And also, the being-home thing is a little bit of a white lie. The parents will be home, but they have their own wing, and they promised to stay there the whole time.

"Uh-huh," Mom says, waiting for me to go on.

I turn to face her. I look her right in the eyes, so she believes me. My mom is really big on eye contact. "So I can give you their number. Lizzie is really normal."

And I may be white lying a bit here, too. Because I'll give my mom Lizzie's cell-phone number . . . and I'll have Lizzie prepped about the whole thing.

"Ryan," my mom says to him. "What do you think?"

"I think it's fine," he says.

"And?" my mom asks. "Do you have anything to say to your sister?"

"And I appreciate Kaylan's effort."

Wow. This is the nicest thing he's said to me since last April. I know Mom had to pull it out of him, but it was still nice.

I smile. "You're welcome."

"I could've told you all of that, though," he says. "You don't listen to me, Mom. You realize that, right? You're always so quick to say no to me. But to Kaylan, you're like *sure, whatever.*"

She shakes her head. "That's not true."

"It is, Mom." He talks with his hands. "Dad took me seriously. But you don't; you never did."

She looks at him and then puts her hand over her eyes and starts crying right there at the kitchen table. Tears are streaming down her cheeks and down onto her chicken parmesan hero.

I don't know what's sadder—the fact that she's so broken up right now or the fact that her sandwich is going to taste salty. Like, really salty. And soggy, too. She's ruining a completely amazing sandwich!

I reach over and put an arm around her. "Mom. It's okay."

I nudge my head toward Ryan and mouth, "Say something."

He jerks his head at me, like I'm a nuisance, but he's the nuisance. He just ruined this, when I had it all figured out for him.

"Mom. It's okay," I say again.

Finally, Ryan says, "I'm sorry, Mom. I didn't mean that. I know you try. But it's like super-sucky without Dad here."

Ryan, I mouth again. That was clearly the wrong thing to say. She knows it's super-sucky. She didn't want Dad to leave. She's like the saddest mom in the world now, even though she tries to pretend she's okay. . . . I mean, I think that's what she's trying to do.

So he continues, "And I know it's hard on you, too. And um, like, I think Kaylan and I can be more supportive. I'm sorry."

She looks up and wipes her tears away with the sleeve of her sweater. "Thank you, Ryan."

I'm not sure if I should say sorry because honestly I feel like I've been pretty good lately and haven't been causing too much trouble. But it's one of those moments where maybe I should just say it to be nice and be on the safe side. Also, I'm just sitting here, not doing anything. I finished my sandwich, and I don't think this is the time to ask my mom for a bite of hers. I could eat around the salty, soggy parts. . . .

I feel both my mom and brother look at me, so I say,

"I'm sorry, too. I can definitely be more helpful. I should set the table without you having to ask, and um, make my bed more often than I do."

My mom nods, waiting for me to go on, but I think I'm done.

"Anyway, I'm glad I solved the party problem," I tell them, and start clearing the table.

"I'll drop you guys off," my mom says. "Maybe I can say hello to Lizzie and Craig's parents."

Ryan and I stare at each other.

Wait. What?

I should've known it couldn't possibly have been this easy.

"Don't worry, Mom," I say, putting some plates in the dishwasher. "We have this under control." I turn around so I can see them. "Look, you have so much going on. You don't need to concern yourself with some dumb middle school party. And besides, I'll post pictures to Instagram, so you can follow the whole thing from home." I smile.

"Kaylan," my mom says, like she sort of finds that funny. "You and Ryan are my concerns. My only concerns."

She stands up from the table and tells us she needs to do some work on the computer, and we tell her we'll take care of the cleanup.

"Oh, that's so nice. Thank you."

When she's in the den and I'm confident she can't hear us, I turn to Ryan and say, "Feel better?"

"Yeah. Whatever."

"Don't be all *yeah, whatever*," I say. "I helped you."

"And I said thank you," he says. "Now leave me alone."

"Ryan." I tap him on the shoulder while he's loading the dishwasher. "Stand up. We need to recognize what just happened."

He hesitates, but then stands and faces me. "Go on."

"We just conquered Mom on this party issue," I remind him. "Together. You and me."

He tilts his head and glares at me. "Kaylan. Do we need to put our arms around each other and sway like we did at that church retreat last year?"

I crack up and cover my mouth. "No. But we can admit we did it, right?"

"Right." He puts his hand out for a low five. "We did it."

I go upstairs and text Lizzie and tell her about the drama with my mom.

She writes back a few minutes later. **I get it. My mom is crazy, too. I'll have her text your mom. Okay?**

Me: **Uh, okay.** ☺

Okay, so that's settled.

Now all I have to worry about is Tyler.

And the talent show.

And figuring out a way to make peace with Ari. I kind

of wonder if she'll be at the party, but I don't think so.

And finishing the 11 Before 12 List.

And figuring out my Whole Me Makeover.

And maybe a birthday party.

Easy peasy.

THIRTY-FIVE

JASON: I'M AT THE BBALL game with my dad. Have fun at the party!

Me: Thanks! I will. I think I will . . .

Jason. You will. Going to get fries now. Later!

Me: Bye.

My mom agrees to drop us off at the end of the block and not in front of the actual party. The weird thing is that other parents are dropping their kids off and it's not a big deal, but Ryan is pretty freaked out about it.

"So you're set, Mom, right?" I ask her before I get out of the car. "You have Lizzie's number? My phone is on. So is Ryan's." I look at her and she smiles.

"I got it. Thanks, Kay-Kay." She turns to the backseat. "Ryan, have fun. Okay?"

He nods hesitantly and seems like he almost doesn't want to get out of the car. He was the one who was begging to go to this party in the first place. I guess he forgot that part. So I get out of the car and then I wait for him. A few seconds later, he gets out, too.

He's really letting me walk in with him? We can hold our heads up high, and be this cool brother-sister duo.

But then he says, "I'm gonna go on ahead, okay?"

I nod, even though it feels like my skin is crinkling up. Walking alone into a party is scarier than flying on a plane by yourself. At least on a plane, you have a flight attendant to look out for you.

I slowly walk down the sidewalk, and I look at my phone a few times, too. I debate texting Ari or calling her. I probably should have asked some of the girls at my table if they were going, but I didn't. It felt mean because if they weren't invited, it would be like rubbing it in.

I finally reach the front door, and I stand on the front steps for a few minutes before I go in.

"Hey, Kaylan," Lizzie says, and I quickly thank God that she's there, right by the door, to greet me. My hands are sweaty so I wipe them on my jeans and give her a hug. We're not really hugging friends, but at this moment, it feels right.

"Come downstairs," she continues. "Everyone's down there."

We walk down a hallway covered with photos of

school picture days and weddings and vacations. And then we reach a steep staircase.

It sounds loud down there. Music is playing and people are talking and the air smells like fruit punch. My stomach twists and turns around itself. I think I should go home.

I might barf.

I stop midstaircase.

"Are you okay?" Lizzie asks me.

"Um, yeah, I think so."

"Don't worry. Nothing that crazy is going to happen. I promise."

"Okay, thanks." I pause and wonder what she thinks I'm worrying about.

When we get downstairs, a big group is sitting on a wraparound couch. The guys are sitting back, drinking soda, and the girls are sitting on the edge, half talking to the guys and half talking to the other girls.

I look around, double-checking who else is here while Lizzie runs back upstairs to get more cups.

In the corner by the foosball table, I see the bikini boobage girls from the pool, and I immediately look away. I don't want them to see me. I mean, I don't even think they know who I am. But I still don't want them to see me.

Tyler is nowhere in sight.

I pour myself a cup of Sprite and take a handful of

pretzels, and I stand near the couch with my back to the wall. I look at my phone a few times, to keep occupied, and I pray that someone I know shows up or that Lizzie talks to me or that Tyler appears. It feels like we've been here for three centuries. Time may be moving backward right now.

If only Jason were here, and we could laugh about clementine peeling or astronomy.

"Where'd he go?" I hear someone say, and of course I know the voice. Tyler.

It's unmistakable. At least it's unmistakable to me because I've been eavesdropping on him for so long. I don't know who the "he" is that he's referring to so I look up and smile, and hope that we'll make eye contact.

"We have your drink, Ryan," Tyler sings, and I look around, but I don't see Ryan. And then Tyler holds up a baby bottle filled with milk. "Ryan, your bottle's ready."

Where did he get a baby bottle?

Finally Ryan appears, coming out of the side room. "Ha-ha. Very funny."

"Drink it. Drink it!" Tyler starts shouting. And then others join in.

I don't understand what's happening here. I get the joke—that they think Ryan's a baby. Kind of lame, but whatever. But why do they think that? And why do they care if he drinks the milk? It's just milk. Then I start to worry—what if it's laced with something? Some kind of poison? Not poison that will kill him, but something that'll make him throw up or have diarrhea for days.

People are still chanting, "Drink it! Drink it!"

Something bubbles up in me—I'm not sure what. This crazy, spiky, fiery feeling that I need to protect my brother. I've never felt it before.

I stand up and shout, "NO!" It comes out louder than I'd intended it to. Like the words are doing what they want to do and I'm not controlling them.

"Kaylan?" Ryan asks, and then he walks over to me and grabs my arm. Through clenched teeth he says, "What are you doing?"

I lead him into the side room to chat and people say "Ooohh," which is totally, totally gross. Do they realize he's my brother? Whatever. No time to deal with that now.

"There could be something in that milk," I say. "You don't know what's in there. Can you trust these people?"

Ryan looks into the big room and people are saying, "What are you, chicken?" and "He really is a baby!" and "Scaredy-cat."

Then he looks back at me and shakes his head. He doesn't say anything.

"What?" I gasp.

He wipes his eyes with the sleeve of his shirt. He's crying. Ryan is crying right here, right now, at this party, and the kids are chanting things and I have no idea what's going on.

I came here to see Tyler, but he hasn't even said hi to me yet. All he's done is torment my brother.

"Tyler. He was my best friend. But something changed this summer. He's buddies with this kid George who just moved here from Queens and this other kid Derek that we never talked to before."

"Yeah?" I say, so he knows I'm listening. And I nod, encouraging him to continue. "But Tyler's at our house all the time," I remind him.

"Yeah, whatever, but he's constantly putting me down and stealing my stuff. It started at the beginning of the year," he says. "They think I'm a baby because I wouldn't steal cans of soda out of Mr. Carlton's car. And because I wouldn't give them my answers for the math test a few weeks ago."

What? Who steals soda?

All of a sudden Ryan is telling me stuff and opening up to me, and it feels like someone dumped a bucket of water on my head when I wasn't looking. It's like I want to help, but I also kind of don't. I feel like I'm frozen.

I wanted to have fun tonight. Not deal with this terrible stuff. But this is my brother, my older brother. I don't have a choice.

"We gotta get out of here," he says. "Think of something. You're the one with the big ideas."

Ryan is asking me to help him get out of a party we begged to go to.

I want to erase this, start over, make this whole situation go away. But he stares at me, and I know I need to help him escape. And then I need to stay and tell everyone that Ryan left because he's going to another party. And I need to tell them that they all suck. Especially Tyler.

I look around and try to come up with a game plan.

"Kaylan, please."

He pleads with his eyes, and I know I have to help.

"Okay," I start. "I'll distract them with the crazy story about Mr. Tucker and how he was sleeping on the lounge chair on his front lawn and how he got really sunburned."

"That's your best story?" Ryan laughs, and I'm grateful that he's laughing. Laughter is good. Especially in times of distress.

"I'll figure something out. And then while I'm going on and on about this, you need to sneak behind me. Like superfast."

He nods but doesn't say anything. I can't tell if he agrees.

"Okay?"

"This sounds risky," he says.

"Risky. But doable."

"Okay."

So I go out there, and the whooping and chanting has stopped and everyone is focused on a game of Spin the Coke Can.

To be honest, I didn't know people really played these

games at parties. I thought it was all made up for movies and TV.

But it's happening.

And this is going to help me.

"Hey, guys," I say, really loud, so Ryan knows I'm starting and he should get ready to book it.

"Oh, uh, hey, Kaylan," Tyler says. "Come join the game." He looks around at his friends, and they all smile, and maybe I'm making this up, but I think he wants to kiss me. I really do.

Too bad for him I don't kiss doofus boys like him, especially doofus boys who taunt my brother and assume all girls wear makeup and laugh when kids are made fun of. And also, I don't kiss someone who thinks terrible parodies like his are actually funny.

"Oh, sure. In a second. First I have to tell you guys this crazy story." I realize that I can't sit down because then it'll be even easier to spot Ryan as he makes a run for it.

"What's your crraaaazzzyyy story?" this eighth grader asks. I don't know his name. But he's one of Tyler's people, one of the ones that was chanting for my brother to drink the baby bottle. And now he's mocking me? No way. Not a chance.

"So, did you guys ever hear about the time these kids were walking by the middle school, and they found Mr. Tucker on a lounge chair in his bathing suit, completely asleep, on the lawn?"

Everyone stares at me. Mr. Tucker is this beloved teacher at school. He only teaches the eighth graders but everyone knows him. I pretend I'm back on Petey G's show, making everyone laugh, and all the kids at this party like me, and want to hear what I'm going to say.

"At first people were freaked. Like, is he breathing and stuff? But he was fine. So then they started pouring water on him. He still didn't wake up." I pause. I think they're listening. I cough a few times—my signal to Ryan that it's time to go. Then I hear his feet shuffling and I know he's making a move toward the door.

"What are you talking about?" one girl says. And Lizzie pats the floor trying to get me to sit down.

"Did someone put something in her fruit punch?" another kid asks.

I hear Ryan moving behind me and I think he's almost in the clear when the floor creaks. I'm midsentence talking about Mr. Tucker's sunburn and how it was actually for some kind of science class, when I hear Tyler say, "Dude. Where do you think you're going?"

I turn around.

Ryan is standing there. Frozen. His mouth agape.

"Uh," I start to talk and then Ryan interrupts me.

"I'm getting out of here," he says, sounding more confident than I've heard him sound in pretty much forever. "You think you're just gonna treat me like this and I'm gonna hang around?" He shakes his head. "No way. I'm done with you losers."

He looks at me, and inside my head I'm cheering so loud. I half smile and wait for him to say more.

Everyone is staring at us—sort of half laughing and half whispering to each other. I can't make out what they're saying. It looks like they think we're kidding, but are also curious to see what happens next.

"I have another party to get to," he says. "Come on, Kay. We're out of here."

I nod. "By the way, that story was totally, completely made up." I look at them. "Losers. Not you, Lizzie . . ."

She gives me a crooked look and I whisper that I'll text her later.

Soon Ryan and I are out in front of the house, and the cold wind is hitting our faces. He's running in place a little bit. I think partially to keep warm and partially because he's excited.

"Wow," he says.

"Yeah." I start running toward the end of the block and he follows me.

"I feel amazing."

I'm surprised he's admitting this. He's been silent and sulking and weird to me for so many months now that I've kind of gotten used to it, I think.

"You should, Ry," I say, all out of breath from the excitement and the cold.

I decide to sit down on the sidewalk, and hope that he

joins me. "When they spotted you, I was almost positive you were going to totally clam up and not say anything or freak out or something. But what you did was perfect. So amazingly perfect."

"Thanks for your help," he says. And he's being sincere. Really, he is. "I'm sorry you had to leave the party. You could've stayed, ya know."

"Yeah right," I scoff. "With those jerks."

He glares and then sits down next to me finally. "Come on, Kaylan. I know you have a thing for Tyler."

I can't look at him now.

He continues, "It's okay. You don't have to be embarrassed about it."

"Yeah, I do have to be embarrassed about it," I reply. "Because he's so rude to you. How could I like someone who's so mean? And also so stupid."

"Eh." He brushes it off. "I mean, he was my friend, too. I dunno. I'm sorry I've been such a jerk to you."

"At least you can admit it now! Progress!" I laugh a little, bumping his shoulder with mine. "You've been the jerkiest of jerky jerks."

I wonder if I should bring up the jam band and tell him what I did or ask him what I should do about Ari. But I decide not to. We just survived a major social calamity.

That's enough for one night.

We call my mom and she picks us up and we all go out for ice cream. She doesn't ask too many questions about why we left the party, and I'm grateful for that. I think Ryan is, too.

"Well, you guys seem to be getting along well," she says, taking the cherry off her sundae. We're not cherry people. "Maybe you should go to parties together more often."

Ryan and I look at each other and smile, and then crack up.

"Hey, Mom," he says. "Do you want to hear a crazy story about that teacher Mr. Tucker?"

THIRTY-SIX

ME: **MEET AT HARVEY DELI at 12?**

    Cami: **YES!**

    June: **Yup!**

    Saara: **See u there!**

After I group-text to confirm the plans with my lunch table friends (it doesn't feel right to keep calling them the Whatevers now that we are at group-texting levels and have actual plans), I ask my mom if she'll drive me over to the Harvey Deli.

"Did you make up with Ari?" she asks on the drive over.

"No." I turn up the music. "I'm meeting some other friends."

"Well, that's nice." She smiles, and I can tell she's trying to contain her enthusiasm.

My mom drops me off in front and tells me to call when I need to be picked up. "Please don't leave the shopping center on your own. And if you do go back to someone's house, call and let me know where you are." She leans her head over to kiss me on the cheek. "And have fun."

"Thanks, Mom." I get out of the car, and I get that bubbly nervous stomach I get whenever I'm in a new situation. I've never hung out with these girls outside of school before. What if we don't have anything to talk about?

I walk inside and they're all already there. Did they come together? Maybe. They do all live kinda close to each other, pretty near here.

"Hi," I say, and do some kind of over-the-top dance to the music playing in the deli.

"Kaylan!" Cami squeals, standing up. "You're the funniest. I'm so glad you're here." She runs over and pulls me into a hug.

I walk over to the table, and all of us squee and say hi, and Saara offers me a sip of her black cherry soda. "It's the best, and they only have this kind here!"

I've never seen Saara so excited about anything, and it pumps me up.

"So, should we order?" June asks.

We nod and hop up and go over to the counter.

"Two Dr. Johnny Fevers and two Blanches?" I ask. "And we'll all share?"

"Um, duh." Cami laughs.

"And four black cherries," Saara adds. "I want another one!"

We go back to the table and wait for our food. I debate telling them about what happened at the party last night, but I don't want them to feel bad that they weren't invited in the first place. And I don't want to think about how horrible it was (before we left).

"Soooo, guys," Cami sings. "What's new?"

I shrug. "Nada. Just getting ready for the talent show," I say. "You guys?"

"That kid Chris texted me," June says. "We may hang out again!"

"First Kiss Chris?" I ask, cracking up.

"Yeah, First Kiss Chris," June replies, laughing, too.

Saara turns quiet then and sips the rest of her black cherry. "I had a first kiss miss," she starts, and we all startle, shocked that she's talking about this.

"What?" Cami shrieks.

"I was at this party at my cousin's house, and all these kids were in the basement, and then this boy Aiden and I were playing mancala." She looks up at us. "You know that game?" We all nod, and she goes on. "And of course I beat him, but whatever, and then out of nowhere, he leaned in to kiss me!"

"Saara!" I shout, and everyone in the deli turns around. I shake my head and mouth *Sorry*. "So what happened?"

"I just backed away." Her cheeks turn red, and she glances over to the counter to see if the food's coming. "It was too weird! I didn't even know him!"

I nod. "Yeah, that is super-weird."

"Mega-weird," Cami adds.

Finally the food comes, and we all eat our sandwiches.

"Best sandwich ever," Cami says between bites. "Agree?"

"You know I agree," I add.

"We agree, too," June says. "Right, Saar?" She nudges her with her elbow.

We spend the rest of the meal talking about the sandwich—the crispiness of the eggplant, the crunchiness of the cucumbers, and the creaminess of the mozzarella cheese. It's a masterpiece.

We walk around the shopping center, browsing in the card store, picking out the matching necklaces we're going to buy each other for Christmas and Chanukah.

"I can't believe it took us this long to hang out," Cami adds when we're waiting for our moms to pick us up. "It's like we were destined to be friends."

I smile, but my throat stings. "Yeah, I agree."

I've moved on from Ari, I guess. I have my own friends. They like me, and I like them.

But, the thing is, I still miss her.

THIRTY-SEVEN

I SPEND THE REST OF Sunday worrying about Monday.
Are people going to be talking about the whole escape-
from-the-party situation? And then will June, Cami, and
Saara be mad I didn't tell them about it?

There's only one thing I can do to take my mind off of
the agita: planning a new party! My birthday party! Well,
Ari's, too.

If Ryan and I can make up, then most certainly Ari and
I can.

I try to compile emails for all the kids we'd want to
invite—June, Cami, Saara, Lizzie, Ari, Marie and the
other-end-of-the-lunch-table people, Jason, other random
stragglers we know from different places. Ari's Hebrew
School friends. I don't know their names or emails, but I

can always find out from her mom or Gemma. She still likes me, I hope.

I try to pick out the perfect online invite, but I can't decide on my own. They all look nice. There isn't really a design that seems to work for two BFFs who aren't talking but are still going to have a joint birthday party.

I write an email to Joey, the pool director. It's the only place I can think of where we can have the party. I don't want to have it here. Our house is too small, and Mom and Ryan would be annoying.

Dear Joey, I wondered if we can use the party room at the pool. When I say we, I mean me and Arianna. We are planning a joint party for our twelfth birthday. You know the pool is our most favorite place on earth. Maybe you can even run a Freeze Dance competition for our guests? ☺ I figured since summer is over, the room will be free. Please let me know. Thank you, Kaylan Terrel

Planning a joint birthday party by yourself is really depressing. What if Ari and I get to the party and don't even talk? What if Ari doesn't even show? If the pool thing doesn't work out, I'll just have a smaller hangout.

That could be fun and low-key.

I decide to text Jason to see how he's feeling.

Me: **What are you up to?**

Jason: **Painting the basement with my mom. Want to come help?**

Me: **I can't right now, but that's supercute. Text me a picture! Will you help me plan my and Ari's bday when you're done?**

Jason: **SUUURE**

And then it hits me. My Whole Me Makeover. It's all about taking a negative thing and making it okay, maybe even positive. Not being knocked down by bad stuff or even if you are, not staying down for too long. Being able to get back up.

There are only two weeks until this talent show.

Two weeks until my birthday.

And I do want to plan that party. But not by myself. And not even really with Jason, even though it's nice to know he's willing to help out. I want to plan that party with Ari.

I can't go on with life without Ari. It's too hard. It's too lonely.

Something has to be done.

And I have to be the one to do it.

THIRTY-EIGHT

TYLER'S WAITING BY MY LOCKER when I get to school Monday morning. My heart doesn't do that pat-pat-flutter-flutter thing it usually does when I see him. It feels more like a growing flame of anger moving throughout my insides.

"So that didn't go the way I thought it would," he says.

"What are you talking about?" Sometimes you need to play dumb because you need time to figure out a response for later on in the conversation. It's hard to think so quickly so early in the morning.

"The party," he says like I'm really dumb, slicking back his hair. It's pretty much soaking wet. "I mean, Kaylan, I thought . . ." His voice trails off, and I think I know where he's going with this. The problem is, I'm totally disgusted. I thought I liked him. Really, really liked him. And now he just grosses me out.

"You thought?"

I'm gonna make him work at this one. He can't get away with being shady and rude and just an all-around bad person.

Helping humanity starts with one person. One person at a time.

"I thought we, ya know, liked each other," he says. "And then you just left."

The bell rings and I gather my books, close my locker, and start walking away. He follows me.

"Where are you going?"

I stop walking and turn around, and that superhuman strength bubbles up again, like how I felt when I stood up for Ryan at the party and when I was on Petey G's show. My words take over. I stop overthinking and just talk. "I'm going to class. And Tyler, how can I like you if you're that big of a jerkwad to my brother? I mean, come on. Don't you even know about human decency?"

He stands there, looking dumbfounded.

"Do you?" I ask again. "Do you even know what it means to be a good person and not a complete turd?"

He doesn't say anything.

I'm kind of shocked I said the word *turd*, but whatever. Too late now. "That's what I thought."

I keep walking to class, my head held high. Because even though I left my first-ever cool-person party, and the guy I thought I really wanted to be my first kiss turned out to be a major jerkburger, and I don't have my best friend anymore, I really do think I'm making a difference in the world—one mean boy at a time.

Later that afternoon, I'm home in my room attempting to do homework.

All I can focus on is how to win Ari back, how to prove that my Whole Me Makeover was a success—we went through a rough time, but we're gonna get back to the way we were before, maybe be even better.

I look over at the 11 Before 12 List tacked on my bulletin board, and the only two things left to accomplish are: kiss a boy (I have no idea how I'll accomplish that in one week, now that Tyler's a complete jerk) and kayak to Arch Island, the little island across the lake.

Our parents always said that when we were twelve, if they thought we were ready for it, Ari and I could kayak by ourselves. But there's no way Mom will let me go by myself at night.

The other problem is that my dad was the main kayaker in the family, and he took his kayak with him. My mom's kayak has a hole in the bottom, so I can't use that one. Ari's parents have a kayak, too, so we could use theirs.

I want to show up at Ari's door, all prepared and ready to go with my water shoes on, and I imagine that I'll look so ridiculous that she won't be able to keep herself from laughing and then I'll convince her that we need to make up and be best friends again. We'll hug and catch up on all the things we've missed in each other's lives.

And I'll convince her that the first thing we need to do now that we are best friends again is finish the list.

And then I remember something—Mrs. Etisof has a tandem kayak for when she and her daughter want to paddle together!

That's even better than me and Ari being alone in our own separate boats! We can really, 100 percent, paddle together!

I run downstairs and yell to Ryan that I'm heading out for a bit.

"Where are you going?" he yells back.

"I need to make peace with Ari," I tell him as I'm out the door. "Tell Mom I'll be home for dinner."

"Okay. . . ." he says. I'm not sure if he's hesitant that I'll be able to make peace with Ari or hesitant that I'll be home for dinner.

Either way, there's no time to dwell on that now.

I run next door to Mrs. Etisof's house. She's doing some stretches on the porch.

"Where are you rushing off to, missy?" she asks me. "You're never out at this time of day."

"Actually, I have a favor to ask you," I tell her.

"Yes?"

309

I sit down on the rocking chair, and pull my hood down over my ears. I seriously have no idea how she's out here when it's this cold. It's not even winter yet, but there's a chill in the air. Come to think of it, how are Ari and I going to kayak when it's this cold? Our fingertips will freeze off!

Another thing we probably should have thought of when we made the list.

Too late for that now. Must move forward.

I think the biggest thing I've learned in my two months of middle school is that there's really no purpose in dwelling on the past or mistakes or regrets. The only thing we can do is try and learn something and then move on.

"Can I borrow your tandem kayak?"

"You'll need another person to use it, you know that, right? Or you'll just paddle yourself in circles," she says. "I'm happy to go with you—"

"No, um, it's just that Ari and I made this list . . . and we need to kayak together to Arch Island, and we need to do it before we turn twelve and . . ." I go on and on about everything, leaving out the part that something calamitous will happen if we don't complete the list. I think that level of superstition will be hard for others to understand.

"Wow." She stops stretching. "There seems to be a lot going on inside that head of yours."

I nod. "So, can I borrow it?"

"Of course you can, silly!" She bops me on the head. "As long as your mom says it's okay. And are you sure you're not running away from home and setting up a colony on Arch Island? I hear there are werewolves there."

We laugh together for a few moments and talk more.

"Do you think Ari and I will make up?" I ask her. "Did you ever fight like this with your friends?"

She puts her head back. "Oh, honey. Of course I have. I still do." She laughs. "Don't get me started on my friend Bev. Oh boy, we have had our fights!"

"You have?"

"Yes. Life is long, my dearie, if you're lucky," she continues. "And these things happen. As long as you don't hold on to anger and you're able to let some things go, all will be well. But—" She pauses and raises a finger. "You also have to tell people when they've hurt you. Sometimes they just don't realize it."

I nod. I'm not going to tell Mrs. Etisof all about our plan right now.

"Just talk to her. Tell her what you're thinking," she instructs. "And then listen to what she has to say as well."

By the end of our conversation, my cheeks are painted with tears, and it's almost dark out.

"I still see one problem, though," she adds. "You can't kayak in the dark, my dear."

I nod. "But can I borrow it tomorrow?"

"Of course. Whatever you need," she says.

"Thanks for listening, Mrs. Etisof," I tell her as I'm getting up. "But you should go inside. It's really, really cold now."

"The cold is energizing. Woo-hoo!" she says, waving her hands in the air like she's at a concert.

I walk home, a little disappointed that I talked for so long and wasted the opportunity to take the kayak and make up with Ari. But it just felt so good to talk, to let everything out. And Mrs. Etisof is such a good listener. She barely says anything; she just sits there and nods when she's supposed to nod, and smiles when she's supposed to smile.

I should recommend her to other kids who are struggling and need to talk about stuff. She likes to have people come and see her, and everyone needs someone to talk to. It's really a perfect match.

When I get home, Mom is scooping spaghetti and meatballs onto plates. She knows Ryan likes his spaghetti on the side without sauce, and she knows I like my meatball right on top with as much sauce as possible.

It's amazing how moms can remember all these simple details, in addition to all the other stuff they have to do, like work and pay bills and buy us clothes.

"Hi, Mom," I say as I take off my shoes and jacket. "How was your day?"

"Tiring," she says, and turns around with a smile. "And yours?"

"It was good," I tell her. "I'll take care of cleanup tonight. Ryan will help."

"Thank you." She smiles and puts our plates down and pours tall glasses of water and tells me to go get Ryan for dinner.

"Come down for dinner," I say through Ryan's doorway. "Mom's waiting."

"Okay, coming." He closes his computer and follows me down the stairs.

We sit and eat our spaghetti and meatballs and talk about our day, and even though so many things are still so unsettled, I start to feel better about things. It feels like life is easing up. Maybe. Just a little bit.

I look at the window and I see snowflakes. It's only late October. How can this be?

"It's snowing!" I exclaim.

"It is?" Mom shrieks. The three of us run over to the window, and a feeling of coziness washes over me.

There's something about snow that always feels like a fresh start to me. It's all perfect and clean and beautiful when it's falling and when it first lands. Like the grass underneath gets a rest, and the snow protects it.

It's inspiring, too. A new beginning, a new season.

I make a mental note to think of this first snowfall when I talk to Ari, to think of the freshness and the clean slate.

This can be a fresh start for us, too.

THIRTY-NINE

SINCE I CAN'T TAKE MRS. Etisof's kayak to school, I print out as many pictures of kayaks as I can find, and I put them in those plastic sleeves that my mom bought for Ryan and me to use for reports. And then I put the sleeves in an extra binder I found in the basement.

My plan is to take the binder to school and put it in Ari's locker with a note, right before lunch. And then we'll meet at our secret place: outside the darkroom on the third floor.

We set up our special meeting spot at the beginning of the year, but then we had our falling out, and so there weren't many occasions when we had to meet there.

After I get dressed and eat my breakfast the next morning, I put the binder in my backpack and head for the bus stop.

My main obstacle in this whole plan is how I'll be able to get it into Ari's locker without anyone seeing. Especially Ari. She usually arrives at school early, but she hangs out in the cafeteria before the first bell rings.

But there's also another obstacle: What if she's changed her locker combination since our fight? Then I guess I can just stand the binder up outside her locker, but someone might see it. Or maybe I can find her in the hall and hand it to her.

My stomach rumbles.

I'm suddenly regretting this plan. Maybe showing up at her house with the kayak is a better idea, but I have to stay after school for science extra help today. And it just seems risky. What if she's not home? And then I'm dragging a kayak around the neighborhood.

I tell myself to buck up. I can do this.

I get off the bus, hold my head high, and walk straight to Ari's locker. The bus got to school earlier than usual, so I don't think Ari's here yet.

I put my backpack down and look around.

Good. The coast is clear.

My hands are shaking, but I very carefully try to open Ari's combination lock. It's 11-1-2 for our birthdays.

It works. I'm in. I silently do a little cheer for myself and then realize I'm actually breaking and entering and could probably get suspended for this or at least get detention. But I've already checked that off my list.

I slide the binder onto the floor, so she'll see it when she opens her locker. I gently close the door. I throw my backpack over my shoulder and hustle up the stairs to the third-floor darkroom. I have approximately nine minutes before the first bell rings and that means I have thirteen minutes before I need to get to class.

By the time I get up there, I'm sweating and huffing and puffing and realizing I really do need to get more exercise. I probably should have stuck with yoga.

I stand outside the darkroom door. Who decided to have a darkroom on the third floor of a building? How do they even keep it dark? They should probably call it the Sorta Darkroom. Or the Oh Well, We Tried to Make It Darkroom.

I start pacing, back and forth, back and forth. This whole experience kind of feels like the try-something-you'll-hate yoga class—I know it'll be good once it's done, but the getting-there part is really, really painful.

No sign of Ari. Where is she?

The first bell rings, and the second bell rings, and I rush to class.

I can't believe Ari didn't show up.

Maybe she's sick today and she didn't even get the binder. Or maybe she's running late and she went straight to class.

Or worst-case scenario: she got it and she's ignoring me.

I'm running to class when I hear someone yell, "Kaylan!"

I turn around and there's Jason, standing there in his dark jeans. They look freshly ironed. And he's wearing an orange sweater. So bright and cheerful. It makes me think of his orange bathing suit that he wore to the pool this summer. That feels like forever ago.

"I'm late to class. Really, really late," I say, and the tears are bubbling up behind my eyes. They're coming out of nowhere. I didn't feel sad. At least I don't think I did.

"We have a study hall, it's okay to be late," he says. "No astronomy. Mrs. Bellinsky is absent today."

"What?" My heart pounds and I start to feel dizzy. "I need to sit down."

I plop to the floor in front of a row of lockers and brush the sweat from my forehead with the sleeve of my shirt.

Jason opens up his backpack. I peek inside—it's entirely filled with clementines.

"For extra practice. Come outside with me," he says, his voice sounding shaky. "To practice. And also, I want to tell you something."

"What? It's so cold," I remind him. "Can you tell me here?"

"It's not that cold. Come on." He grabs my hand and we walk out the side door into the little garden behind the cafeteria.

To be honest, I have no idea what's about to happen, but it seems like bad news. I look around, expecting one of the teachers to find us, or the hall monitor, someone to tell us we're doing the wrong thing.

That's how life feels these days, like someone is always finding me and telling me I'm doing the wrong thing.

"Jason, I really should go and try to find Ari. We need to make up," I say, trying not to make it seem like I'd rather be hanging out with someone else.

"Okay, yeah, look at this tree for one second." He laughs, but nothing's really funny. "Doesn't it kind of look like it has magical powers?"

"Umm, maybe?" I don't even know what he's talking about.

"Okay, so do a quick clementine peel. I'm ready to time you."

"Uh, okay . . ." I'm so lost in my thoughts and worries that I peel and don't focus too much on it. I'm midpeel when I'm completely and totally thrown off guard.

I don't even have time to prepare.

Jason kisses me. Mid–clementine peel!

Well, it's kind of a kiss.

Our teeth crash. Part of his lip ends up on my nose.

Right there, in the garden, behind the cafeteria of West Brookside Middle School.

Jason is kissing me.

His lips are on my lips, kind of.

My lips are on his lips, kind of.

I pull away. "Wait. What just happened?"

He stands back a little bit. "I had to do that. I just had to."

"Why did you have to?" I ask, about to cry again.

I pause for a moment and then I realize what he's saying. He had to do it because he knows the timing for the list is running out.

A pity kiss is worse than no kiss at all.

Though it does make Jason a really great friend. That he thought of that. That he would do that for me.

"I just wanted to, Kaylan," he says. "I've liked you since that first day at the pool."

"For real?" My smiling turns into laughing because I'm nervous and because I haven't finished peeling this clementine and it's getting mushy in my hand. And I'm laughing at everything, mostly from the most awkward first kiss in the history of the world.

In fact, I cannot stop laughing.

"Why are you laughing?" Jason's forehead turns red and he covers his cheeks with his hands. "I'm sorry. I shouldn't have said all that."

"No. Stop." I put a hand on his shoulder. "I like you, too. I laugh when I'm overwhelmed sometimes."

"I'm sorry that first kiss was bad."

"I'm glad you kissed me," I tell him. "It wasn't that bad. . . ."

"Yes it was," he replies. "You don't need to lie. It was a bad first kiss. But that means there's always a chance for a redo."

A redo. That sounds pretty good to me.

FORTY

I TRY TO PAY ATTENTION during my classes, but I can't stop touching my lips. It still feels like they're buzzing. I wonder when it will stop. But I kind of don't want it to. I kind of want my lips to buzz forever.

I walk to lunch in a daze. I drop my backpack at the table and walk over to the salad bar. It's like all around me stuff is happening but all I can think about is that kiss. Do I look the same? Can everyone I tell I kissed a boy today?

I'm midscoop in the tomatoes when I feel a tap on my shoulder. I turn around. It's Ari.

"Can we talk?" she asks.

"You didn't come to the darkroom," I say.

"I know. Can we talk?"

"Um, yes. Of course." I feel like I've been zapped alive

again by the fact that Ari wants to talk to me.

I don't know what to do with my tray, so I bring it over to the table and leave it there.

"What's going on?" June asks me. "Are you okay?"

I nod. "Um, I think so." I laugh a little. "Are crazy things happening to you guys today?"

They look at each other. "Not really. Unless you count the fact that Arjun Johar did a cartwheel into math third period," Cami says. "That was kind of crazy. Who knew he was such a great gymnast?"

I shrug. "I had no idea. I'll be back soon!"

Ari and I walk outside into the hallway, not talking. The four-second walk feels like three hundred years.

"You broke into my locker, Kaylan."

I had a feeling this might happen, but I'd hoped she would be so pleased with my gesture, she wouldn't think about that part.

"In all fairness, you told me the combination," I remind her.

She crinkles up her eyes like I'm a complete idiot, but then laughs a little.

I don't think I meant it to be funny, but I guess it is. I'm not sure. I don't know what I'm sure of anymore.

"I've missed you so much, Ari," I tell her. "And I shouldn't have gotten so mad when you invited Marie to do the list. I can't believe how much time has gone by and we haven't been BFFs."

"I've missed you, too." She looks down at her feet. Does this mean we can be BFFs again? I want to ask, but I also don't want to ask. I want her to say it, to reassure me.

"We have so much to catch up on," I remind her.

"Can we start fresh?" she asks. "Like, do things differently?"

My heart pounds. I wait for her to say more, and chew the inside of my cheek. I don't know how to do this. I don't know what she means. Will we still be BFFs in this new, fresh version of us?

"Kaylan?" she asks. "Are you there?"

I nod. "What do you mean, differently?"

Kids spill out into the hallway because lunch is ending, and my whole happy feeling drifts away. Agita is back and feels like it's settling in to stay for a while.

"Just stuff. We'll talk," she says. "I mean, you're not the only one who gets agita and needs help figuring things out and calming herself down. Ya know?"

I think about it for a second. "I know."

"Let's meet after school," she says. "We'll talk more. Meet in the main lobby."

"Sounds good," I say.

FORTY-ONE

AFTER SCHOOL, I GO TO science extra help and then I sit on the edge of the bench, waiting for Ari.

"Let's get ice cream," I say as soon as I see her.

"Um," is all she says at first, standing there, arms folded across her chest. "Kaylan, it's freezing. It's supposed to snow again tonight. We never have this much snow in October. It's like the weather is freaking out or something."

"I know." I stand up, shuffling my weight from foot to foot. "But, ya know," I stammer. "It's never too cold for ice cream. Come on. We'll bundle up."

We put on our coats and scarves and mittens and walk to the Ice Cream Shop. That's what it's called. It's like they got so tired from coming up with all the ice cream flavors that they just gave up on giving it a more creative name.

It's only around the corner from school, but the walk feels like forever. It's too cold to talk, and I don't know what to say, anyway. After you have a fight with your best friend, you can't just go back to talking like you used to.

It's like everything you think to say feels like the wrong thing. And everything I put on my list to talk to her about feels like it'll make things worse, like nothing is the right thing to start with.

We get to the Ice Cream Shop, and my cheeks are freezing and chapped, but the rest of me feels warm from the walk. We both get scoops of chocolate Oreo with chocolate sprinkles, and we fill a million mini cups of water because ice cream always makes us thirsty.

And then we sit across the table from each other.

I try super-hard to think of the right way to begin this talk, and all that comes to me is what Mrs. Etisof said about being brave and telling someone when they've hurt you, and being ready to listen. I think back to the Whole Me Makeover and the list and the doing-something-you-think-you'll-hate thing. I think this can also fall into that category.

"I was so sad when we weren't talking," I say. "And I missed you so much, but you really hurt my feelings. And I just needed to tell you that."

"Go on," Ari says.

"The whole thing with Marie. I felt like I was being replaced. And then I called you and you never called back," I tell her, holding back tears. "And it was like you didn't need me anymore or miss me or anything."

She looks away, toward the ice cream counter, like she can't really make eye contact with me. "I'm sorry about all of that. I did miss you. But sometimes I feel like you don't want me to have other friends. And I love you so much, but the more the merrier, ya know?"

I laugh a little. "I know. I just had to tell you that I was hurt, or it would, like, dig a hole in my heart that would just get bigger and bigger." I sigh. "I feel relieved that I spoke up and said how I'm feeling."

"Good," Ari says, eating a bite of ice cream. "And can I tell you one other thing?"

"Of course. What is it?" I ask.

"Your agita—it gets to be a lot sometimes, ya know?" Ari looks down at the table and then up at me. "I want to help but sometimes I don't know how to, and it's just, like, stressful. And also, you're not the only one who gets agita."

I nod, wide-eyed, waiting for her to continue.

"I get agita, too," she says. "I know I don't always talk about it, but I do."

"I'm here for you, Ar." I reach over and touch her arm.

"We can just, like, be there for each other, and that'll make everything seem more manageable. Ya know?"

"I agree." She smiles. "Anything else we should talk about?"

"Um . . ." I wonder if I should bring up the list or the party or first kisses or the Whole Me Makeover. "I'm really sorry if I made you feel like you couldn't have other friends."

"Apology accepted." She pauses. "I have big news. Like, really big."

"What?" I ask. I feel a little sting of jealousy, like she's about to tell me something really awesome—like she's been discovered and she's going to be in a movie.

"I kissed someone," she says.

My first instinct is to say *me too*, but I don't want to steal her thunder or take away her moment.

A part of me feels sad that we each accomplished this part of the list without the other one's help. But maybe kissing someone is a one-person operation. Well, two because of the person you're kissing, but maybe it doesn't necessarily involve your best friend.

"Noah?" I ask.

"What? How do you know?" She pulls back a little.

"Let's just say I eavesdropped . . . a bit." I smile. "But I don't know anything about him!"

"Okay, well, he moved here last year, but I just met

him. He goes to Hebrew School with me."

"Yeah?" I ask, picking a sprinkle off the top of my ice cream.

"He goes to East Brookside."

"Uh-huh . . ." I smile.

She finishes her spoonful of ice cream and then talks with her hands. "So we had this Hebrew School bowling day, and I know that sounds so dorky, but whatever. It was kind of cool. They had amazing french fries at this bowling alley. It's, like, twenty minutes away. I'd never been there." She leans forward onto the table. "So anyway, we were bowling and then Noah and I went to check out the vending machines. And we've been friends, like, since the beginning of the year. And, like, I think we knew we both liked each other, but I wasn't sure." She pauses.

"Get to the kissing part!" I yell, and a table of high school girls turns around and starts laughing at us, but I don't even care.

"Right! Well, I forgot to tell you that we sat together on the bus ride there, and talked the whole time, just about random stuff," she says. "And it's, like, he actually thinks about the stuff we talk about in Hebrew School. He was asking me if I believed in God. On the bus ride!" She laughs. "But it didn't feel weird, really. It was, like, normal and interesting. So anyway, we went to get some of those gummi snacks out of the vending machine, and we were standing side-by-side, and then he just kissed me! Right there!"

"That's amazing, Ari," I tell her, feeling super-excited about this story, but also like I might explode. I need to tell her my kissing news, too! "Really amazing."

She sits back in her chair, and looks around. "That was, like, two weeks ago, and we haven't kissed again, though. But we haven't had a chance, really. We can't just kiss in the middle of Hebrew School while we're practicing the prayers for the service! And who cares? I completed it for the list!"

"I did, too," I say.

Her mouth falls open. "You did?" she asks.

"I did."

"Okay! So tell me!"

I go into the whole story about how it was actually really awkward and bad, and we need a redo, but then I realize I didn't tell her who it was, and she goes, "Who's the boy? God. You're so bad at telling stories!"

"Sorry! Sheesh." And then it occurs to me that maybe it's weird that I kissed Jason. He was in friend territory and now he's in kiss territory, and I'm not sure that was even allowed. I know we made the rules ourselves, but it's still confusing.

"Please tell me it's Tyler. Please tell me you finally kissed Tyler."

"Tyler? No. That's a long story." I roll my eyes.

"Oh, right, duh, the party . . . I heard about that."

"You did?" My heart flops a little. "It was Jason," I say. "We like each other."

"Jason? As in our Jason?"

I nod and look away, like I suddenly can't make eye contact with her. *Our Jason?* I guess he is our Jason. But he's a little more mine now. I guess a lot more mine.

She sits back in her seat a little. "I didn't expect that," she stammers. "But, um, that's cool."

I wonder if he told her he liked me. I guess he didn't, since she seems so surprised.

"He's so great, Ar." I lean forward on the table. "Honestly. I mean, remember when we met him and he was just so friendly? Sometimes friends turn into more than friends."

"I know that," she defends. "He lives across the street from me. Remember? I just didn't expect Jason to turn out to be more than friends because he's, like, friends with both of us. Ya know? And he never mentioned that he likes you. . . ."

"Yeah. But he can still be friends with both of us," I remind her.

"I guess." She shrugs. "It'll probably be a little weird now."

"I don't think so," I argue without meaning to be difficult. "Honest."

"Well, I guess we'll see. I think it's gonna be weird for the three of us to hang out. But I'm happy for you." She forces a smile. "Anyway, I pretty much did everything on the list. I counted playing piano at my great-grandma's retirement community as helping humanity," she tells me. "I heard what you did. Climbing into someone's house through a window to get them inside—very daring of you. I bet you didn't even have agita about it because you were helping Mrs. E."

I smile. "And I heard about how you got on TV. Doesn't that community service day with Sydney count as helping humanity, too?"

"Maybe. I dunno. I also did yoga a few more times with Marie. I still don't really like it." She laughs and looks away for a minute, but I can't tell what she's thinking about. "Anyway, tomorrow after school, come to my house, and we'll go over the list to make sure we have everything."

"Sounds like a plan," I say and drink another mini cup of water. "We don't have that much time."

"I know."

"And we still have to plan our birthday party!" I yelp and look around, worried that I just scared the few people here. "We forgot the most important thing. I mean, I didn't forget. I tried to make an online invitation, but I didn't have everyone's emails. And I tried to see if the room behind the pool was free, since my house is so small, but Joey said it's under construction. So basically, I failed at party planning."

Her lips curve upward. "Actually, I did a pretty good job with it."

My heart sinks. Ari planned the party herself and invited everyone herself. It's all figured out. I'll have to do my own party the next week or the week after. A little belated is okay, I guess. Jason can help me plan.

Fire burns inside my heart but I push it away, like tiny little sprinklers inside my chest put out the flames.

I don't want to be mad at Ari. I don't want to be in a fight again.

"I planned it. I invited your friends," she says.

"Well, that's nice that you invited my friends to your party," I say, trying to take the attitude out of my tone, but it's hard. The attitude is still there. It seeps out whether I want it to or not.

"To *our* party, goof," she explains, shaking her head. "I hope you're not mad that I planned it all. But I had a feeling we'd be made up by now, and I didn't want everyone to be busy. Ya know?"

I nod. Ari planned our party. She knew we'd make up. The fire in my heart turns into sweet relief, the feeling you get after you've been sick for a few days and you're finally feeling better.

"There's still stuff to plan, though," she reassures me.

"I'll need your help coming up with a playlist and a snack list. Tomorrow after school. We'll go over everything."

I scrape the sides of the cup to get every last drop of ice cream and then put it down. I reach over and give Ari the biggest hug I've ever given her.

We throw out our cups, put our coats on, and walk home in the freezing cold. It doesn't matter, though; I really don't feel it.

"So we're okay, right?" I ask. "Mrs. E says it's good to talk, and also good to listen."

"Yeah," she replies. "It is good, I guess. But I don't know."

"I don't know, either." I laugh.

She shoves her gloved hands in her pockets.

We walk quietly for a few moments after that.

"So I think we're okay now," I say. "It feels like we're okay, right? We're, like, whole new versions of ourselves now. Our Whole Me Makeover is a success, I think."

"You're right. We are definitely okay." Her scarf is over her mouth. But I can still see her cheeks curve up from smiling. "We can keep talking about things, when we want to. . . ."

"Wait!" I stop in the middle of the sidewalk and grab her arm.

"What?" she looks around, scared.

"JHH," I explain. "For all of the stuff we did apart."

"Wait, you're not afraid to look goofy in public any-more? Maybe you can go back to freeze dancing!" Ari squeals.

"Oh yeah, I am definitely freeze dancing next summer!"

We jump in the air, high-five with gloves on, and hug. And then we continue walking.

I feel so warm inside that the outside temperature doesn't even touch me.

FORTY-TWO

ARI AND I SIT IN the middle of the lunch table between the girls formerly known as the Whatevers and Marie and the others. It feels kind of nice. Like we're two groups, still. But we can all be together.

Jason's at our table, too. At first I really don't want him to sit with us because it's an all-girls table, and I think it'll be super-weird. And after the awkward first kiss, I'm a little on edge. Like will he try and kiss me again and do the redo when I'm not expecting it, like, in the middle of the cafeteria in front of everyone? Is a redo something we plan or something that just happens?

Lunch turns out to be okay at first. But then Saara, June, and Cami get all giggly and they start to ask Jason goofy questions.

June goes, "Hey, Jason, would you rather be a red

pepper or a piece of asparagus?" She cracks up, and we all eye-bulge at her. But we're laughing, too.

Ari adds, "Definitely red pepper." She covers her face and says under her breath, "The pee thing."

Jason says, "She's right. The pee thing."

We all start laughing. My cheeks are as red as a red pepper now, though. The boy I kissed is at my lunch table, and we're talking about the asparagus pee thing.

Cami adds, "My uncle is a doctor, and he explained it to us at Thanksgiving." She pauses. "Do you want to know why asparagus does that?"

"No," June shrieks. "I'm still eating. Cami, stop!"

"Okay, on that note, I'm going to get more water. Anyone need a refill?" Jason looks around. Everyone shakes their heads and laughs like it was the funniest question in the world.

They laugh at everything Jason says. I mean, he's funny. But come on!

When Jason's refilling his water, they all turn to me and smile.

"What?" I ask.

"He's the cutest boy in the school," Cami says.

They all echo with "totally" and "you're so lucky." My cheeks feel like they're going to burst open.

Ari groans. "Okay, people. Come on! He's going to hear you. . . ."

"So you guys know about the party, right?" I ask,

trying to change the topic.

They nod. "We've known for, like, a week," June says. "But Arianna said to keep quiet about it."

"They listen to whatever I say." Ari nods, with a half-kidding *I'm so great* face on.

It still throws me off that they call her Arianna, but I get it. She's Arianna now. I need to get used to it.

Jason comes back with our drinks.

"So I guess you knew about the party, too?" I ask him.

"Of course I did." He leans over the table to high-five Ari. "We're BNFs. Best Neighbors Forever."

"For sure," Ari says.

Later that day, we're at Ari's house, lying on our backs, side by side on her bed, going over the list. I turn on the Holiday Jams playlist on my phone, and we're singing along. *All I want for Christmas is you . . .*

I know it's early for Christmas music, but when it's this cold out, and there's snow on the ground, it's hard to wait for the best music season of the year.

Ari holds her laminated list, and I look over her shoulder.

Eleven Fabulous Things to Make Us Even More AMAZING Before We Turn Twelve

1. Make a guy friend. ✓

2. Do a Whole Me Makeover. ✓

3. Get on TV for something cool we've done (not because we got hit by a bus). ✓

4. Help humanity. ✓

5. Highlight our hair. ✓

6. Do something we think we'll hate. ✓

7. Fulfill lifelong dream to kayak at night to the little island across the lake. (First step, find a kayak.)

8. Kiss a boy. ✓

9. Get detention. ✓

10. Have a mature discussion with our moms about their flaws. ✓

11. Sabotage Ryan. ✓

"It's hard to believe that we've really completed everything," I say. "Well, except the kayak trip."

"We may have to wait until the lake melts a little," Ari says. "Did you hear the weatherpeople talking about the lake icing and how it's so unheard of for this time of year? But don't worry. Nothing bad is going to happen to us."

"I know, because of our list." I raise my eyebrows. "So your parents are okay with us having the party here?" I ask.

The only thing we have left to do is kayak, and I know we're going to do it. But I don't have agita about when it's going to happen or how it's going to happen. The Whole

Me Makeover thing helped with that—I try not to worry about silly stuff. That way I'll have much more energy for the important stuff.

"Of course." Ari pops a sucking candy in her mouth. "We can use the basement. My mom ordered soda and chips and stuff."

"Oh, and Cami said she can get us a discount on subs from Harvey Deli—ya know, from her neighbor," I tell Ari. "How fab is that?"

"Superfab!" Her phone buzzes on the bed, and she picks it up. "Noah."

She shows me the phone. **Hey, Ari. So psyched for the bday party.**

"Eeeep!" I squeal. I grab Ari's hands and we dance in place. "Noah is so excited! And you invited everyone we know?"

She nods. "I didn't want to leave anyone out; I don't think everyone is coming, though."

"So we have the talent show Friday night, *your birthday*, and then our party Saturday night, *my birthday*," Ari says. "This is going to be the best weekend ever!!"

"What do you think is better?" I ask her. "A weekend birthday because you don't have school or a weekday birthday because you do have school and your friends can decorate your locker and stuff?"

She pauses to think. "I don't know, actually. I guess both are good."

"Yeah, I think it's good if they alternate. You don't want a weekday birthday every year, ya know," I tell her.

"Totally," she agrees.

"You just reminded me—I gotta practice for the talent show. Got any clementines?"

"What?"

"That's my act for the talent show. You didn't know?"

"Peeling clementines?" She cracks up. "Okay, I knew. I was trying to pretend I didn't. I don't know why—"

"Do you have any?"

"Yeah, let's go downstairs." We walk into the kitchen and she grabs the crate off the kitchen counter. "Knock yourself out," she says.

I've never really understood that expression, but her dad says it all the time.

"My act is clementine peeling and singing," I explain. "Please get a stopwatch."

"I'll use my phone." She gets it out of her pocket and rolls her eyes at me. "Is that okay?"

I nod.

"Ready?" she asks.

"Ready!"

I complete the peel in nine seconds and keep it all in one piece.

"Impressive," Ari says. "How many are you gonna do?"

"As many as I can while singing a short song," I say, and then I come up with a genius idea. "Hey! Why don't you be my assistant? You can be the person who hands me the clementines!"

She clenches her teeth together. "I don't know. . . ."

"Why not?" I take another and practice my peeling and eating.

She eats one, too. "I don't like to be onstage. You know that."

"But all you have to do is hand me clementines. It'll be so funny."

"I'll think about it, okay?"

"Okay." I need to back off and not pressure her. I can't expect Ari to always do whatever I need her to do, without thinking of her feelings. She gets agita, too; I know that now.

A big part of friendship is meeting people on their terms, I'm realizing, and not expecting them to be someone they're not.

Just because you're BFFs with someone doesn't mean you're exactly the same as they are.

And that's okay.

That's probably better, actually.

FORTY-THREE

"I'LL DO IT," ARI SAYS, startling me at our lockers the next morning. She's not back to taking the bus yet, and she's not offering me rides, either. I guess it takes time to get back to where you were before a fight, but the fact that we're talking again makes everything feel safe and exciting all at the same time.

I whip around. "Huh?"

"I'll help you with your act in the talent show," she says. "I thought about it, and I think it'll be fun."

I bounce on my toes. "Really? Yay!"

She looks a little confused that I'm this excited but proud, too.

"Really. Let's meet after school and practice," she says. "I want to make sure I know what to do and everything. Okay?"

I nod. "Sounds good."

Marie meets Ari at her locker, and they walk arm in arm together down the B corridor to history.

Half of me stings with jealousy. I don't like that Ari is walking arm in arm with Marie. But the other half of me doesn't feel jealous at all. I mean, they have class together—why shouldn't they go together?

I push the jealous half away like a disgusting cafeteria lunch, and focus on the nice side.

Maybe that's the most important thing to do, the most important thing to remember: focus on the nice.

I walk down the A corridor to math, feeling pretty great about everything, when I run into Tyler in the hallway. We've been ignoring each other since the whole discussion after the party. And he's never at our house hanging out with Ryan anymore.

I plan to just keep walking and ignore him, but then he stops me. "Hey, Kaylan," he says.

"Hey," I mumble. "I'm late, and I need to get to class."

"I just wanted to say that, um, I'm sorry about stuff, and I'll see you at your party," he says. "Maybe you'll give me a second chance?"

My heart starts pounding so fast and so loud that I'm debating a trip to the nurse and maybe even the hospital.

I stand there, still, in the middle of the hallway, like I've stepped in a barrel of bubble gum and can't move.

"Will you at least think about it?" he asks, before I've said anything else.

"Uh, okay."

Why did I just say okay? I have no idea. I don't want to give Tyler another chance. I like Jason. But when Tyler talks, he throws me for a loop, and I can't say anything. I don't know why he has this power over me. I don't even like him anymore!

"I'll see you at the rehearsal," he says, smiling.

I nod and mumble out a "bye," and force myself to keep walking to class.

Ari invited Tyler and didn't even tell me? I don't understand what's happening here. I explained the whole situation; she should have mentioned it.

When I get to class, all I can think about is the Tyler situation and how I can disinvite him to the party. He's like this little bug that keeps buzzing by my eye. I swat him away, but then he just buzzes right back.

FORTY-FOUR

I GET TO LUNCH AND grab Ari by the arm before she gets on the line for the salad bar.

"What?" she screeches. "I'm hungry."

"Tyler. Our party. Hello?"

"Hello what?" She looks at me like I have seven heads.

"Hello, he said he'll see me at the party, and he wants a second chance. And I don't want to give him a second chance. And hello—" I nudge my head toward the back of the cafeteria to where Jason is sitting. "Jason! My first kiss. The boy I like. The one who will also be at the party."

Ari puts her hands on my shoulders, probably in an effort to get me to shut up. "Calm down."

"I. Cannot. Calm. Down." I breathe in and breathe out and then breathe in and breathe out.

"I invited him before I knew what had happened," Ari

explains. "I thought I was doing you a favor because of your massive crush." She bulges her eyes at me, and pulls my arm, and leads me out of the cafeteria.

When we're safe in the quiet of the hallway she says, "Well, we can't disinvite him now," she says. "Or is it uninvite? I don't know."

"I don't know either." I fold my arms across my chest. "I'll just say that I think we're better off as friends, and I kind of like someone else now, and maybe he'll feel so embarrassed that he won't even want to come."

"Good. Go for it." Ari nods with encouragement. "Can we go eat lunch now?"

I shrug. "Sure."

"I'm going to have to tell him he's no longer welcome at the party," I whisper to Ari as we're walking back in. I hate to whisper in front of other people; they'll think it's about them.

"Kaylan, I know you're stressing," she says. "But I'm starving and I need to review the vocabulary words before the test. Let's discuss it this afternoon when no one else is around."

Jason finds me on the hot lunch line. He puts an arm around me, and then pulls it away, and then puts it back like he can't decide what to do. "Everything okay?"

"Yeah," I say.

"Doesn't seem like it," he says, grabbing a tray.

"It's a long story," I explain, while the lunch lady

346

gives me some baked ziti.

Jason waits for me to start telling the long story, but instead I stay quiet. My stomach flips around and I'm not sure I'll be able to eat this ziti. It's really hard to tell someone you don't want to give them another chance.

The thing is, Tyler isn't very nice, but I still don't want to hurt his feelings.

It's weird when you realize stuff like that. I always expect that I'll want revenge and I'll want to get back at people. Those who make others suffer should suffer themselves. Stuff like that.

But when it comes down to it, I really don't want to. I don't want to hurt Tyler's feelings.

I tell Jason I'll try to explain later, hoping he'll simply forget about it.

"See you in astronomy," he says.

Then I go back to my lunch table. Jason's sitting with his other lunch table today, Andre and those boys.

June, Cami, and Saara are eating their salads and studying for the science test at the same time. Ari, Marie, Sydney, and M.W. are talking about trying out for the tennis team in the spring. But I don't feel like joining that conversation; I don't even play tennis.

I sit there at the table, forcing down bites of baked ziti.

I'll talk to Tyler after lunch. He eats next period, so there's a good chance I'll see him. I'll tap him on the shoulder and explain everything, and that way if he's really upset, he'll have the whole lunch period to feel better.

Mr. Nowdon stands up in front of the cafeteria, trying to get our attention. I didn't even think we were that loud today, so I don't know why we're getting in trouble.

"Quiet please. Quiet please," he says. "Just an announcement for everyone in the talent show. Reminder that the final run-through will be today after school."

I tap Ari's hand across the table.

"I forgot it was today! We won't have time to go over the act before the run-through," I tell her. "But really, all you're doing is handing me clementines. I think you can handle it."

"I think so, too." She smiles and I'm relieved. For a moment I thought she was going to get all weird and freaked out about it.

"So you get that you're going to be doing this in front of a lot of people, right?" I ask her.

"Yeah, Kaylan, calm down." She shakes her head. "It's gonna be great. You'll be there with me."

FORTY-FIVE

AFTER SCHOOL, WE ALL GATHER in the auditorium for the talent show run-through. Ari and I sit in the front row waiting for everything to start. She taps my knee every three seconds asking me about everyone's acts.

"It's so fun to have you here," I say. "Like, none of this felt as exciting when I was doing it alone. But now that you're here—it's like a big moment. Like something I'll remember forever."

She smiles. "I know what you mean. Things are just better when we're together." Ari grabs my hand and we sit there like that for a few seconds until we look at each other and say "this is weird" at the same exact second and crack up.

I didn't see Tyler before his lunch, and when I hear him and his boys coming in to the auditorium, I try not to notice. I try not to pay attention. But it's hard. His voice is so loud, and they're constantly high-fiving each other.

How can that many things be high-five-worthy?

Finally, Mrs. Bellinsky comes to the microphone. "Does anyone have any changes to their acts?"

I raise my hand. "Arianna here, my BFF"—I point to her next to me, and she waves—"is going to be my assistant and hand me the clementines."

"Lovely. Noted." Mrs. Bellinsky looks down at her clipboard, and then calls on the next person.

"I would've done that for you," a voice behind me says. Tyler.

I turn around. I had no idea he was so close to us. I say, "Yeah, well, thanks so much. But also, no thanks."

He rolls his lips together. "Kaylan, you can just tell me to my face you don't like me. A million girls in this school want to go out with me," he says.

My throat burns. There are kids in the seats around us, and they're all hearing this. "First of all, there aren't a million girls in this school. You're really bad at math," I reply. It's the only thing I could think to say. "But must be nice to think so many girls like you."

"It is nice for me," he answers. "You're dumb not to realize how awesome I am."

My whole body clenches in disgust. Who does Tyler think he is? Clearly someone great, I guess, even though he's the opposite. I'm mad at myself for ever liking him at all!

Ari nudges me with her shoulder, so I turn to face her. She opens her mouth, and puts her finger toward it, the universal symbol for about to barf.

I almost crack up, but then I see Tyler again and I want to scream at him, tell him he's a jerk and a bully, and I don't care. That I'm not dumb.

But instead, I just sit there for a second, and then Ari and I get up and walk away.

He doesn't even deserve a response.

Back at my house after the run-through, Ari and I are up in my room, trying on different outfits for the party.

"You rocked it today," I tell her.

"Thanks, Kay, but really—all I'm doing is handing you clementines." She spins around to show me how much her skirt twirls.

"I know. I know. But it's great!"

I'm trying to compliment her; I wish she could see that.

"I can't believe Tyler said all those things," she says, admiring the way my shimmery skirt fits her.

"I'm over it," I tell her. For a second I wonder if I'm just saying that, but then I know that I actually feel nothing when I think about him. Not anger, not love, not that pitter-patter-heart feeling. Nothing. I know I'm over it. I'm over Tyler.

I've heard Mrs. Etisof say many times that people will show you their true colors again and again, but sometimes it takes a while to really see them, to really believe them.

I'm glad I can see it now.

"Your brother isn't friends with him anymore, is he?" Ari asks.

"No. I don't really get what was going on," I explain. "Maybe he was always a jerk, and I just didn't realize it. Like maybe he was a jerk that was only nice to me. . . . Ya know?"

Ari sits up and puts down the mirror. "How are things with your brother?" she asks. "You guys are getting along again?"

I nod. "Yeah. Pretty much. I mean, he can still be a doofus sometimes."

Ari replies, "All boys can be a doofus sometimes."

"Would the plural be doofuses? Or doofi?" I ask and then we both start cracking up, completely cracking up. We're like that for a while, laughing about something so silly until our stomachs hurt.

Our phones buzz at the same time. "Text from Jason," I say, looking at my phone first.

Party prep? Talent show prep? SO MUCH PREP.

What r u guys doing?

"We should tell him it's girl time, so he doesn't expect to be invited over," I suggest. "Or will that make him feel bad?"

She stops to think for a second. "Let's give him a job for the party, so he feels needed," she says. "What could it be?"

"Doofus detector," I suggest. "If someone starts acting like a doofus at the party, he has to tell us!"

Ari falls back on my bed in a laughing fit. "No! That's too silly."

"Chip refiller? He keeps an extra eye on chip bowls, and has to refill immediately!" I laugh through my words.

"No, no," she says, still giggling. "Something he can do now, goofbrain!"

"Oh!" I do a little dance. "He can make a playlist!"

Kaylan: **Can you make a playlist for the party? Think pool Freeze Dance songs . . .**

Ari: **But make it better. Okay? Thanks!**

Jason: **On it!**

We fall back on the bed, laughing, about nothing, really.

Even though things have changed a little, we can still laugh even about the most ridiculous things.

I overheard my mom on the phone once. She was talking to her best friend, Gwen. They've known each other since eighth grade, but Gwen lives in Canada now, and they don't see each other so much.

Anyway, my mom said something like, "It's over when the laughing stops. That's how you know."

I think she was talking about Gwen's new boyfriend, but I could be wrong.

It stayed with me. I don't remember when Mom and Dad's laughing stopped, but maybe it's better that I can't remember. If there was one moment, I'd replay it over and over again, trying to figure out what we could have done differently to make sure the laughing continued.

The thing I know for sure: mine and Ari's laughing hasn't stopped. I have a feeling that thirty years from now, we'll still be laughing together.

FORTY-SIX

I CAN'T DECIDE IF I want next week to fly by so that we can get to the talent show and our birthday party, or if I want it to slow down because I'm actually pretty nervous about the talent show and the birthday party. I'm not even going to think about Halloween. I'm so glad my lunch table decided not to dress up this year.

The thing about time, though, is that it doesn't really matter if you want it to go fast or if you want it to go slow. It'll go however it's going to go.

The school week goes medium fast, and we finally decide on outfits for the party.

Ari's borrowing my frayed-edges jean skirt and my sparkly black tank top. I'm borrowing her black dress with the cutout shoulders and her knee-high boots.

It feels more exciting to wear your BFF's clothes.

We finally make it to Friday, my birthday. June, Cami, Saara, and Ari decorated my locker with wrapping paper and ribbons.

I'm organizing my books for the day when I feel Jason come up behind me. He puts his hands on my shoulders, and starts to give me a massage.

It sends shivers down my back, but not in a good way.

I start to wonder if I'm losing interest in Jason. We had the whole awkward-first-kiss thing, and then we were going to have a redo, but it hasn't happened yet.

Maybe we've waited too long.

Maybe if a first kiss is awkward, it's a sign that the relationship won't work out. Maybe he is just a friend.

"Happy birthday!" he says.

"Thanks! What's up?" I ask him as we walk to class.

"Nada," he says, shifting the straps of his backpack on his shoulders. "Ready for the talent show?"

I nod, not looking at him. "I think so. I'm kinda nervous."

"Don't be," he says, elbowing me. "We've practiced your act so many times."

I laugh when he says that because my act is actually such a joke. "I hope people find it funny, and not too ridiculous."

"I know three people will find it funny: me, Arianna, and you."

"Well, that's something," I say, smiling. "Just make sure you laugh, like, really loud so it sounds like everyone is laughing even if they're not."

"I'll practice my loud laugh." He stops talking and walking and tries to laugh as loud as he possibly can.

I put a hand on his shoulder, looking around at all the kids staring at us. "Thanks. That was a tremendous effort!"

He bows, and we start walking again. "I'm excited about your party," he continues. "Did you find out if Tyler's coming?"

"I doubt it. He knows I don't like him."

All of a sudden it feels like the hallway is shrinking, like Jason and I are in a closet and it's so tight and I can't breathe.

I need space.

"Listen, Jason, I need to go talk to a teacher before class," I lie. "I'll see you later."

He says, "I can walk you there," but I shrug him away.

I don't understand what's happening.

I like Jason.

At least I thought I liked Jason.

When lunch rolls around, I get to the cafeteria and find Ari on the hot-food line. I've gotten much better at spotting her in a crowd; I have, like, Ari-finding GPS.

"I need to talk to you," I tell her.

She gives me a look of concern, but continues getting her food.

"Now," I say.

"I'm starving, Kaylan. I'll meet you at the table."

I huff away, wishing she'd drop everything and go outside and talk to me now.

I make it to my table, and everyone's already eating their lunch. They look up, smile at me, and then go back to eating, and discussing what songs the orchestra is doing for the winter concert. I stare at my turkey wrap, but I don't take any bites. My stomach feels like a gravelly sidewalk.

Finally, Ari taps me on the shoulder, in the middle of a bite of her apple. "Are you okay?"

"Can we go talk in the hallway?" I whisper.

She nods, and we walk out as quickly as possible trying to avoid the lunch monitors.

"What's up?" she asks when we're in the hallway.

"I don't think I like Jason anymore," I announce.

"What?" she screeches.

"I don't think I do."

"Kaylan." She puts her hands on my shoulders and looks me straight in the eye. "You're just nervous."

"I don't know," I explain. "It feels different."

"This is high-alert agita levels," Ari says. "Like, mega-agita: the talent show, your birthday, our party; you're overflowing with so much agita you can't even feel your other feelings."

I laugh at that. "I guess."

"Trust me," she says. "Just take deep breaths. You're worried about the first kiss redo. But don't be. If it happens, it happens. If not, it's not meant to be. Or not meant to be right now."

"You think?"

She nods. "Definitely. Jason likes you. And you like him. Not everything is neat and organized and figured out. As much as we want it to be. And we can plan and plan and make lists. And do all sorts of stuff. But it's still gonna be a little chaotic."

"You're always so calm and wise. How do you do it?" I ask her, and then crack up. "I don't know why I'm laughing. I'm being totally serious right now."

She glares at me. "First of all, nervous laugh. Second of all, I'm not calm and wise all the time. Just sometimes. Hello—remember the beginning of school? But I realized that even though these weeks without you have been really crazy and sad, we can get through the crazy and sad times, and things can work out."

"Hug?" I ask her.

"Of course," she says.

So we stand in the hallway, and we hug it out, and I feel better. At least for right now, for this minute, I feel better.

An hour later, I could feel totally different.

But I guess I just have to accept that's the way middle school is going to be. It's a three-year-long seesaw ride, and there's no getting down early.

FORTY-SEVEN

ARI AND I DECIDE TO wear all black for the talent show. We don't want the outfits to detract from the act itself, and all black just looks so theatrical.

We plan to meet at the front door to the school twenty minutes before the show starts.

Me: **On the way! Eeep!**

Ari: **Me too! Double eeep! HAPPY BIRTHDAY!!!!!!!!!!!!!**

We're halfway to school when Ryan tells us that he's doing some kind of jazz duo thing with new kid Brian.

"Wait, what?" I ask. "You're just telling us now?" I turn around from the front seat to look at him.

"I kind of wanted it to be a surprise," he says.

"You never even went to rehearsals!" I look at my mom. "Did you know about this?"

"Nope," she says, turning down the radio.

"We just decided on Friday," he tells me. "Mrs. Bell-insky said we could join at the last minute. Brian just moved here, like, two weeks ago!"

"Brian and Ryan!" I crack up, looking at him again.

"Stop, Kaylan," Ryan says. "Not funny."

"Fine." I turn around and face forward. "It's my birth-day; you have to be nice to me!"

"He was rejected from the jam band at his old school," he says. "So we're starting our own thing, recruiting some other kids, too."

"I love that, Ry," Mom says. "Proud of you for being so innovative!"

Maybe getting rejected (ahem, my sabotaging) wasn't such a bad thing after all, even though I still feel guilty about it.

We're almost at school when Ryan says, "I invited Dad to come tonight."

"What?" I gasp. "What is with you and these sudden surprises?"

We haven't seen my dad since early last summer, and I haven't missed him. I know that sounds mean, but we're finally getting into a groove, the three of us. Dad's not coming back. I don't want to get my hopes up. I don't want him to upset the order of things now.

"I wanted him to come," Ryan says.

"You could have told me!" I yell. "It's my birthday, doofus!"

"I am telling you right now!" he huffs.

"Kaylan, please relax," my mom says. "It will be fine. Your father will enjoy the show. He'll be happy to see you perform, especially on your birthday."

I don't understand how she can stay so calm about this.

"I'm not going to talk to him," I say.

No one responds to that. I take it as a sign that they're okay with it, and I put this whole conversation out of my head. I pretend it never even happened.

I need to peel my clementines and get the whole audience to crack up. I can't be focused on anything else. I think back to Petey G's show—where it seemed like all of my words just clicked and everyone laughed and I was, like, crushing it.

I need to do that tonight. I need to make that happen again.

My mom drops us off in front of the main entrance to school, and we run in and head straight to the backstage area. I only look straight ahead. I don't want to see my dad lingering anywhere. I don't want to see him talking to anyone.

Thinking about my dad makes my stomach hurt. And I do not want my stomach to hurt right now.

My phone buzzes and I look down to see a text from Ari.

Ari: **Mrs. Bellinsky asked me to come backstage, so meet me there!**

Me: **OK!**

I walk through the double doors and the lobby, looking straight ahead, not making eye contact with anyone.

I get backstage and Ari asks, "Are you ready?" as soon as she sees me. She's biting her lip.

"Not yet. But I will get there."

Ari grabs my hands. "You have to get there now."

"What?" My heart pounds. I put my hand to my chest to calm it down. "Why?"

"There was a last-minute change. Mrs. Bellinsky wants us to go first."

I gasp. "Are you serious?"

I kind of feel happy about this because at least it means we can get it over with. But I also hate that I was excited about this, and now all I want to do is get it over with. Life shouldn't be a series of things that you need to just get done.

"You girls ready?" Mrs. Bellinsky asks us. "I'm about to go introduce myself and start the show!"

Ari says, "Yup!"

I'm frozen all of a sudden, unable to talk. I stand there and stare at Mrs. Bellinsky.

My whole body feels shaky.

"You okay, Kay?" is the last thing I remember hearing.

✳ ✳ ✳

When I open my eyes, I'm lying on the floor backstage, and there are kids all around me.

"What's going on?" I ask.

"You passed out," Ryan says.

"I did?" I sit up and feel dizzy, and Ari hands me a cup of pink lemonade.

They all nod.

"For how long?" I ask.

"Like, ten seconds," Ari says.

"Luckily the nurse was in the audience," Mrs. Bellinsky says. "She's coming to check you out."

I hear murmuring in the audience, and I feel terrible for delaying the start of the show, and causing all this chaos.

I guess my nerves got the best of me. The agita actually won.

"What's happening here?" The nurse bends down and checks my pulse and feels my forehead at the same time. She smells like flowery perfume. Like way, way, way too much of it.

I almost gag but I hold it back.

"I think I just got nervous, Ms. Sellers," I tell her. "I pass out sometimes. I think that was in my health file."

"I seem to remember that." She looks at me. Takes my blood pressure, my temperature, asks me to move my head around, my arms around.

"She's fine." Ms. Sellers stands up. "Rest a little, Kaylan.

Maybe go on toward the end of the show?"

"I'm fine," I say, and I think I mean it. I'm almost positive I mean it. "I can go on now. Really."

"You sure?" Mrs. Bellinsky asks.

I nod. "Let's go, Ari."

"You sure?" Ari asks the same thing.

"Yes!" I shout.

"Wait! I need to introduce you!" Mrs. Bellinsky runs through the curtain and out onto the stage. She says, "So sorry for the delay, everyone. We're all set now. I'd love to start off our show with one of the most unique acts I've seen in the twenty-three years I've been running the West Brookside Middle School Talent Show. Without further ado, please welcome Kaylan Terrel and Arianna Nodberg."

"Ready?" I whisper to Ari.

"Ready!" She grabs my hand and we walk out on the stage, waving. It feels like we own the world right then. Like we own this talent show and this stage, and it's all about us. We're going to show West Brookside Middle School just how awesome we are.

"Hi, everyone!" I say into the microphone.

"Thanks for coming!" Ari says.

I ask, "So most people love clementines, right?"

There's murmuring, clapping, laughter.

"But I challenge anyone out there tonight to do what I'm about to do—peel as many clementines as I can in the time it takes me to sing 'Here Comes the Sun' by the Beatles. And I will keep every peel in one piece." I pause. "Ari, I mean, Arianna here will be handing me the clementines. I could not do this without her!"

Then more laughter.

Making other people laugh is the ultimate best feeling in the world.

"So without further ado, whatever that means." I pause for effect. "Arianna, please hand me a clementine."

She bends down and gets one out of the crate and hands it to me.

I hold it up.

I do a quick, successful one-piece peel, as I start singing the first line of "Here Comes the Sun," and then—in an unexpected addition to the act—Ari sings the *doo, doo, doo, doo* part.

We sing together, "Sun sun sun, here it comes."

She hands me another clementine, and then another, and another.

Twelve one-piece clementine peels! It's a record! We grab hands and bow.

There's cheering and clapping, and I'll admit—being onstage with Ari feels so good. Not only am I making people laugh, I'm having fun, and I'm doing it all with the help of my BFF.

"I loved your *doo, doo, doo, doo*," I whisper as we walk backstage.

"I had a feeling you would," she says. "I thought about doing it the other day at the run-through, but I wasn't ready yet."

"You rocked it, Ari." I pull her into a hug.

"No, *we* rocked it," she says.

FORTY-EIGHT

THE WEST BROOKSIDE MIDDLE SCHOOL Talent Show turns out to be a mixed bag.

Some acts are good (Triona Hanely singing songs from Disney movies was amazing) and some acts are terrible (I wouldn't say this to his face, but Elliott Chafer is really not so good on the clarinet). My brother's jazz duo actually sounds pretty awesome, and I'm proud of him for that. He's been practicing more, and it's really helped with his chords.

As for "Cool Tyler," well, he isn't as cool as he thinks he is. His voice cracks, his wig falls off, and he forgets some of the words to his "Mad Mud" parody. Oh well. Karma's a real thing. Better learn that sooner rather than later, Tyler.

When the show finally ends, I turn to Ari. "My dad is here."

Her eyes look like they're about to pop out of her head. "Really? What are you going to do?"

"Escape before he sees me," I tell her.

"Maybe you should talk to him," Ari says. "But on your birthday?"

"I don't want to. I'm nervous. Can I just avoid?"

"I don't think you can." She shakes her head. "But don't worry, I'll stay with you."

Ari grabs my hand, and we start to walk out of the auditorium. We don't make it very far because people keep stopping to tell us how great our act was. They ask how I got started, how I thought of it, if my hands have turned orange.

I almost feel like a celebrity.

And then, right as we're turning out of the auditorium, passing the water fountain and the glass cabinet that displays students' art, I see my dad.

I try to look away, but our eyes lock.

He smiles his closed-mouth smile. My heart pounds.

This is my dad. He shouldn't make me so nervous. But when I see him, all I can think about is him leaving. All I can think about is how sad Mom was, and still is, and how she tries her hardest to be strong, how I hear her quietly cry at night when she thinks we are asleep. All I can think about it is that he'd rather be away from us than with us. Seeing him makes me think that terrible things are going to happen. One after another.

"Happy birthday, Kay-Kay," he says. "And great job!"

I wish he wouldn't call me that. We're past the point of nicknames. Nicknames are for people who like each other. People who stand by each other.

"Hey, Ari," he says, all cheerful and friendly. "Or I guess you're Arianna now, huh?"

She smiles, and then looks down at her feet. "Yeah. Arianna."

We stand there staring at each other for a second before he asks us questions about how middle school is going, if we're excited about our birthdays, stuff like that.

I answer as quickly as I can and don't offer much information.

I want to get out of here. I need to get out of here.

He left us. He can't expect me to be his best friend.

I fold my arms across my chest, not looking at him as he tries to make small talk. I try to stay calm, but my insides feel like they're being scraped with sandpaper.

Doesn't he see that he made this choice? That he is the one who made everything so painful and awkward? He was the one who decided to move to Arizona. He was the one who thought that leaving us was better than staying. Doesn't he see that he broke my heart into three zillion pieces, and I can't put it back together? Nothing will ever be the same again. Nothing will ever be the way I wanted it to be.

Ryan comes around the corner, a stack of chocolate chip cookies in his hand. "Want one?" he asks us.

Ari and I shake our heads. Like we'd really want a melty cookie from Ryan's gross, sweaty hands.

My dad takes one, though. Maybe he's trying to be nice.

"So, I'm sure you guys are busy tonight," he says. "But maybe I can take you all out for ice cream next week." He looks at us. "I'll be here for a few weeks, for work. I'm really glad the timing worked out, so I could see the show."

I wait for Ryan to respond.

"Yeah, sure, sounds good," he says. And I guess he means it. He sounds like he means it. Ryan looks at me, and I look at him, and there's an ease in his face that hasn't been there for a long time. It's a look of calm, relaxed peace.

I guess Ryan needs our dad in his life.

I don't know if I do. That would mean forgiving him. And I'm not sure I want to do that. Not yet.

"Sure," I say. "Ari and I have to go now."

"Okay." He smiles. "Have fun."

"Thanks for coming." I turn away. Ari links arms with me, and we start walking.

I hear Ryan and Dad making small talk, and I guess that's good. They're going to the diner for a snack, just the two of them.

We find my mom in the front lobby. "Ready, girls?" she asks.

"Yup!" we answer at the exact same second.

We walk out of school into the freezing November night. We pull our hoods up and run to the car.

"Ice Cream Shop?" my mom asks.

Ari and I look at each other in the backseat, and it feels like my mom is our chauffeur, which makes us totally crack up.

"Ice Cream Shop!" we yell.

It's freezing outside but it's definitely a night for ice cream with your friends. Performance nights, parent drama—all call for ice cream. And they have french fries, too. So maybe we'll get both. Salty and sweet.

We are celebrating, after all.

"I'll text Jason and tell him to meet us there," Ari says. "He did help you with your act. And he is our friend." She laughs.

Our friend.

It has such a nice ring to it.

FORTY-NINE

"HAPPY BIRTHDAY!" I SQUEAL AS soon as Ari opens her front door. "Happy birthday to you! Happy birthday to you!"

"Thank you." She bows. "I am so psyched to set up for *our party!*"

"Me too." I follow her down the hallway.

"My dad got these," Ari says, showing me these cool rainbow lights as soon as we get down to her basement. "I think they're meant for a dorm room or something. But they're cool, right?"

I nod. "I picked up streamers and balloons," I tell her.

"I know we've been talking about it for months now," Ari says as we're stringing the lights around the room, "but I still can't believe we are really twelve!"

"Me neither," I say. "When I was, like, seven, all I wished for was that I was twelve. How dumb is that?

But the thing is, twelve always seemed so grown-up, so mature. Ya know?"

Ari nods. "Totally. But is it?"

"I don't know," I reply. "How do we know if we're grown-up and mature?"

"No clue."

"So then maybe we're not," I tell her. "Maybe we'd know if we were."

She shrugs. "I think we are. We've done Whole Me Makeovers. That just screams mature."

"That's a really good point."

We stop talking for a bit and continue stringing the lights. Soon, Ari's mom comes down with bowls of chips and pretzels and bottles of soda.

"Thanks, Mom," Ari says.

"Pretend I'm not here," Ari's mom sings as she puts out the snacks. "I'm not here. I'm invisible."

I look at Ari, slightly perplexed.

"She's trying to not meddle so much in my life," Ari explains. "After we had that whole talk."

Then I remember—another thing on the list we did separately.

"How did your talk go?" I ask her.

"Well, my mom kind of understood what I was saying. I mean, I think she did. She's tried to stay out of my business, while still kind of being in my business. If that makes any sense."

I grab a handful of pretzels and put some glow-in-the-dark stickers above the doorway. "I think it does."

"She was kind of upset, though," Ari admits, standing back to inspect her work.

"Really?"

"Yeah, she cried a little, saying she knew this day would come, and she understands and gets it, but it's hard that I'm not her little girl anymore." Ari rolls her eyes. For some reason my throat stings a little, and I feel bad for Ari's mom. I guess that means I feel bad for my mom, too. "I guess she's glad she still has Gemma."

"Who still has me?" Right at that second, Gemma comes bursting down the basement stairs, licking one of those giant gobstoppers.

"Gem! Were you listening at the door again?" Ari shrieks.

"No! I came downstairs to get some DVDs. Mom and Dad told me I'm banned from being down here tonight." She glares at us. "Thank you very much."

"Get your DVDs and go," Ari says, doing her best to sound forceful.

Gemma smiles at me, and I smile back. She's so cute with her blond curls.

"I'm glad you and Ari are friends again," she says, propping herself up onto the railing. "It was so boring around here."

"Get out of here!" Ari shouts, and then Gemma jumps down and scurries up the stairs.

I start to wonder if we should prepare Gemma for what's to come. And maybe it's more than prepare— maybe it's help her realize how good she has it now. Maybe we should be reminding her to savor her youth, to really appreciate it.

And then maybe when Gemma reaches middle school, we can help her, so everything doesn't go crazy the way it did for us.

Ari shakes her head, sprinkling hot pink confetti all over the table. "Gemma does not understand what things should be said aloud, and what things should be kept inside her brain."

I laugh. "Well, give it time. She's only in third grade."

After we're done with all the decorations, we stand back to survey our work. I put an arm around Ari. "It looks great," I say.

"Better than great," she adds. "You have your playlists ready?"

"I do!"

"Let's JHH," she says. "I know this wasn't technically on the list, but we set up and it looks so good, we need something to mark the occasion!"

"I agree completely."

✳✳✳

We told people to come at six, but it's 6:06 and no one is here yet. My stomach churns. What if no one shows up? Or worse—only, like, two people show up?

"Where is everyone?" I ask Ari.

"No one comes on time," she explains. "It would look lame."

"Why? I don't get that. I like to be on time."

She shrugs. "I know you do. But it's a thing—coming fashionably late. Just trust me."

"Well, what should we do in the meantime?" I ask her, glancing up the stairs to see if anyone is coming in.

"Let's just look busy," she says. "Put on music. We'll start the snacks."

I turn on our Birthday Party playlist, and we sit down on the couches and drink cups of Cherry Coke and munch on chips. I'm not even hungry. In fact, my stomach hurts and I don't want to eat, but I need to physically do something so I don't completely freak out from agita overload.

"'Cause baby, you're a firework," Ari and I sing at the same time, using our fists as microphones.

Finally, at 6:12, we hear the doorbell ring, and muffled voices, and then Ari's mom tell some kids that the party is downstairs.

I grab Ari's hand, and we eye-bulge at each other. All the Cherry Coke sloshes around in my stomach. I'm afraid I might burp when I'm about to say hello to someone.

Marie and a few of the girls from the other side of the lunch table come down the stairs, holding brightly colored packages.

"Hiiii," they all sing at the same time. "Happy birthday!"

"Surprise!" It's Jules from the pool. She continues, "Sydney told me about the party, and I figured it would be okay, right? What's one more person?"

Ari and I look at each other.

"Sure," Ari says. "Welcome!"

Marie, Ari, Sydney, Jules, M.W., and I all do an awkward group hug, but I'm glad to be included in it.

Pretty soon after that, June and the friends formerly known as the Whatevers arrive, and they're so peppy and happy-seeming. I can't believe they ever seemed *whateverish* to me.

"It looks amazing down here, you guys," Cami shrieks. "Seriously amazing! My mom dropped all the Harvey Deli subs upstairs, BTW. Your mom is getting them ready."

Ari smiles. "Great, thanks so much for bringing those!"

June, Cami, and Saara are all wearing matching glittery eye shadow and pink flare-y skirts.

"We decided to match," Saara says. "Cute, right?"

I nod. "Definitely cute."

"Oh, and I found these on sale at the Dollar Store," June explains, holding up some bizarre decorations of neon cats. "I don't like cats, but they're just so weird, I had to bring them."

One cat is wearing sunglasses and another is wearing a toga. They may be the oddest things I've ever seen, and maybe it's my nerves or these ugly cats—but I start laughing hysterically. June does, too.

"Ugly cats," June, Saara, Cami, and I say again and again.

I think this is our first private joke.

Soon everyone arrives. The basement is crowded and loud, and there are a thousand conversations happening all at the same time.

I pull Ari to the side. "This is happening," I tell her.

"I know!" she squeals.

"Everyone came here for us."

"I know!" she squeals again. "But Noah's not here yet. . . ."

"He'll come," I say, looking around. "He said he'd be here."

This moment feels big and happy and I want to make sure I appreciate it, make sure I remember it and take notice.

Then, in the middle of my happy, appreciative hug with Ari, I feel a tap on my shoulder.

Ari raises her eyebrows at me; it lets me know exactly who is standing behind me.

I turn around. "Hey, Jason," I say. My eye gets all twitchy, but I hope it's only something I can feel and not something he can see.

"Hey," he replies, a little out of breath. "I brought these." He hands me a box of the smallest cupcakes I've ever seen. They're all different colors and almost too adorable to eat. "Happy birthday. Again."

"Thank you," I say. "These look amazing."

"They're the best," he says, looking around. "Especially the green ones; they taste like candy apples."

I nod, and it feels like there's nothing else to say. I'm scanning my brain for something, anything, to talk about, and zero results are coming up.

But then he says, "This is way better than the rec room at the pool, by the way."

I shrug. "Yeah, probably. I can't wait to see what it looks like after the renovation!"

"Me too," he says. "Maybe you can teach clementine-peeling classes there next summer!"

I laugh. "Maybe. You're the one who suggested that awesome act! I never would've thought of doing that."

He takes a bow.

Taylor Swift's "Shake It Off" comes on, and soon everyone at the party is dancing and singing along.

It's like I got this music in my mind, saying it's gonna be all right.

My skin prickles and I pull my hair up into a messy bun. I'm singing along and dancing, and Ari's basement feels like the happiest place in the entire world.

We're all dancing in a circle, and then Jason grabs my

hand, and we're dancing like that, bopping up and down and holding hands, and it feels so silly, but I don't even mind. During the chorus, he twirls me under his arm, and I don't care if anyone is watching us, but I don't think they are. They're all having fun and dancing, too.

I, I shake it off, I shake it off.

When the song ends, we're all out of breath, and everyone runs over to the drinks table to refresh.

"Your playlist is awesome," I whisper to Jason.

"Of course it is!"

"Subs will be out in ten minutes," Ari's mom calls down the stairs.

I look at Ari to see if she's embarrassed, but I think she's having too much fun to even care.

"Jason, come here," I say, after I refill my cup of Cherry Coke. He looks up and raises his eyebrows, like he doesn't know what's going on.

"I want to show you something."

FIFTY

I LEAD JASON TO ARI'S laundry room. There are a few drying racks stacked in the corner. A box of dryer sheets. And the biggest bottle of laundry detergent I've ever seen.

Guaranteed to fight stains.

I picture the detergent literally in a battle with a stain—armed with a shield and a bow and arrow or something.

I'm laughing a little to myself, which I know makes me look totally crazy. Jason turns to me and says, "So what's up?"

His hair is a little slicked back and parted on the side, all perfect. He smiles his sweet, little-boy smile, and I can't resist smiling, too.

"Just in case a game of hide-and-go-seek breaks out," I start, trying to act all serious, "this is the absolute best hiding spot."

"Good to know," he says, taking a sip of soda. We hear music playing—an Ed Sheeran song that Ari and I were obsessed with last summer.

"So," I say, nervous about what I plan to say next.

Everything in my heart says to say it, but everything in my brain says not to, because I'm so scared. I don't want it to be bad again. I don't want it to be awkward.

"So," he mimics, and soon we're both giggling, and he holds up a bottle of Spray & Wash like he's about to spray me.

"The redo?"

He nods, and we're still laughing about nothing and everything at the same time.

We both lean in a little, and then Jason's lips are on my lips.

They taste like root beer.

His lips are on my lips, and they stay there for a second. But they're there! They really are. It's not awkward like last time—with half a lip on my nose, and my tooth cutting into his lip.

This is the redo. And it's going well.

We're kissing. We really are.

Finally, he pulls away. We look at each other, and I cover my mouth because I feel like I'm about to start laughing again.

"So?" he asks.

I nod. "That was a good redo."

"It was definitely a good redo."

"So what happens now?" I ask him.

"What happens with what?"

I hoist myself up onto the washing machine, and Jason sits next to me on the dryer. It's hard to take yourself that seriously when you're sitting on boring household appliances. And it's hard to talk to someone after you've kissed them. Your lips have touched. How do you just go back to normal chatting?

"I don't know. With us? Now that the redo went well, what do we do now?"

He shrugs. "I guess we do whatever we want to do."

"That's a good plan," I say.

"I still like you," he announces.

"Well, that's good." I smile. "Because I still like you, too."

He puts an arm around me. "Well, now that that's settled . . ." He hops down and smiles at me for a second. "Can we get more chips?"

I nod. "Definitely."

FIFTY-ONE

I SMELL THE SUBS AS soon as Jason and I come out of the laundry room and everyone rushes up to the table to get them.

"These look amazing, don't they?" Cami says, putting an arm around me, admiring the platters like she made them herself. "Harvey Deli buddies forever!"

"Forever!" I say back.

I'm making sure we have enough of everything when Ari comes up behind me. "Noah's here with a bunch of kids from Hebrew," she screeches in my ear. "The ones from the trip." She nudges her head in their direction.

"Happy birthday, Arianna!" one of those girls says, pulling her in for a hug. "You look amazing!"

"Thanks." Ari smiles.

"Yeah, Ar," another one says. "You should totally wear that outfit for the Chanukah party next month."

Ari shrugs and says, "Oh, good idea!"

I think back to that trip; it feels so long ago now. I can't believe those girls were so mean to her at first.

When they walk away to go get food, Ari puts a hand over her mouth and whispers in my ear, "Noah came so late. I honestly thought he was gonna bail!"

"See, I knew he was coming," I say quietly. "And he's here now. That's what matters."

"I guess."

I turn to whisper in her ear. "We had the redo."

She steps back. "And?"

I give her two thumbs-up, and we walk over to the drinks to refill our cups.

We're standing by the soda when Noah comes over to us. "Did you ever mix Cherry Coke and Sprite together?" he asks. I assume he's asking Ari, since he's never met me before, so I stay quiet.

"No. I don't think so." She laughs a little. "Is it good?"

"Yeah. It should definitely be its own soda flavor. I can't believe I'm the only one who thought of it!" He pours a cup. "Here, try it." He hands her the cup and then looks at me. "You want one, too?"

I nod. "Sure."

I feel like Ari should introduce me, but she's just standing there, shuffling her feet and biting her lip.

"I'm Kaylan, by the way," I tell him as he hands me the cup.

"Oh, the other birthday person? Cool!"

I wonder if Ari's told him about me, or if he knows we're BFFs, or that we had a fight, or made the 11 Before 12 List.

Noah makes all these unusual soda concoctions and has us sample them—root beer and Cherry Coke; Sprite and orange soda; Dr Pepper and Coke.

My phone buzzes in my pocket.

Can I come down with cake now? It's Ari's mom.

"Did you see this text?" I ask.

Ari shakes her head, laughing. "I think she only texted you! Write back that it's okay."

Me: **Sure!**

Three minutes later, Ari's mom comes down with a birthday cake with twenty-four candles: twelve for me and twelve for Ari, and I'm only a little bit worried that the guests are going to get too close to all the flames.

We sing "Happy Birthday" and "Are You One, Are You Two?"

I put an arm around Ari, and she puts an arm around me, and we blow out the candles together.

"Don't tell me your wish!" we say as fast as possible, at the same time.

"Jinx!"

Ari's mom and dad cut up slices and pass them out.

"Best cake ever," Marie says, after a gigantic bite.

"Well, yellow cake, chocolate frosting," I tell her, realizing this may be the first conversation we've actually had, just the two of us. "It's the only way to do birthday cake."

"I totally agree," she replies.

The party goes on, longer than we expected it to, but that's always a good thing—everyone is having so much fun, we don't want to kick them out. But we do have something we need to take care of, something we've been waiting to do together for so long. Something we need to make sure happens before the end of Ari's birthday.

The kayaking.

"Ari, it's almost the end of our birthdays," I remind her when we're having a second piece of cake. "We gotta do this."

"I know," she says. "We need to kick everyone out if they don't leave soon."

Finally, at ten thirty, everyone is gone. Well, almost everyone.

Jason is still here. I mean, he lives across the street, so it makes sense. He doesn't need a ride home or anything.

We're sitting next to each other on the couch when he says, "This couch is so comfortable." He leans back, all over-the-top.

"It is. But you need to leave now." I smile, so he doesn't think I'm mad.

He moves away from me a little bit. "What did I do?"

I laugh for a second. "Nothing. Why do you always think you did something wrong?"

"I mess up sometimes," he admits.

I shake my head. "Jason, you didn't mess up! But our birthdays are almost over, and Ari and I promised we'd do something, so we need to do it," I explain.

He crinkles his face. "The list again, huh?"

I gently nudge him off the couch. "I'll talk to you tomorrow."

I walk him to the door, and Ari says, "Bye, Jason. Thanks for coming."

"Later, birthday girls." He hugs both of us, and then runs down the driveway, and across the street toward his house. My cheeks hurt from smiling so much.

"Okay, we need to make this quick," Ari says, as we change into our wetsuits and water shoes. "I think it's really dangerous to kayak at night. But I had the Curtins, who live right on the lake, turn on all the outside lights, and stand guard to make sure we're safe. I'm going to text them and let them know we're on our way."

"It's really dangerous?" I ask. "Maybe we should do this tomorrow."

Ari interrupts me. "No, it's not that dangerous if some-one is looking out for us. Tomorrow our birthdays will be over! We're doing it today. Tonight. We're living on the edge!"

"Girls," Ari's dad calls out to us from the den. "The tandem and paddles are already by the lake. I dropped them off for you, so go! And have fun! And come back soon!"

As we walk over to the lake, I ask Ari a million questions. "Do you think Noah is your boyfriend?"

"I don't know," she replies. "How does anyone ever know if someone's their boyfriend?"

"I have no idea!" I shriek. "I guess one day you discuss it or something. . . ."

Finally, we get there, and we're all suited up in wetsuits plus our coats, hats, mittens. We push the tandem toward the edge of the lake and climb in.

"We are doing this," I say. "We are making it happen."

"This is hardcore," Ari replies. "Probably the most hardcore thing we've ever done!"

"Yeah, because we're twelve! This is going to be the most exciting year of our lives," I remind her.

It feels like our toes are freezing off inside our water booties, but we paddle and we paddle and in a few minutes we're in the middle of the lake.

The Curtins are on their deck waving to us, shining the brightest lights we've ever seen.

"Ari!" Mrs. Curtin yells. "You're okay?"

"Yes!" Ari yells back.

"This feels like we're on some kind of reality show, doesn't it?" I ask Ari.

"Kind of."

After a few minutes of quiet, taking in the sounds and smells of the lake, I say, "I'm glad we made the list."

"Me too," Ari says. "It drove us apart, but then it really did bring us back together."

"And maybe we needed to be driven apart a little bit," I say. "Sometimes people need space to really appreciate each other."

"You think?" Ari asks.

"Yeah, I do. Also, it sounds good. Doesn't it?"

"Definitely." Ari laughs.

We paddle for a little while longer and we make it to Arch Island. It's starting to snow so we don't get out, but we make sure to touch the land with our oars. The list was specific. We sit in the kayak laughing for a few minutes and then Mrs. Curtin yells, "It's starting to snow! You girls should really go home now."

"When we made the list, this isn't really how I imagined it," Ari says. "The kayaking, I mean. My mom said we could only do it if the Curtins kept an eye on us. I didn't want to tell you that. I wanted you to think that I was all daring now, and really into living on the edge. A whole new Arianna."

"Ari, I'm happy the Curtins were looking out for us," I admit. "It would be so totally scary out here if it were dark. I wanted to be the one to wait until tomorrow, remember?"

"I guess we still need our moms sometimes," Ari admits. "To help us figure things out, and make situations safer, and to talk to sometimes, too."

"I know." I smile, imagining my mom all snuggly, reading under her afghan on the couch. As soon as we get home, I'm going to cozy up right next to her.

"I think we need to finish this whole thing with a major ritual," I say.

"Jump in the air, high-five, and hug in a boat?" Ari asks. "That seems hard. And kinda like we might tip over."

I nod. "You're right. I didn't mean *that* ritual, actually. I was thinking something else. And I came prepared."

"Huh?"

I grab my backpack and take out two of these eco-friendly paper lanterns I found online.

"What's happening right now?" Ari asks.

"Just you wait, my dearie," I reply, in my best slightly spooky witch voice.

I reach deeper into the backpack for a lighter. I felt a little silly buying it at the convenience store around the corner. But you gotta do what you gotta do sometimes.

"So we'll light the candles, and then we'll release the lanterns," I tell her. "I saw this done at a wedding once."

"Okay . . ."

"They'll fly up in the air. And it's like we're releasing all the negative feelings and struggles of this year. So we can focus on the positive. And focus on the future."

"The Curtins are staring at us," Ari reminds me. "I feel like we're going to get in trouble. The whole playing-with-fire thing . . . literally."

"It's okay," I reassure her. "I know what I'm doing. And plus, these are eco-friendly. And totally safe. Have no fear, my dear!"

It feels good to be comforting Ari, to be the one in control, the one who doesn't need the comforting for once. I guess I helped her with that at the talent show, too. Maybe I'm more calming than I realized.

"Ready?" I ask her.

She nods, tentatively.

I light both candles and hand Ari a lantern. We lift our arms up and release them into the sky.

"Good-bye, eleven," I say. "Good-bye, Arianna and Kaylan in a fight!"

"Good-bye, lunch table drama and getting lost at school," she replies.

"Good-bye, stupid crushes on jerky boys like Tyler!" I yell.

"Good-bye, super-extreme agita!" she screams.

"Hello, twelve!" I yell out into the night sky. "We are ready for you!"

"We are more than ready for you!" Ari yells out.

The Curtins shine a flashlight. "What is happening,

girls? We're getting nervous. Are you okay?"

"We are great!" I yell as loud as possible.

"Better than ever!" Ari raises a paddle in the air.

As we're paddling back to shore, when we can't see the lanterns anymore, I say, "Well, we released all the bad stuff."

"I feel so light," Ari says, laughing. "I think I'm a whole new person. We really did get a Whole Us Makeover. Everything we did was part of our Whole Me Makeover."

"And we need to remember that we survived the beginning of middle school. That's a major accomplishment. That place is scary!" I laugh, and Ari does, too.

"I'm proud of us," Ari says.

"Me too. There isn't anyone else in the world I'd rather turn twelve with," I tell her.

"I feel the exact same way," Ari replies.

We're quiet for a moment, almost at shore, when Ari says, "I just realized something!"

"What is it?" I ask, feeling the thump that we're back on land.

"I have something to add to that ritual," she says, looking right into my eyes. "I'm starting a new list!"

"A new list?" I ask. My heart jumps.

"There's just one thing on it for now." She lifts her eyebrows.

"Oh? What's that?" I ask.

"Keep our friendship strong!"

I reach out to hug her. "Of course. That's not even a question."

"Friends forever?" Ari asks.

"Best friends forever and ever and ever and ever . . ."

We laugh as we get out of the kayak, and walk arm in arm back to our houses.

We've only been twelve for less than twenty-four hours, but so far it feels good.

Definitely worth waiting for.

ACKNOWLEDGMENTS

Utmost love and appreciation to Dave for being the best husband, partner, and person in the world. Thank you for supporting me, encouraging me, and challenging me to always do my best. Extra thanks for doing bedtime all of those nights so I could finish this book.

To Aleah and Hazel—I love you both beyond words! You add sparkle and smiles to every day.

To David and Max—you are the best brothers and the best friends I could have ever hoped for. I am thankful for all of your help, support, love, and laughs. You are my heroes.

To Bubbie and Zeyda—thank you for being a 100% consistent source of strength and love throughout my entire life.

To Mom and Dad—thanks for putting up with me when I was eleven.

To Maria, Katherine, Rebecca, and the whole team at Katherine Tegen books—thank you so much for all of the enthusiasm, excitement, thoughtfulness, and hard work you have put into this book.

Alyssa Eisner Henkin, thank you for all of your guidance and editorial feedback. I am so lucky to have you in my corner.

To Aunt Emily, Aaron, Karen, Ari, Ezra, Maayan, Elon—thanks for the love and enthusiasm.

To Rhonda, Melanie, Maddy, Kathleen, Rich, Alex, and the whole BWL Library team and community—thank you, thank you, thank you!

To Athena, Jason, Mike, Cindy, and all the staff at the Dream Hotel—thanks for knowing my favorite lounge chair, putting up the umbrella, asking me how the book was going, and being so kind to me. I literally could not ask for a better office.

To anyone who has ever read one of my books—I am so grateful.

Kaylan and Ari's friendship continues
in Friendship List #2:

12 BEFORE 13!

"WHAT DO YOU MEAN YOU made a list?" Alice asks
me. We're at the water fountain in center camp and I'm
refilling my water bottle. Somehow my shirt is getting
drenched in the process.

When it's full, I snap the cover back on, take a sip and
say, "we made a list of eleven things we had to do before
we turned twelve, and now we're making a new one of
twelve things to do before we turn thirteen."

Crinkling her nose, Alice says, "but why? Just, like, for
fun?"

I laugh a little. "Um, kind of yeah, but also because it
helped calm us down before middle school. And now it's
a tradition and we don't break traditions."

Alice throws her head upside down and pulls her red
curls into a messy bun on the top of her head. "I like it.
It's cool." She links arms with me. "Seriously, Ari, how
have I only known you for two weeks? I feel like we've

been friends our whole lives."

"I kinda do too," I say. "I should've come to camp earlier. My mom always suggested it, but I never really wanted to go."

"Lamey McLamerson," she says. "But wait, I'm confused—how much water do you really have to drink?"

"Just enough to keep the glowing complexion." I turn my head to show her both sides of my face.

"You're hilarious. What's the next thing you're—"

"Girls!" We hear someone yell behind us. It's Sari, one of our counselors. Her voice is pretty much unmistakable—high pitched and squeaky. "You're going to be late!"

"Sorry!" Alice and I say at the same time, laughing and running to the Beit Am. It means *house of the people*, in Hebrew.

I may be fluent by the end of the summer, but hard to say for sure.

We get there just in time, and plop down on the wooden floor. Most of our unit turns around to look at us, and we shrink down, still laughing behind our hands. I know we're late, and I know we shouldn't be, but with Alice, things like lateness, and being sort of in trouble don't feel as bad.

"So." Simon our unit head looks out at all of us from the front of the room. "What does it mean to be a leader?"

Alice and I look at each other, rolling our eyes and groaning as quietly as possible.

"Haven't we already done this?" Alice asks under her breath.

"Alice!" Simon yells out. "You seem to have an answer. Come on dowwwwwwwnnnn . . . .." he says like he's a game show host, gesturing with his hands.

In a way this kind of feels like school when you get in trouble, but not exactly. Here it just feels funny and laid back, and people are laughing but they're not really laughing *at* Alice. They're more laughing with her. I make mental notes of all the things I have to write to Kaylan later. We've been trying to write every day. She's way better at it than I am, but in all fairness she has more time.

"Um, hi." Alice says from the front, her arms folded across her chest. "A leader is someone who gets things done."

Simon nods. "I like it. Good job. Now call someone else up."

Oh God. She's going to pick me. I know it. And I'm not sure I have an answer.

"Okay." She looks out and raises her eyebrows at me, and I nod to let her know it's okay to call on me. "Arianna, come on dowwwwwnnnnn . . . "

I hop up from the floor, and think about what to say as I walk up to the front. "So . . . " I start. "A leader is someone who can organize other people and get them excited to be part of the project or work or whatever is, um, happening."

"Excellent!" Simon says, high-fiving me. "Your turn to call on someone."

I could pick someone from my bunk, or one of the girls in the tennis elective, but this feels like an opportunity, a chance to do something different. And that's the thing about camp—you can be whoever you want to be here.

"Um, I pick Golfy." As soon as he stands up, I run back to my seat and Alice pulls me in for a squeezy hug.

"That was a fab answer," she says.

I watch closely as Golfy walks up there (his real name is Jacob Stanberg, but everyone calls him Golfy because of an answer he wrote on a camper questionnaire when he was nine. That golf was his favorite sport, or something like that.

He stands in front of the group with his hands in the pockets of his cargo shorts. His curly hair is sticking up in a million different directions and I feel like my heart is exploding through the v-neck of my faded gray t-shirt.

"A leader is someone who thinks about the greater good. And makes things happen. And generally just crushes it every single day." He shrugs and half-smiles.

Golfy. He may be the most perfect boy in the history of the male species.

I've only known him for two weeks but I think I love him. Really and truly love him.

More great books by LISA GREENWALD!

The Friendship List

TBH

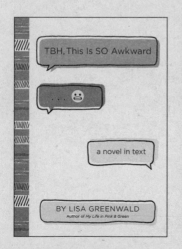